Pinky Promise

HJ Bellus

A pinky promise
is forever
xoxo
Bellus

PINKY PROMISE

Edited by: Emma Mack

Formatting: HJ Bellus

Cover Designer: Cassy @Pink Ink Designs

Dedication—

To the Miss Tami's all over the world who love unconditionally. Love is powerful. And to all the children of the world who have the power to break vicious cycles.

Chapter 1

"State." I push open the door hanging on its hinges to his room. "State, are you in here."

"Baylor?" His voice comes out shaky.

"Yes, where are you?" Fear grips me and I hate it, but it happens.

It happens every single time there's chaos around us, which is happening more and more every night. The warm liquid runs down my legs and I begin to shake even harder.

He appears from his closet and holds a hand out to me ignoring the mess between my legs. "Come on."

Our two trembling hands connect and he pulls me back into his closet sliding the doors shut. He digs through some things until he pulls a pair of his shorts from the mess.

"Here."

"Thank you," I whisper still trembling.

I edge to the furthest corner of the closet and slide off my wet clothes and glide his gym shorts on. Pulling the drawstrings as tight as possible so they won't slip down, I toss my disgusting clothes out into his room and carefully slide his closet doors shut.

I scramble on hands and knees back to him and snuggle into his side. Stayton Blake is my best friend and has been since we were toddlers. Our mothers were the same way until mine was killed in a drive by shooting on the streets of Kings. His mom took me, well, I should say State took me in. She's too strung out on Meth, and having sex with men to pay for it, to worry about us kids.

His dad is one of the biggest dealers on the street and my own dad runs for him. We know way too much at the young age of eight, but it's the life that we are forced to exist in.

"You okay?" He whispers wrapping his pinky in mine.

I nod in the dark space, but know he can feel it on his shoulder. My silent tears roll down my face. State never cries or shows fear. He's my protector and best friend. And even though we're the same age, he towers over me. His hands are twice as big as mine, along with his shoulders. You'd never know we were only born a few days apart. State always brags how he's so much older than me.

"What happened?" he asks.

I brush off the tears with the back of my hand and rub them on my shorts.

"I was coming to get you to go to the park and then shots went off," I sniffle again. "I ran, State, ran fast as I could. The shots got closer and I even think one hit my house."

He squeezes my pinky until it hurts. "I told you that I'd come get you."

The tears of fear and panic are back. "I know, but some women and a weird man showed up at the house to talk to my dad."

"Did they hurt you?" He turns to face me.

All I can make out are the whites of his eyes. I shake my head no.

"Baylor."

"The guy made me feel weird like that one…" I trail off, fighting to not let that night take over me. "That did hurt me really bad."

"The one that made you bleed?"

"Yes," I whisper.

I've never told anyone the full story. Not even my momma when she was alive and definitely not State. I've seen how everyone looks at the girls in Kings who get raped. I'm not sure I even know what rape is, but what that man did to me was bad, really bad. Late at night, when I'm not with State, I feel the ripping.

"Okay, I forgive you for not coming here first." He lets up on my pinky.

"Should we call the cops?"

I hate my dad, but I'm scared and don't want to lose him. If I do, I'll go to the state like some of our other friends already have. I'll be torn from State and that can't happen.

"No."

Before State finishes, the front door of his house slams open. I bury my face in his chest and feel his face fall to the back of my head. It hurts knowing he's always protecting me. Shielding me from the ugly facts of our world on the streets and even in school.

It's me gripping his pinky this time. The shots come closer and then the sound of his bedroom door being ripped off the hinges fills the air. I sob out loud and feel the wetness between my legs flow again. State covers my mouth making it hard to breathe, but I know what he's doing.

I have no idea how long we stay in that closet, but we do, huddled together.

Chapter 2

"I have a twenty."

"State." I shove his shoulder.

"Dad was passed out around a bunch of strangers and I just grabbed it."

"You'll get beat."

My body begins trembling because State gets beat a lot, until he bleeds and can't see out of either of his eyes.

"They won't know. There was wads of hundreds."

"Are you sure?"

He takes my pinky in his and continues down to our ice cream shop.

"I'm sure."

"I love ice cream."

"Me too," he smiles at me. "I'm getting a triple scoop waffle cone."

"You're a pig."

We push open the door to the ice cream shop and I inhale the glorious scent of sweets. It's a rare treat for both of us. We're use to hoarding the bag of canned foods our teacher sends home with us on the weekends. We've become professionals at hiding it and rationing it out through the week. I hate packaged noodles, but when it's your only choice you learn to love them.

State orders his ice cream with confidence. He's always doing the talking and taking care of us. Our older siblings don't care much about us anymore; they're wrapped up in the business that Kings has to offer.

When it's my turn, he looks down to me and I shake my head then whisper to him.

"It's okay. I don't want any."

I don't like to talk to anyone but State. Miss Tami at school has been trying to work with me to talk to the teachers and other students, but I can't, it's too scary. Every time I attempt to open my mouth my voice never comes out. The streets of Kings have stolen it from me.

She even told me the teachers were threatening to separate State and I next year when we go into fourth grade. She explained all the reasons why and that it's important for me to make an effort. I only peed myself and cried.

"She wants one scoop of bubblegum in a cup please." State has turned back to the pretty woman behind the counter, and I have to hide my smile because that's exactly what I wanted.

We watch her scoop the ice cream from the tubs in the cooler. My lips smack together — so excited about this treat.

"It's our birthday presents to each other."

"Our birthdays were almost three weeks ago," I whisper.

"So." He shrugs. "We didn't get anything, so now we are."

A feeling of fear circles in my stomach knowing that if his dad finds out State will be beaten, badly. I don't like those days because I don't get to see him. His daddy will lock him in his room until most of the signs are gone. I hate not having my best friend during those days and I hate it even more that I don't get to help him be better.

State lets go of my pinky while he pays her and grabs our ice cream. He hands me mine and then clutches my pinky again. He knows I'm scared. The bell above the door rings with new customers walking in. It's the mean boys from school. They're a couple of years older than us and they are evil. I try to pull my pinky from State's but he only squeezes harder.

"Pussy boy with his little sister." One of them calls out, alerting his friends to us.

"State the sister fucker," Antonio, the ring leader, sings out.

I feel State's shoulders puff out and know he's going into attack mode. They know how to play him to set him off into a fit of anger. He may be a couple of years younger than the bullies, but he towers over them, same as he does over me. He's always in the principal's office for fighting.

"Don't," I whisper up to him. "Let's go to the park."

"My uncle said you're a smart boy because he's had Baylor, too."

I don't do it very often, but I know exactly who his uncle is, so I spit in the boy's face then kick him in the boy parts. State has taught me to always hit there if need be.

"Leave us alone." I shock myself when my voice comes out steady, without any fear in it.

I drag State past them and finally relax when he's out on the sidewalk with me. The group of bullies roar in laughter, forgetting about us. State must be shocked because he doesn't say a word as I drag him down the sidewalk. Our spot is only about three blocks away. We found it two years ago and it's the safest place in Kings.

We eat our melting ice cream in silence, sitting on our favorite rocks. It's not until every lick is gone before either of us talk.

"You were full gangster back there."

I laugh, but then correct him. "I'll never be a gangster."

"Neither of us will," he corrects me.

I want to be a doctor, for several reasons, and State thinks he'll be a pro player in the NFL. We dream about the money, the nice houses, and crime free places we will live in. We're going to be neighbors, with no fence between our mansions, and buy an Xbox and all the games we want. My house is going to be pink, because pink is the best color ever, and States' royal blue.

"We are halfway there."

"Uh?" I ask looking up from the cloud scene I'm coloring on the cracked sidewalk. I've found a certain rock that makes faint white lines.

"We're nine, Baylor, we only have nine more years until we get our houses."

A huge smile spreads across my face. "Half way there."

Chapter 3

"Uno," I squeal and slap down the handmade paper card.

"Cheater," State accuses.

"I didn't cheat."

"You made the cards from your notebook."

"Sore loser," I taunt him.

He continues to draw from the stack and finally places down a yellow seven, and I follow suit by laying down a wild.

"Boom."

"I'm done with this. Let's play catch out back."

"If you hit me in the forehead with your ball, I'll kick you in the crotch."

He chuckles, and I know he'd never hit me on purpose, but damn State can throw a ball and catches even better.

"Promise," he says.

"Pinky promise?" I ask, laying down the law.

He holds his pinky up and clutches it with mine.

"Pinky promise," he says.

State's football is his only prized possession. No other toys or games, it's all football when it comes to him. I hate playing catch with him, but there's no one else since he spends all of his time with me. I stretch my fingers out, knowing my hands will be sore for days. His never hurt since his hands are the size of the sun.

We escape to the backyard without anyone noticing us. A few strange women linger in his house, but it's nothing new to us. The fence between our yards lays in crumbles with rusty nails poking out in every direction.

"Let's go on this side of my house," he points to the opposite side of the fence.

"If you hit me with the ball I'll kick you so hard and won't even care that it was your birthday, State."

"Okay, chicken pants. Stand in front of me and hike the ball."

"The bend over thing where I huck it back to you?"

"Geez, you need to at least act like you know football, Baylor. I mean, I will be a world champion one day."

I roll my eyes and bend over, ready to huck the stupid ball to him.

"After I yell out play calls and say *hike*, then throw it to me."

I look through my legs at an upside-down State and say, "You mean huck it?"

"Yeah, huck the bastard."

"State, language," I scold him. I refuse to think that either of us will grow up to be like the uneducated and cruel people who surround us, but the older we get, the more he cusses.

"Sorry, Baylor, after I holler hike, then huck the butterflying ball."

"Okay."

He's lucky that the PE teacher has taken him under his wing and lets him watch football movies during lunch. I always pick at my nails while the two go into depth about the stupid ball.

We spend hours of me bending over and hucking the ball, while State lives out his fantasy on a perfect green field with screaming fans. I only manage to nail him a few times where the ball shouldn't have gone.

I collapse, hungry and very thirsty, on the grass plucking at my crusted bare heels.

"You okay?" He asks.

"Tired. Very tired."

"Yeah, football isn't for normal wussies like you."

"Uno is." I smile at him and kick him in the knee.

"Do you ever think about…"

"What?"

"Us being separated." His voice is sad, and I know my clinginess wears on him.

"I'm trying to be better, State."

"No, it's not that."

I look at him confused.

"I'd die if we were separated."

He laces our pinkies together and we lay back, calling out shapes in the clouds, having no idea that this would be our last night together in our childhood homes in Kings.

Chapter 4

State fell asleep on my bed and I snuggled right up beside him. Both of our places were deserted and it's those nights that are the best. Just me, him, his football, and our dreams to escape Kings to our side-by-side mansions.

I roll awake when loud voices enter the tiny house. It's not a party, but angry shouts. I try to shake State to wake him up, but he's out. I tip-toe from the bed and peek through the sliver of the door opening.

Three men hold guns up pointing at my dad, State's parents, and few other strangers on the couch. He's yelling for his money and all their drugs. Their faces are covered with black masks. The wetness between my legs runs when I see the fear in my dad's eyes. One shot fires. The flash of it causes me to stumble back, but not before my dad's head flops back on the couch with his brains flying all around him.

More shots go off and I scramble to State who's sitting up in dazed confusion. I clutch his hand and pull him under the bed. He tries to ask questions, but I cover his mouth. Our pinkies latch together and I cry until all the noise ceases. The men rifle through the house looking for something and when my bedroom door flies open, I pee again.

They never find us. It's light by the time we look up into the eyes of police officers. I scramble to race into their arms, but State holds me back until he makes sure it's safe. They ask question after question before taking us down to the station. We are fed really good food, and I eat like a raccoon I saw feeding from a trashcan in a documentary once.

I refuse to talk until they bring State to me and that's when I tell him what I saw. The kind woman with blonde hair is nice when she talks to us. State asks them to get Miss Tami to help ease my fear.

She rushes down to the station, and that's when I finally talk and cry reliving all the pain. The officers tell us all of our parents are dead. It's the first time I see my best friend sob in his hands. Everything we had, as evil as it was, was stolen from us that night.

***

The food is amazing here, but I only get to see State at school and during TV time before bed. I have to sleep in the girl's dorm and him in the boy's. My eyes hurt every single day from crying and no sleep.

No one will listen to State or Miss Tami, the foster house doesn't seem to care. I've been pictured with a profile of all my favorite things listed and State told me he'd had the same thing too. The workers have been very honest with us, telling us we're now in the system and waiting on our "forever" home.

"Baylor, you have to eat." State pulls a bag of chips from his gym shorts.

I only shake my head side to side. I live in greater fear now than on the streets of Kings. At least there I knew the way of life and had State always by my side.

The days go by, endless and hopeless. State finds me whenever he can, grabbing my pinky and I finally learn to enjoy the moments we get together. It's been months.

I wait on the couch, saving his spot with my leg so none of the other kids will screw with me. I've been labeled as a mean bitch and have never stopped the rumor that was started of me shooting my dad. They're afraid of me and I like it that way. No one bothers me.

Our favorite episode of Scooby-Doo starts and ends with no sight of State, so I go and search for him. He rounds a corner shoving me into the ground. When the world quits spinning, I look up to State who has tears rolling down his face.

It's only the second time I've seen him cry, so I know it's bad.

"I'm sorry, Baylor." He holds a hand up bringing me to him.

His right eye is swollen from a fight at school last week. The wound is a product of State standing up for me once again.

"Are you okay?" He hugs me tight to his body.

"What's wrong?"

I feel his tears rain down on my shoulder, but he doesn't respond. I fight to push him back, but he doesn't move.

"What's wrong?" I scream.

Still no response.

"I'll knee you in the balls. Talk."

"Are you ready, State?"

I look over his shoulder to see one of the social workers standing with a man and woman. The woman is nervous, wringing out her fingers, and the man holds her tight to his side.

"No. No. No." My last no comes out as a scream.

"I told them no, but I have to go, Baylor."

"You can't, State."

"It's time, State." The social worker taps his shoulder.

"Please don't leave me." I hug him tighter than ever before, feeling my world finally crumble.

"I don't want to."

"He doesn't have a choice." The social worker pries us apart.

State clutches onto my pinky. "I asked and begged them to take you, Baylor."

"Please, God, please. No." I sob, so terrified I don't even recognize my own voice.

My knees slap the hard tile floor, still holding onto State's pinky. The woman pries us apart and I can't watch him go. I bury my face in my hands and completely fall to the floor, screaming loud and violent. I can hear State yelling my name, but it fades off into the distance until he's gone forever.

"Call Miss Tami. It's in her file, and she's the only person besides State who can calm her down."

Chapter 5

Years Later...

"Rowe, you have to get dressed." I plant my hands on my hips and stare her cute little face down.

"I'm playing princess today." She sticks out her tongue and goes back to dressing her stuffed hamster in her latest Princess Elsa dress.

I kneel down before her and cup her face in my hands. "School isn't an option, buttercup. You have to go. I promise, after school and when I get off work, we will play hamster princess as long as you want."

She sticks her bottom lip out and tries to pout. We've been working on transition periods with Rowe. She's the perfect, prettiest barely seven-year old alive, with a bright soul and a tender heart. Rowe never lets her disability get in the way, so by damn, never tell this girl she has down syndrome.

"I'm going to pull my hair back and you better be ready for school, Missy." I tap the tip of her nose.

"Oh, oh, oh." She jumps up and down. "Let me."

"Only if you pledge to be a little princess and go to school."

"Promise." She covers her heart.

I cringe. I hate that word. Have never used it since that day so long ago. I turn and let Rowe drag a brush through my thick brown hair and cringe each time I feel hair being plucked from my scalp. She sings and hums while brushing through it, and then mangles my hair into a ponytail. Well, I'll be sporting this pony until I drop her off and will have to pull it up again in the car.

She rounds me in her pajama top and princess tutu and covers her mouth. "You so beautiful, Baylor."

She sits in my lap and wraps her little legs around my waist, cupping my cheeks. "I hope I'm as pretty as you one day."

Her voice is hopeful.

"Rowe, I have a secret." I bend to her little ear.

"You're already prettier than I'll ever be, inside and out."

"I love you, sister."

"Love you, too, Rowe."

She hops from my lap and skips into the bathroom down the hall. I pluck her hand held princess mirror from the floor and check her masterpiece. I have to stifle my laughter, Rowe doesn't miss anything and I don't want to hurt her feelings. It appears a very healthy rat has nested in the right side of my hair while the rest of the family has nestled in other places.

My hair is a bitch and not one to easily tame. It's a dark brown, thick with a layer of curls on the bottom, and more than halfway down my back. It either has to be straightened, which takes hours, or I have to use lots and lots of products to make it look wavy, so ponytails are my go to.

"Rowe get hold of you?" Miss Tami sits in her recliner working on her daily crossword puzzle.

"What would make you think that?" I twirl in my pajama bottoms and tank.

"At least the make-up didn't come out this time."

I laugh hard, picturing Miss Tami and I all painted up by the hands of an over exuberant Rowe. That shit doesn't wipe off.

"What are your plans today?" I kiss her forehead and pat her leg, taking a seat at her feet on the floor. She hates the old habit, but it's one I've never been able to break.

"Have lunch at the senior center and then pinochle club until four."

"Wild momma. Any men on that schedule?" I begin massaging her swollen ankles.

"Smart ass."

"I don't like you going to that senior center." The word rolls off my tongue in disgust.

"My friends are there."

"I don't care. I hate that place." My hands rub deeper into her skin.

"Kings is both of our homes. I know we don't live there any longer, but my friends are there."

"Yeah, we are a whole whopping six miles out of the hood." She winces with a deeper roll of my hands. "One day I'll get us further."

"We are just fine here, Pissy Polly. Rowe has settled in quite nicely. I love our home and my girls."

"I know you do. You've always been a sucker."

"I love you, Baylor."

"Love you, too, Miss Tami."

"Where's my chariot?"

We both turn to see Rowe with a matching rat nest ponytail centered smack dab on the top of her head, her hot pink tutu, red shimmery leggings, and favorite princess t-shirt on.

"Get me my backpack, bitches."

Miss Tami kicks me. "I told you *The* Heat wasn't a good movie for her."

I can't help the laughter. I know it encourages her, but, my hell, that's the funniest shit I've heard and seen in a long time. I pop up from the floor and grab her hand.

"Rowe, you can't say those words remember."

She shrugs. "I know, but it felt so smooth."

"You're going to think smooth, little munchkin, now come give me some loves." Miss Tami holds her arms out wide.

I stand back and watch her hug Rowe while whispering in her ear, telling her how smart and beautiful she is. It's the same thing she used to do to me. And on really bad days she still does. She lets go of Rowe and then opens her arms to me. I bend over hugging the life out of her.

"Now make sure you talk to that cute principal," she winks.

"Mr. Moore loves Baylor." Rowe sings out.

"You two." I wave them off and roll my eyes. "I don't have time for men, nor do I want to make time."

"You deserve it," Miss Tami says.

I give her *the don't you dare bring up this topic* stare and she only smiles back.

Rowe has her favorite jam on, rocking out in the car with her oversized aviators. She doesn't miss one word to *Party in the U.S.A.* by Miley Cyrus. She holds my phone up to her mouth to belt out the chorus. My heart clenches in my chest because I hate dropping her off at school. Actually, it's more than a hate.

Rowe Abott was one of Miss Tami's last students she worked with. She raised me, and it was only thirteen months ago when I met Rowe and learned of her circumstances. My stomach becomes violently ill just thinking about what the poor baby has been through.

She was more than abused by neighborhood boys, and her parents were too disgraced by Rowe's disability to give two thoughts about her being hurt. The sickest part of the whole situation was that they were high school boys and the football coaches even knew what was happening, but not one of the motherfuckers stood up for Rowe.

Rowe grew up in the better parts of the King's project. She'd wait for her older brother to get out of practice every day, even though she was a young pre-kindergarten student. It only takes one evil soul to bring hell on everyone. The team captain decided it would be great fun to torture Evan, her older brother, he was just a freshman, so they took it out on Rowe.

Easiest target with her age and disability. Awful and horrendous things were done to the sweet girl, but it wasn't until an object had to be removed from her rectum that something actually happened. It wasn't the coaches, older students, or even her brother who finally spoke up. It was the school nurse who noticed poor Rowe in pain.

Miss Tami was on the verge of retiring, but knew she had one last person to save before she quit. She'd moved to that school years before, after she took me from Kings. She let me go to school in a better part of the city, but told me it was her mission to stay there and help children.

I shudder recalling the incident, but what really makes me sick is the slap on the wrist the boys received. No jail time, just an expulsion from school and a scaring from the police.

"You okay, sissy?" Rowe places her hand on mine.

I take a second to look down at her while at a red light.

"Only because you're with me."

And it's the God damn truth. This girl has made me feel and come to life more than anything else. I'd do anything for her. She's slowly teaching me to live again.

"When do you get off work?" She asks.

"Around six, Rowe. Miss Tami will pick you up at 4:10, okay?"

My vision focuses back on the road and wait for her response.

"Why don't you call Miss Tami *mom*?"

That answer is easy. "Because she's way more than a mom."

"I thought so."

We pull up to the school parking lot and Rowe waves out to everyone who will look.

"You're going to walk me in, right?"

"Yes, baby."

She asks the same question every morning and I respond the same way. She's so full of life it's hard for it not to be contagious. She bounces next to me with her Cinderella backpack on, giving everyone high fives as she walks by. This school loves Rowe, and she loves them. Well, that's unless it interrupts her princess playtime.

"Princess Rowe." Principal Moore kneels down and opens his arms wide, waiting for her leaping hug.

She lets go of my hand and rushes into his chest, hugging him tight. She's never said it out loud, but I'm pretty sure she looks up to him like a Prince Charming.

"How's the fairest princess in the land?"

He holds her back a bit taking in her outfit and hairstyle. *Shit.* I remember our matching do's and try to run my palm over my own pony mess. He looks up at me and smiles wide.

"Looks like you did Ms. Baylor's hair as well."

"I did. She's beautiful, huh?"

"Very." He nods making eye contact.

What is wrong with me? The guy has hinted so much about asking me on a date, and I acted clueless. He's gorgeous with sandy blond hair, piercing blue eyes, and his smile? Well, his smile reminds me that my lady bits are well and alive. Boyfriend territory has never been on my radar. Ever. In fact, even if he wanted to wine and dine me, I wouldn't have any time between school, work, and my girls.

"She's post to pinch your butt," Rowe tries to whisper, but her whispers always come out as shouts. "Miss Tami said so."

"Well, I wouldn't want to have to put that pretty lady in detention now."

Rowe's shoulders slump. "You'd never hurt her. Would you?"

He knows her background and has a double Master's in counseling and administration. He always, always, handles her with grace, kindness, and respect.

"I'd never hurt a soul, but students who don't follow the rules have to serve detention."

"Right." She perks up. "Pinching butts is bad."

She shakes her head side-to-side with huge eyes. Her teacher joins us before Rowe schools us any further in butt pinching 101. She gives me a quick kiss before bouncing off to class. I wait, knowing what her next move will be. She stalls, making her teacher stop, and blows me a kiss. I pretend to catch it and blow her one back.

She's much more excited about catching mine, doing a leap in the air and flailing her arms.

"Hard to have a bad day around that one, eh?"

I look over to Mr. Moore and admire his light blue-pinned striped buttoned up shirt before responding.

"She's a blessing."

"Good at hair too." He points to the nest on my head.

"I could never hurt her feelings. I fix it on the way to school or work, and by the time my day is over it looks like this again."

"Florida humidity."

"Yeah, and a nervous tick, not a good combo."

"Pharmaceutical, right?" He asks, rubbing his strong jawline.

I tilt my head in shock.

"I'm not a stalker. Rowe brags how you'll be able to hand out pills."

I slap my hand over my mouth. "That girl, but yes working on my Pharmacist degree. It's years out, but I'll get there before I'm sixty-six. Right now, I work at a diner and do massages on the side. I mean I'm a licensed masseuse not a..."

Baylor, foot in mouth. Foot in mouth, stat!

He lets out a deep chuckle like he's reading my thoughts. A young boy runs up to him tugging on his sleeve.

"Juan is hurt. Hurt real bad."

"Talk to you later, Baylor," he nods to me quickly while paying attention to the distressed young student. But he turns to me before rushing off. "I'll be in for a massage one day. Let you get in Miss Tami's request."

Oh God. I blush one hundred shades of red with embarrassment. Then, like an idiot, I send him an awkward wave before getting in my car.

I flip down the visor and look at the glorious rat's nest on the top of my head and think how funny life is.

Chapter 6

After four massages this morning at the small space I rent in a salon, I'm off to my waitress job. Miss Tami insists I work way too much, but I've found I function better when completely busy. It's my weird way of warding off my demons, I guess.

I have an hour to spare between jobs, so I go to my favorite coffee shop off the beaten path, to submit a research paper for one of my online classes. Coffee is definitely my drug of choice to keep the engine running at high speed. The smell of the shop hits me when I walk in. The smell alone is rejuvenating. I order my usual iced caramel coffee and settle into a corner booth.

It's funny the way life works out. Most of my school years, I was placed in special education programs because I didn't talk. Miss Tami fought for me, but I was the problem and never fought for myself. It wasn't until my sophomore year of high school when they ran another IQ test and some random academic ones, that the school finally figured out I was more than capable.

I fooled them into thinking I couldn't even read and that writing was a struggle. When in fact, after Miss Tami saved me, all I did was read. I'd read everything in sight and loved our library visits. I shake off the old memories and fire up my laptop.

It's definitely on its last leg. The screen barely remains attached to the keyboard and I have to prop my backpack up behind it so it doesn't flop back on the table. Miss Tami bought me a new MacBook for Christmas this last year, to replace my pathetic Windows machine, but another quirky fact about me is that when I grow attached to something I never abandon it.

Oh, my abandonment issues are another whole level of nut case. It would take the finest astronauts, scientist, and neurosurgeons to crack me. I let out a light giggle at the thought, and jot down some notes to write in a story that I've been working on. Because, let's face it, fiction is way more entertaining than fact after fact of research papers that I'm currently buried under.

I send off the final research paper and tenderly shut the lid of my laptop, brush my bangs out of the way, and then make it out to my car. It's only a five-minute drive to the sport's bar I wait tables at. It's ridiculous really. Alley's Sports Bar is a good thirty-minute drive from my house, but it makes me feel more alive the further I am from the streets of Kings.

The bar is always hopping and full of sport's enthusiasts. I'm busted with the dull roar of the crowd today when I walk in the back door. I busy myself changing in the back bathroom. I shimmy into my tight orange tank top with Alley's logo on it, then leap into the tight black spandex shorts. We have to wear signature blue and orange Nike tennis shoes.

I re-adjust my out of control hair, smoothing it back into a ponytail. My reflection shines back at me in the mirror. I'm a plain gal who loves make-up and have only been fueled to use more, thanks to Rowe. It's fun to put on make-up, making my brown eyes pop and highlight my cheekbones. It's like my own fantasy of being a princess. Oh, that Rowe has been quite the influence on me.

The door to the bathroom swings open, nearly clipping my booty. "Oh, sorry."

A gorgeous runway blonde giggles.

"It's okay." I tuck my mascara back into my bag and I'm slammed with how fucking not pretty or princess like I am, when staring at the voluptuous blonde in front of me. She's perfect and belongs on the cover of a magazine.

Alley's bar is a good hour from the University of Florida Gators, but she's Alumni and loves that University more than life itself, I swear. She played four years for the women's basketball team and bleeds royal blue. She holds a deep hatred for Georgia and doesn't give a shit if it offends any of her customers.

Alley is a good friend of Miss Tami's and a former case of hers. It blows my mind to think, of the hundreds of students that woman has inspired, Miss Tami is actually who set me up with Alley. Once again, I'm forever thankful for her…even though I hate sports and despise the skimpy outfit I have to wear even more.

It's an unusually calm night, but then again the football season is just on the brink of opening day. And, oh man, do I love football season even though I despise football itself and the memories it holds. Why do I love it? Simple, the tips flow like a rushing river with drunk customers screaming at a television screen. Oh, and it's great entertainment, too.

But tonight most of the patrons are here for our signature burger. The Alley Stackhouse is known state-wide in Florida. So, in the offseason of popular sports, people from all over the state visit us to order one. The Alley Stackhouse is comprised of two handmade patties seasoned with Alley's Secret Seasoning, grilled to the liking of the customers, and then topped with a light layer of blue cheese crumbles, lots of bacon, and a spicy nacho cheese.

I've never tried one myself, but have witnessed several satisfied faces when sinking into one. If I ever eat here, I tend to go for something quick like a basket of fries and onion rings. My eating habits are socially psychotic at best, just another one of my strange ticks I may never overcome. The only time I hide this fact is when around my Rowe girl.

Our in-house DJ begins play *Brown Eyed Girl* and I shake my head knowing what's coming next, but pluck the plates from under the warmer to deliver to the customers.

"What's this?" His voice booms over the beginning of the song. "Did you all know we have our own Brown Eyed Girl in the house tonight?"

All of the staff erupts in a chorus of cheers, causing me to duck my head and an insane amount of heat to rush to my cheeks. Alley is dead set on cracking my shell. She's always setting me up on dates that I supply endless excuses for, and is always embarrassing the hell out of me.

She tells me she won't stop until I'm on top of the bar dancing, or go out on a date. The poor woman will lose this battle. I continue to my table while the DJ pauses the song.

"See we have this waitress who is killer gorge and doesn't seem to know it. So how about you all sing this song along with us to serenade her? Baylor Jones, wave your hand for the good customers of Alley's."

I set down the plates at the small booth and know if I don't wave my hand a few of the cooks will be out soon raising me above their head, so I comply.

"Let me know if you need anything else," I nod politely to the people in the booth and then back away.

"Oh, Baylor, we don't see you."

I back up with my face on fire and wave my hand up in the air.

"There's the gorgeous brown eyed girl. Give us a whirl and little shake."

I bite down on my bottom lip, ready to stick the mic so far up the DJ's ass that he'll never need to use one again, and then I spy Alley behind the bar with a shit eating grin plastered all over her face nodding me on.

I throw up both of my hands and make a show of spirit fingers to appease my pushy boss and then spin around. My ponytail nails me in the eyeball, in a not so glorious act, and I'm wrapped up in arms before I can protest.

It's Joey. He should be a Calvin Klein underwear model, but tends the bar here and brings in more women than should be legal. Joey likes the other team though, which provides comic relief watching women slip him money, phone numbers, and even reveal a boob to him. He gags at just the words, *boob* or *vagina*.

He has me wrapped up and swaying to the song in the middle of the bar. I hear ovaries bust all over the place when his deep voice begins booming out the song to me. Joey kisses me on the forehead, before pushing me away and twirling me around his finger. When he pulls me back in, I lay my head on his chest. I love this place because they're like my family. Always protective and pushing me to my limits.

"Go on, girl. Give them something to look at with that banging booty of yours."

I laugh hard and kiss Joey on the cheek, then surprise the hell out of him when I push back on his chest and shake my booty. It's a rare sighting, but I let go with him near me.

The song comes to an end and the bar erupts in cheers. Joey holds my hand up like I've just won the world champion belt in boxing and I take a quick bow.

"Dead to me." I pat his chest.

"Yeah, Alley sent me out here."

"Rat bastards." I step back cocking my head to the side.

"Baylor, so mean. I'm just a sweet, kind, and lovable man looking for a glorious dick."

I shake my head side-to-side and tuck back a few out of control tendrils that came lose during our fancy-free dance session. I grab another order and all the cooks give me their seal of approval with a round of applause. My eyes roll and then I send them a thumbs up. There's a lot to be said about being in the good graces of the cooks when waitressing. They always have my back getting my orders processed quickly and efficiently, which results in more tips for me.

"You have a table of eight over in the corner," Sally, the hostess, whispers in passing.

Cha-ching is all I can hear. I love these nights when we're still steady as hell with no blaring game in sight. If I'm honest with myself football hurts my heart like nothing else could ever do. Ironic, I work here! But in true Baylor fashion, I've attached to something and will never let go until I'm broken.

I drop off the food with a kind smile, check my other tables, and then grab a handful of menus before making my way to the new table. Mid-step I hear a voice and freeze as it takes back to a place I never thought possible.

It can't be.

Then a deep roar of laughter finally causes me to look up. I'm only feet away. It must have been the dance and me busting a move because I've gone officially fucking nuts. It's the voice I only hear in my dreams. But when I look up it's the mature face that has haunted my dreams every single night.

His brown eyes pierce mine at the same moment my hands tremble, and the menus fall to the ground. I wipe the mirage from my eyes, bend over, and pick up the menus. On unknown wobbly legs, I make my way to the table. The cover model blonde has her hands wrapped around the back of his neck cuddling right next to him.

"Dude, your life is about to change forever with the food, State."

"Yeah, man, can't believe it's taken three years to get you out here."

"You'll for sure clench the Heisman Trophy this year after this shit."

All the men in his booth flood him with comments. I survey them and realize there's seven men and one female. And that female is touching my State. I'm automatically back in the orphanage screaming *no* and wetting my pants as he left my world.

He never contacted me, and I never tried to find him after my entire world was ripped apart. He was my protector, my best friend, and the other half of my soul. He left, disappeared one day forever, until now. Now, he sits in a booth with what looks like college football players and a gorgeous blonde petting him.

Before I have a chance to hand out the menus like I normally do, one of the men on the edge of the booth tears them from my hands.

"State, dude, you have to let me order for you. I grew up on this shit and contribute my fierce pounding and orgasmic power to this shit."

He doesn't look away from me as the table grows silent and all I do is tremble out of control. Alley's lanky arm wraps around me, pulling me to her. My quivers of fear absorb into her tall frame.

"Welcome. What can we get started for you?"

The men hit her up with a full list of appetizers, but State remains still and quiet. I mentally try to remember the list, but get lost in his deep brown eyes staring at me. I fall a bit more into the side of Alley, feeling my legs begin to give out.

State reaches out and grabs my pinky in his. It's warm, nice, and home.

"State." The blonde pulls him into her, noticing our connection.

He's huge. Like when we were kids. He easily towers over the rest of them just in a sitting position. The width of his shoulders takes up nearly half of the booth. He's not all legs and lank like when we were kids. He's stacked with hard muscles, racing up and down his arms, exposed from his tight fitting tank.

The bitch huffs in disapproval when State refuses to let our connection go. And yes, she's a bitch because she's with my best friend. The only one I've ever had. He's mine. Then reality crashes in on me as his buddies enjoy a good laugh about something…I'm no longer in his life or have a place to be.

"I'll go grab the drinks." My common sense finally hits me upside the head and I race off.

My legs no longer shake as I sink down the wall in the back room. My whole body heaves and trembles. I am going to be sick. I scramble over to the trash can near the door and let the contents of my stomach flow out.

"Baylor?" A voice comes and then the door slowly pushes open.

I look up to the face staring down at mine. The tears flow and my past rushes in without warning. It's State.

He sinks down to the floor with his back against the wall and pulls me into his lap. I fit into him just like I use to. I bury my head in his chest and close my eyes, forcing out the current situation and enjoy being lost in my best friend. He curls his finger around mine and I sob harder.

"Baylor."

I don't talk or look up to him. I inhale his cologne. It's a new smell for him and I fall in love with it way too fast. The woodsy scent mingled with a light hint of honey seduces me.

"Oh my God, Baylor, I never thought this would happen."

"You have a girlfriend. Leave please." I blurt it out through my wracking tears without thought.

"You want me to leave?" He pushes my shoulders until I'm forced to look up to him.

I nod without saying a word.

He brushes loose hair from my face. "You're gorgeous, Baylor."

He's not subtle about taking me in from my face down to my huge tits. I feel naked in his lap and don't like it all.

"Quit looking at me." I scramble from his lap. "Go back to your life."

"I don't want to." He doesn't quit staring.

It causes anger to boil up in me. Unanswered anger, and I have no idea where it's stemming from.

"You left me. You have another life. Please leave me alone, State."

He slams his enormous fist into the sheetrock wall sending bits sailing. He's a beast. Huge and demanding, and now pissed.

"Go," I whisper, looking down at my olive tanned legs.

"I didn't have a choice, Baylor." He cups the ball cap sitting backwards on his head. "I fucked up. Beat the shit out of everyone, trying like hell to get back to you, but my mom and dad didn't give up on me."

His last few words grab my attention. "You're mom and dad?"

State brings his knees up to his chest, placing his elbows on them, and bows his head still clutching his hat. "I never wanted any of it, but they didn't give up on me. I just wanted you and to come back to Kings."

"Please leave." My bottom lips trembles as I stand to my feet. "It's clear you have a new life now, State."

"Baylor, please."

I open the door and feel his enormous palm wraps around my ankle.

"Don't leave, please. I've wanted to find you for so long."

I kneel down in front of him and speak the most painful words of my life. "Our time was on the streets of Kings. It's over. I wish you nothing but the best of luck in your life, State."

My hand reaches out and brushes his strong set jawline. The pain pouring from him makes my insides melt. He may have had a great life after leaving me, but it's evident he still loves me.

"It's not like that, Baylor."

"We've never had it easy. It's okay."

I lean forward and brush my lips against his out of greedy need. My body needs just one thing to hold on to before he leaves again. We both freeze at the connection and State moans. His large palm grips the back of my neck, pulling me down into him.

The kisses are hard and needy. The electricity he sends through my being leaves me shattered and whole all at the same time. State darts his tongue out, running between the seam of my lips, and I open easily for him. I shudder when he explores my mouth and forget we are even kissing.

Hell, he's my first kiss and I begin mimicking his actions like a seasoned professional. I soak up all of State letting him fill my soul like he used to when we were best friends.

He pulls back cupping my face in his hands. I moan and close my eyes. Tears leak through my eyelids.

"I love you, State, I've always loved you." I let it all out. "I've missed you every single day of my life. I dream about you every night and our dumb games we use to play. My favorite dream is hanging out with you at our spot in the park. God, I love you, State."

He brushes his thumb over my bottom lip. "Stay with me, Baylor, don't run."

I finally open my eyes and look at him. "You have a new life and deserve it more than anything. I'll always love you."

It takes everything in me to stand up and walk away from the only man I've ever loved.

Chapter 7

The pads of my fingers run over my bottom lip and I want to cry. I still feel him on me. Smell his new scent and see the hurt running through his eyes.

"Baylor, you okay?"

I look over to Miss Tami helping Rowe open her new princess movie.

"Fine, why?" I drop my hand down to my lap.

"Are you sure?" She presses.

I'm a damn fool. The woman can read me better than anyone and there's no way of tricking her.

"We'll talk later," I offer with a half shrug.

I'm thankful she drops the topic and helps Rowe put in the DVD.

"Popcorn," Rowe squeals, clapping her hands together.

I hop up from my State trance and make my way to her. "I'll get it, sweetie."

My arms wrap her up in a tight hug and I kiss the top of her head. A princess movie marathon and Rowe are the perfect distractions from the incident earlier today. I drove around forever after leaving my shift early. Alley, bless her heart, didn't even ask a question.

I holler from the quaint kitchen bathed in salmon pink tiles. "M&M's or no."

"M's." Rowe's excited voice floats through the house.

My phone lights up with a notification while I lean on the counter waiting for the microwave to ding.

Mr. Moore: Have any openings for a massage this week? Had to break up quite the cat fight between two second grade girls today.

I giggle.

Me: Pull a hammy?

Mr. Moore: Something like that.

Mr. Moore: I know I only have your number for emergency purposes. I hope this is okay.

Me: No worries. It's fine.

He's a rapid-fire texter and I forget all about the popcorn, M&M's, and princesses.

Mr. Moore: Great.

Me: I have tomorrow at 4:45. Is that enough time to make it after work?

Mr. Moore: I'll be there. But I'm thinking it's a glute muscle that needs worked on.

Me: Are you sure you just don't want it pinched.

Mr. Moore: I'm pleading the fifth.

I laugh like a lunatic, set down the phone, and fix the popcorn before Rowe busts me. I have no idea why it's so easy to talk to Mr. Moore. Maybe it's because I know there's no chance of anything happening, but he makes me feel halfway normal like a twenty-two year old should.

Me: See you then. Off to a princess marathon with the fairest of them all.

Mr. Moore: So jealous

Mr. Moore: God, that came across needy, eh?

Me: Just working on your prince swagger.

He doesn't respond and there's no sight of the three dancing bubbles in our text thread, so I grab the three bowls and head for the living room. Princess Rowe is in my seat with her hands in her lap and hypnotized by the previews. I give Miss Tami her bowl, but she clutches my hand before I can back away.

"What happened?" She eyes me.

"I, uh, I ran into…"

"Baylor, are you okay. Please just tell me that."

I nod my head up and down. "I'm fine. It's just that…Fuck, I can't say it."

She slaps my shoulder. "Language."

"Ouch, you mean woman."

She raises her eyebrows at me.

"Can we talk in the morning? I don't have it in me tonight."

"I love you, Baylor."

"Love you, too, child hitter."

She slaps me again and I giggle.

"Sissy."

I turn to see Rowe who is now perched up on the arm of my chair. I settle in next to her, extend the recliner, pull her into my lap, and cozy on in. We have our favorite blanket spread across us and both dive into our sweet and salty treat. My phone dings with a text, but I ignore it.

Way too fast, my eyes grow heavy. Seeing Tangled for the thousandth time just doesn't hold my interest. Rowe earned a new DVD since she wore out the last one. And truth be told, I want nothing more than to drift off to sleep to see State again.

Darkness hits me, and I'm magically swept off to dream land and State. We're not little kids anymore, but adults kissing and catching up.

Way too soon sweet little giggles bring me from slumber. When I pry open my eyes Rowe has my phone in her little hands and laughing way too hard.

"What are you doing?"

"Look."

She has my Snapchat app open and a picture of her as a dog with her tongue hanging out. I only have the stupid app for Rowe to play on. It entertains her for hours making silly pictures and videos to send Miss Tami. She's my only contact in the app. I'm not sure who enjoys making ridiculous Snaps more, Miss Tami or Rowe.

My phone chirps with a text and I see Mr. Moore's name at the top.

"He texted back."

"Rowe." I grab the phone from her and scroll up to my last text to him.

Mr. Moore: Sorry, had a school board meeting.

Me: Will you marry me?

Mr. Moore: Rowe?

Me: No, this is sissy.

Mr. Moore: I see.

The next picture text makes me gasp out loud and then shudder in horror. It's of me with my head bent backwards, mouth wide open, and a clear shot of my nostrils.

Mr. Moore: LOL

Me: See it's me.

Mr. Moore: I see.

Several more pictures of me in the same position with popcorn up my nose and balancing on my lips are sent. Mr. Moore must be laughing like a lunatic because he only comments with LOL's.

"Why did you let her do this?" I stare at Miss Tami.

"I told her she could only do it if she spelled everything out."

I look down at the lapsed time between texts and can tell Miss Tami had to probably spell out most of the words and it's probably why Rowe reverted to picture texting.

The last picture is a Snap Chat pic of me with a bright yellow daisy framing my gaping piehole.

Me: This is the real Baylor. Princess Trouble Pants has been having some fun I see.

Mr. Moore: Quite entertaining that Princess is.

Me: Good Night! PS- My phone is going under lock and key.

Mr. Moore: Smart move.

Me: Moon (emoticon)

I only remain silently embarrassed for a few moments, but then busy myself tucking Princess Trouble Pants into bed. There's no way I could be mad at Rowe. Actually, it was funny as hell and would've even been funnier if it wasn't my gaping hippo mouth in the pictures, not to even mention my nose hairs.

"Baylor."

"Rowe." I leap on her bed and snuggle into her.

"Will you sleep with me tonight?"

"Yes." I tap the tip of her nose. "What's up?"

"Just a bit spooked."

"Why? I mean you do have the coolest sister in the entire world."

"Are you sure I'm your sister?"

"Double promise, hop scotch, with butter on top, Pop-Tart princess promise."

"I love you, Baylor, so much." She wraps her hand around my neck and squeezes me tight.

"You make my world perfect, Rowe."

"Tell me one of your stories when you were little. You know the ones you tell me with your best friend?"

I generally love telling her embellished stories about State and I growing up, but tonight it squeezes my heart in all the wrong ways.

"Let me see." I pause for a bit.

"I really love the ice cream one where he was the prince and nailed those bullies in the nuts."

Like I said, they're embellished a lot. I try to open my mouth to share a time at the park, but his scent hits me and his sorrowful brown eyes gut me.

"Did you love him, Sissy?" She asks out of the blue.

"I do love him, so much, Rowe." I squeeze her tight to me.

"Let's go on an adventure and find him. We can get cool spy glasses and take our wands."

"What if he doesn't want to be found?" I ask.

"That boy is going to want you and your big butt."

I laugh hard this time at her frank honesty. I do have a big ass.

"Okay, one time we were at our favorite magical forest, set in a corner of a park on King's street. I was boiling up a witch's brew to give the mean kids in the class."

"What kind?" She perks up.

"The kind that makes them grow goat horns and oink like a pig when they say mean things."

"Ooohhh."

"State was busy shining his armor and sketching out…"

I never bring up football in front of her. It's an automatic trigger for her.

I begin again. "Sketching out his next enemy raid. We waited for hours in the magical land and passed the time by playing tic-tac-toe on the cement. State threw a fit when I kept winning, always claiming I was cheating. I pulled out my paper UNO cards and whipped him in another game."

Rowe's grip around me loosens and her little lids flutter off to dreamland. I'm thankful because every word about State hurts. I smooth down her messy hair and kiss her forehead.

"I'll give you the world, Rowe, you deserve it and so much more."

When I study her relaxed and sleeping features I see so much of me in her. I didn't have a disability, but just inverted in my own self and refused to talk. We were both hurt by others with no one to fight for us until Miss Tami.

I love this girl so much it pains me. A reflection of a young Baylor stares back at me and tears leak down my face. I cry for all the lost children in the world who never had a State or Miss Tami. None of it's fair.

Chapter 8

3:45 and my palms are sweaty. What is wrong with me? This is my job not a damn circus show. I fight to finish up my last massage before Mr. Moore comes in. I should be excited and a bundle of nerves for him and the potential outcome, but the truth is my heart belongs to someone else.

It took me running into State to realize it. I've never felt whole since the day he left the orphanage. I know it wasn't his fault and in all actuality my life was saved as well. But it was never the same without him in it. When he held me yesterday, everything melted away in his arms. I was time warped back to our childhood days in Kings. I've never wanted to go back there, but now it's all I can think about.

Everything about State is bigger. His smile, his muscles, and his pull on me. When we were little he was never handsome to me because he was always just State, my best friend. But yesterday I saw the most beautiful man I've ever seen. His body is an empire of perfectly sculpted muscles bound together with beauty.

I shake him from my thoughts and clean up my small space for my next appointment. There's about thirty minutes to wait, so I work on an assignment. The intense assignment fades away yesterday and the thoughts of going back to work.

"Baylor." A light knocking and my name rolling out in a deep voice catches my attention.

I readjust my "Superman" style glasses on the bridge of my nose and look up to Mr. Moore.

"I'm so sorry." I stand running my hands down the front of my thighs. "I lost track of time."

He points to my laptop.

"School work," I offer.

"Good girl. Makes the principal in me happy." He shines with a friendly smile.

The man is really nice on the eyes and is genuinely kind to me.

"I'm always juggling," I joke and follow it up with a weak laugh.

"Living the dream, I see."

"Yeah." I brush back my hair, feeling nervous all of a sudden. "Well, you didn't come here for chit-chat. Let me grab you a robe and get you set up."

"We could grab coffee if you'd prefer."

"Oh, that's too nice of you, but sounds like you're need of a good massage."

"That I am." He grabs the robe from me and heads for the bathroom in my area.

I slap my forehead causing a loud smacking sound. Damn, could I sound like a bigger idiot? I'm so awkward and attribute it to my odd desire, or the lack there of, for the opposite sex. It's easy talking to him at school with Rowe's hand in mine and even easier texting.

When Mr. Moore appears from the bathroom in a white robe, I shake a bit. His tan skin is a great compliment to the bright white robe.

"I'm a virgin here. I left my boxers on, is that okay?"

I fumble for words before something coherent comes out. "Uh, yeah. I'll, um, work on your back and shoulders today to ease you in."

"Perfect." He smiles at me like he's sensing my nervousness.

I relax a bit when he lies face down on the table. I didn't even realize he took off the robe before he laid down. My mind begins comparing him to State. His shoulders aren't as broad and his muscles aren't as well developed. Mr. Moore is packing some buns though. Holy hell!

"Do you prefer a scent?"

"I don't think so." His words are a bit muffled. "Am I laying right? I've only seen this in movies."

"Perfect. Are you comfortable?"

"Yes."

I queue the calming music, dim the lights, and lather my hands in a new coconut oil rub I've just bought and begin to lightly massage his shoulders. They're incredibly tense and will require some deeper work in a later appointment.

"Let me know if anything hurts, okay?" I continue working my hands over his skin. "I'll try to loosen some of these muscles."

"Damn, that feels good."

I blush with his compliment. It's all really stupid, he's just another client, and hundreds have told me the same thing.

"Excellent. Just relax and enjoy."

I pay attention to both of his shoulders, tying my hands together down his back. I'm thankful when he stays silent the remainder of the time. It avoids all kind of weird conversation and awkward feelings brewing in me. Toward the end, I'm pretty sure I hear light snores coming from him.

I wash my hands and sanitize the area while he dresses back into his button up shirt and khakis. I have everything put up and ready to go before he exits. I texted Alley earlier this morning asking to switch shifts at bar. There's no way in the hell my heart can handle seeing State two days in a row. I mean, it's not like he's going to come back for me or anything. It's just a chance I want to avoid if, there even is one.

"There's going to be a lot of unhappy people when you get that degree, Baylor."

I look up from twiddling fingers to Mr. Moore dressed in all his glory.

"Thanks." I give him a half smile. "It will be a while, trust me."

And that's the fucking truth, at this point I may never get my degree with my pace of classes.

"I doubt that. You seem to go after what you want."

I laugh out loud at his last comment because he really has no idea who I am. I've grown up to fool the world, with the help of Miss Tami, but I'm polite back.

"Thank you," I say.

He pulls his wallet from his back pocket and digs around in it.

"This one is on me for always taking such amazing care of Rowe."

"Nope." His one word reply is certain.

"Seriously, I mean it. I can never tell you how much I appreciate it."

"It's not a hard job at all, Baylor. I love that little girl and, honestly, every morning that she runs up to me makes my day a bit brighter."

"She definitely has that effect." I smile, all of a sudden missing her.

"Baylor?" He runs his hands through his sandy blond hair leaving it standing on end.

"Yeah." I can't make myself look him in the eyes, so I busy myself fiddling with my teal chevron messenger bag.

"Would you like to have dinner with me sometime?"

Chills run up my spine. He's a nice guy, but I have no desire to entertain this thought. "I really don't get much free time these days."

"Yeah, you're right I don't either." He's defeated and I feel like an asshole.

"I'll let you know if I ever have an opening," I offer.

"Great. I'll work on Rowe to see if you can get an opening."

"Sorry, I didn't mean for it to come out that way." I shrug hopelessly. "And you know if you tell her she'll have our wedding planned out with matching crowns and tiaras."

We both share a good laugh as we walk out in to the parking lot and before we part ways he grabs my hand.

"Baylor, I'm very serious about wanting to take you out."

"Okay." I look down at the scuffed up tip of my favorite black pair of Converse.

He brushes the hair dancing in my face back, cups my cheek, and guides me to look at him.

"I'm trying not to be too forward here, but Baylor you're gorgeous with a huge heart, and I'd love to get to know you better."

"You won't like what you get to know."

"That's my decision, Baylor, not yours."

"You're not going to give up, are you?"

"Doesn't seem like it." He pulls his hand back since I'm staring at him. "But I'm not a creeper or stalker in any way. I'll always respect your boundaries."

"Okay, let me think about it, and just know it has nothing to do with you and everything to do with me."

"I get it." He takes a step back. "Give my princess a hug for me."

"Will do." I wave to him and then slump in my car knowing the date will never happen.

I feel as broken and shattered as I did the day State left me and I can't control it.

Chapter 9

"Damn the tips were on fire tonight," I say, giving a portion of mine to the bartender and cooks. Just keeping the cycle positive and well-oiled.

"Baylor, can I talk to you?" Alley peeks from her office.

"Yep, let me finish stocking the napkins and I'll be there."

I know I'm not in trouble, but can't force the fear out of my belly. Just like every time I was called to the principal's office in grade school. I was never in trouble, but always felt like I was.

I wipe my hands on my shorts after filling the napkin dispenser and peek into her office. "Hey."

"Have a seat Baylor?"

I take the one across from her in her sports decorated office. "Am I getting fired?"

"Hell to the no, dumbass." She laughs hard at my question.

"Well, you're scaring the shit out of me, Boss Woman."

"One, if I ever fired you, Miss Tami would cut my lady nuts, and two, you're one of my hardest and most productive workers. Three, everyone loves you here."

"Then spill already. I'm about to stroke out here."

Alley leans back in her chair and kicks her feet up on her desk. "Let's get real for a second here, Baylor. I'm not going to hold back."

I swallow hard thinking these words might be worse than actually being fired.

"You know that man that had you so shook up a few days back?"

My world spins and I want to bolt, but I'm caught in a trap, so I only nod.

"He's been back here twice looking for you. He wants to know where you live, but see, I can't give out that information."

"Okay." I clutch to the hem of my shorts, letting my fingernails dig into my flesh.

"Who is he?"

"Nobody," I answer quickly.

"Bullshit. I'm not your boss right now. I'm your friend. The joint is closed and we are sitting here as friends."

I shake my head side-to-side, feeling the tears well up in my eyes. "He's nobody."

"I could go to Miss Tami, but wanted to talk to you first. If you could look in the mirror right now you might convince yourself he's not a nobody."

"He's my past."

"How past?" She asks.

"Kings' past. He left me."

"The second time I had to turn him away, he was teared up just like you are sitting there. He beat the shit out of guy in the parking lot. His buddy begged me not to call the cops."

"Why did he beat someone up?" I ask.

"He's pissed and wants to find you. His buddy said he has quite the temper that he struggles to control."

"He does," I admit while drifting back to all the times he protected me with his fists.

"Friendly advice from a person who has been around the block a few times. Hear him out."

"I can't."

"Why?" She presses.

I blow out of my seat with my hands flying in the air and tears streaming down my face. "Because he's my past. He WAS my best friend and we were torn apart. He has a new life and I'm not in it, nor do I belong in it."

"That's not your choice, Baylor. The man needs you."

"I needed him time and time again, but he left." I fall to my knees and wail out the hatred. Yes, hate for the way things went down between State and I. Alley wraps me in her arms, soothing down my hair, and rocking me until I'm able to drive home.

Chapter 10

"Alley called me last night." Miss Tami begins picking up the table.

"Nice," I reply, trying to act cool.

"She's worried about you."

"It's fine." I grab the casserole dish helping her with dishes.

I've escaped the topic of State until now and it seems the time has come to spill. Miss Tami will be pissed if I don't tell her. She loved State as much as I did, and she'll also be disappointed in me for running from my problems. What can I say? It's a bad habit I can't kick.

"Want to talk?" She asks, turning on the hot water to the sink.

"No, there's nothing to talk about. It's a closed book."

She bites her bottom lip, keeping in the words she really wants to say because Rowe just rushed in.

"Spoon. Spoon." She reaches her little hand up to the Jell-O salad.

I hoist her up to the counter and scoot her back until her heels are on top. I hand her the spoon and push the nearly finished Jell-O bowl towards her. Rowe is her own dishwasher with certain dishes.

"We're not done talking about this," Miss Tami warns me.

I slam my hand on the counter and don't miss the fact I startled Rowe. "We are."

My voice is harsh and hurtful, and I immediately regret it. Rowe begins sobbing and I feel like an even bigger piece of shit.

"I'm sorry." I ball my fists at my side. "I'm sorry, Rowe, I shouldn't have done that."

"Don't be mean, that scares me." She wipes the tears from under eyes.

I go to her and pull her to my chest. "I'm so sorry. That was wrong of me."

I stare at Miss Tami while talking to Rowe.

"Let's just finish cleaning up." Miss Tami turns her back to us while busying herself with the dishes. "You girls put stuff away in the fridge."

"Can you help me with that?"

She sniffles. "Yes."

I'm thankful she doesn't bring up the topic again, and before bathing Rowe I apologize to her and do my best job of explaining my reasoning. It's foolish I know, but where I'm at right now.

The doorbell rings.

"I'll get it," Miss Tami sings out. "Delores is bringing over a new yarn for me tonight."

I hear her open the door and greet the person into the house. Delores has a very deep and muffled voice. Miss Tami squeals loudly and I know something is off.

"I'll be right back. Get dressed in your PJs." I kiss the top of Rowe's head before leaving the room.

When I round the corner, I freeze in my step with the sight before me. It's State hugging Miss Tami with one arm and a huge bouquet in the other.

"I swear my eyes are playing tricks on me," she squeals practically hanging from his neck.

His hearty chuckle fills the house and warms my insides. He's here. State is really here in my house.

"Sorry, I would've called, but didn't have a number."

"You never have to call, State, you're family. Come in." She closes the door behind him and that's when we lock eyes.

His smile goes on for days while his eyes bore holes in mine. His scent hits me from across the room. He's dressed in gym shorts and a University of Florida football t-shirt with a gator chomping on a football.

"Baylor." His deep voice hypnotizes me. "I got these for you."

"Those are gorgeous." Miss Tami claps her hands together. "I'll put them in water."

She takes them and rushes into the kitchen.

"What are you doing here?" My words are cold.

"I have to see you, Baylor."

"No."

"Yes." He takes a step closer to me. "Why are you avoiding this?"

"Because you have a new life."

He clasps his hands behind his head and grows pissed off. "Are you an idiot?"

His insult hurts and cuts deep. He's never said a cruel word to me, but I don't show the effect it has on me.

"I guess so if that's what you want to call it." I shrug. "You have a new life and world. Go live it."

I leave out the girlfriend part, but aim loaded to throw that in his face too.

"There's no life without you. My world has been black and white since the day we were torn apart. You color my world. You're my second half, Baylor."

"You never looked for me."

"You don't know that." He steps in closer until his chest is pressing into me. "I looked. You didn't."

"You're right, I didn't. You're better off without me and our past."

"You're wrong. I need you. You complete me." He cups my face in his huge palm and I melt into it.

Like so many times before when I burrowed into him for protection, loyalty, and friendship.

"My lips can't get you out of my head. I've felt you on me since finding each other the other day."

I close my eyes and feel everything inside of me shatter. All my barriers begin to crumble, the walls fade away, and the buried core of me comes to life. I reach up on my tiptoes needing to feel him again.

"Kiss me, State."

He bends down tentatively and covers my lips with his. It's me this time who moves first kissing him back, darting my tongue out, and taking advantage of his mouth. I moan in pleasure and grow confused with my actions. All I know in this moment is that State is in my house, has me wrapped up in my arms, and is kissing the hell out of me.

We both pull away when we hear Miss Tami rushing back in to join us. State steps back and adjusts the crotch of his shorts. My eyes follow his hand and stay mesmerized on the bulge pushing through the thin material.

But we were just friends.

"Come have a seat, State." Tami points to the couch.

"Princess Sissy," Rowe sings out rounding the corner.

She throws her head to look up to State. He easily towers all of us girls. She scrambles to me, clutching my leg, and begins screaming in fear.

"Hey." I bend down to her and pick her up. She's near the point of not being able to be picked up anymore. She locks her legs around my middle and buries her head in my neck, screaming to high hell.

"Football. Bad men. Football. Hurt Rowe."

Oh shit, the football on his shirt.

"Hey, hey, hey." I bounce her softly and rub her back. "This is State. he's my friend. He's a good guy."

"No. Football. No."

A warm sensation flows between Rowe and me. I can hear the urine dribble down on the hardwood floor. I look up into State's eyes and follow his vision. He stares at the urine and our coated bodies. I'm instantly reverted right back to my younger years of fear.

"Oh shit, I'll go." He holds his hands up with hurt in his voice.

"No." It comes out panicked. I need him right now. "Take off your shirt, please."

He looks at me as if I've lost my damn mind. "Just do it. I'll be right back. Miss Tami will fill you in."

I rush into the bathroom between Rowe's room and mine, and start a tub of water.

"Rowe, you're okay. Look up."

She's still sobbing and yelling out gibberish.

"Baby, look up."

It takes her several minutes to look up from my neck. A wave of relief washes over her features, but her sobs still control her little body.

"He's bad guy."

I shake my head side-to-side, knowing she's in a real panic attack with her short sentences.

"No, he's my friend." I comb my fingers through her hair. "He used to be my best friend when I was your age."

"Bad guys play football."

"No, baby. Remember bad guys can be anywhere."

We've been working with her on this for some time now, but it's her one trigger she can't get past. I strip her wet panties and princess nightgown, and place her in the tub.

"Don't let me go, sissy."

"I'm right here."

"No." She shakes her little head in my direction.

I bend down on my knees and put both arms in the water. "Miss Tami and I will always keep you safe. Do you trust me?"

She shrugs her shaky shoulders.

"I princess promise you on top of Pop Tarts, I'll do everything to protect you." I run my soapy hand up her back. "Football isn't bad, sweetie."

"I'm scared."

"I know, honey, I'm here."

I soap her all up and re-wash her hair before taking her from the tub. I make a show of wrapping her up in her favorite princess towel that has a hood. I sing and hum to her while I dress her, and feel Rowe relax.

Kneeling down, I ask her. "Are you ready to meet my best friend?"

She nods her head slowly. "But hold my hand?"

"Always."

The sound of Miss Tami and State talking fills the house. Her voice is full of excitement and love, and it makes me feel selfish for keeping him from her. She loves him just like she loves me and I was an asshole for telling him to leave at the bar.

"We're back," I announce as we round the corner.

I look down to Rowe who has her eyes covered while peeking between two of her fingers.

"Hey," State says, standing to his feet.

"State, I'd like to introduce you to the fairest princess of this castle. Meet Rowe."

He walks toward us and Rowe steps back widening her fingers to look up at State. The man towers over me by a good two feet, so I can't imagine how he looks to her.

"Doesn't he kind of remind you of Shrek?" I ask, squeezing her hand in mine.

She nods and then giggles.

"Shrek, really Baylor? I'm offended." He splays his palm over his bare chest.

"Hey, Shrek's a good guy," Rowe pipes up.

"Then Shrek is good." He kneels before Rowe.

His broad shoulders fill our space, his romantic manly scent assaults me, and then I realize he's shirtless. Those muscles that I thought were sculpted aren't, because he's damn well chiseled with little to no body fat.

"Nice to meet you, Rowe, I'm Shrek." He holds out his hand to her.

I have to stop myself from bending down and encouraging her interaction. Miss Tami has told me over and over again that we need to push Rowe just a bit out of her comfort zone so she learns how to cope in uncomfortable situations.

I drop her hand and am shocked when she lets go so easily, but she's quick to wrap her little arm around the back of my leg.

"Ouch. That's pokey." She points to my leg and places her hands in front of her.

She jumps a bit when a deep baritone laugh erupts from State. It takes her several more moments before she reaches her hand out to take his. They do the cutest little handshake. State's hand makes her tiny one disappear into his large palm.

"I prefer secret handshakes. Want to make one up?"

She nods excitedly.

"Baylor close your eyes." He looks up at me with a grin.

I make a huff of disapproval, but finally cover my eyes. I hear them rehearsing it and then finally nailing it.

"Where did that football man go?" She asks.

State and I both stall, not knowing which direction to look or even how to handle this. Miss Tami steps in to save us.

"Come sit on my lap, sweetie and I'll explain it."

Rowe rushes over to her, jumping up in her lap still unsure of everything going down. State rises up to his feet and stands by me. He clutches my pinky in his, but I don't have the courage to look up at him yet. All I know is that it feels good. Really good.

"You know how my job used to be to help kids?"

She nods.

"I helped State when he was a little boy. He and Baylor were best friends."

"Are they getting married?" She asks in a nervous voice.

"No, sweetie. State loves football. He loved it when he was little, like you love princesses. He's a good guy."

"Okay." Her voice is so small and leery.

"Is it okay if he watches a movie with us tonight?"

"Will you and Sissy be here?"

"Always."

"I'll try." She finally nods while leaping off of Tami's lap and bounding over to me.

"You have to sit over there on the couch and my sissy and I will sit on that chair." She points.

"Deal." State nods, drops my pinky, and walks away.

A guttural gasp escapes me at the sight of his back. My palms slap over my mouth to cover the noise. State looks over his shoulder and winks at me. He has scars all over his back. Thick, deep, and long ones cover his skin, but those aren't what holds my attention.

It's six letters that are printed across the top of his back in a delicate font that contrast his beastly body. *Baylor*

"That's your name," Rowe squeals.

"That it is."

Chapter 11

Rowe is passed out in my arms only a quarter of the way through *Frozen*.

"State can you pack her to bed and then I'll give you and Baylor some time."

"I got her," I say, trying to stand up and balance her in my arms, but the motion of the rocking recliner makes it a real struggle.

State is up and on his feet in a matter of seconds, scooping her into his arms.

"She's precious," he says, staring down at her.

"Let me be by your side in case she stirs."

He nods. "Lead the way."

He lets out a light growl when I walk in front of him and it confuses me. State is gently laying Rowe in her bed and bringing her covers up to her chin. I give her a light kiss before backing out of the bedroom.

Once in the hall, I whisper thank you to him.

"Baylor, you have no idea how happy I am to be here. None."

I don't know how to respond, so I don't and walk back out into the living room.

Miss Tami is standing at the door. "I'm just going to go on over to Delores' to grab that yarn."

"Are you sure?" I ask. "I don't like you out after dark."

"She lives in a good neighborhood. I'll be fine." She shuts the door before I have chance to talk.

State and I are left in the living room staring at each other. I know he's a grown man now with a new life, but when I study his brown eyes, I see the friend I once knew.

"What now?" I ask, wringing my fingers. "Uno? I have real cards."

He laughs. "You cheat."

"Do not." I push his chest.

"Can we talk?"

I nod and head for the couch, but State cuts me off and plops down on it dragging me into his lap.

"Just let me hold you, please."

His last few words hitch deep in his throat and then I feel tears falling on the top of my shoulders. When I look up to him, he's crying silently.

"Don't." I try to wipe the tears from his eyes.

"I can already tell you hate me, Baylor, I'd take it all back if I could."

"I don't hate you. It's just that I lost you and I hate that."

"You have no idea what I did and who I became to try to get back to you."

"We'll never get the past back." I cringe saying the words because why in the hell would we want to be put back in that hellhole.

"Just let me hold you before you tell me to leave again."

I press on his chest before he has the chance to hug me to him again. "What about your girlfriend?"

He looks confused.

"The blonde who was practically dry humping you at Alley's?"

"I don't have a girlfriend. Never have."

"She was touching you."

"She wants to be my girlfriend. She has since we were freshman."

"Oh."

I collapse down onto his chest and let him hold me. I fight to keep my tears back, all of them, and it's not an easy battle. I take the time to relish in everything State. My mind floats back and forth between the boy who was my whole world, to the man who's sitting here now.

His body has morphed into a castle of perfection, but the remnants of my best friend linger within him. He's still gentle, still has that same dazzling smile, and he still knows me. He didn't forget me, and that thought nails me in the gut.

"You okay?" He runs his enormous palm over my head.

I don't look up at him and only nod into his chest.

"Still not much of a talker?"

With as much courage as I can muster, I look up at him and plant my palms on his chest. "Not since I lost my best friend."

"I'm here." He bites down on his bottom lip. "Don't you see that?"

"I do." I whisper while digging my fingertips into his smooth skin.

"Can I talk?" He hugs me closer. "I'm not sure if you even want me here, but let me talk, Baylor."

"I want you here."

I cringe and have to stop myself from slapping my palm over my mouth.

"Well, that's a start." He brushes my hair back from my face. "Look at me."

I look back up at him and offer up a weak smile. State flashes back a panty melting one to me. My brain swims in confusion with his manly gorgeousness after so many years of passing. The man could be a damn runway model.

"Thank you." He brushes the pad of his thumb over my jaw. "Sorry, I can't quit touching you."

His voice is full of pain and love, and my dumb body and soul have no idea how to comprehend it, let alone speak.

"I fought to get back to you, Baylor. I was kicked out of four schools, went through counselor after counselor, but my parents refused to give up. The more they refused, the more guilt I wore for having a caring home."

"State, stop." I push up from him. "You have no idea how happy I am that you had amazing loving people in your life, or at least that's what they sound like. It's just…" I pause thinking how to word this the right way.

"Just what?" He urges.

"I'm a jealous asshole. I wanted you in my life."

"I'm a greedy prick then, because it makes me feel good to know that."

A nervous giggle escapes me.

"I finally focused all my energy into football through middle and high school, and now college."

"Shocker." I roll my eyes.

"Haven't had a better friend to practice with than you."

"Whatever, you liked crushing my fingers! Damn, I wouldn't dare catch a ball from you now." I let my vision roam up and down the empire of muscles known as State.

"We'll see about that." His fingers dig into my hips making me want to melt into him. "Anyway, I was raised in Tennessee."

"Tennessee?" I had to have heard him wrong.

"Yeah. Baylor, if I was anywhere near here, it would've been easier to find you."

I find the courage to raise my hands to his face, dragging my finger tip down his harsh jawline. "We were kids."

"We were, but Baylor no matter what happens, from here on out, please know I never forgot you. Hell, I talked to the moon every night knowing you're possibly looking at the same one."

"You're weird." I try to break up the way too intense direction our conversation is flowing.

"You're my home. Always have been." He closes his eyes. "The mansion I grew up in and the money that surrounded me, never even came close. Baylor, you've always been my home, my best friend, and you own me."

I speak with authority for possibly the first time in my life. "That means everything to me, State. I've never forgotten us, made any new real friends, or…"

I think about it for a second before blurting it out.

"Loved anyone like I love you."

Both of his large palms clutch to my cheeks and pull me to his face. I don't close my eyes and just stare into the depths of his brown ones. Our lips brush each other before we kiss. It takes me back to King's when I'd hide my face in his chest, fighting to forget the hell surrounding us.

"I'm going to kiss you, Baylor."

I nod my head, letting my lips brush up and down on his. He doesn't lie when he admits to kissing me. I'm flipped down on the couch with my back pushing into the cushions. State's frame envelopes me, but he keeps most of his weight on his shoulders. My palms dig into his back, urging him to put more of his weight on me.

"You're my home, State." I pull harder on his back and he finally gives in a bit.

His lips are on mine, kissing me hard and rough. We spend a long time exploring each other's mouths before pulling back, and we're both left breathless.

"I'm never leaving you again."

Instead of pushing him away this time, my arms snake around the back of his neck, and tug him down closer to me until our lips are brushing each other again.

"You have a new life."

"You do too," he argues.

"You saw it tonight. I have a feeling you're a star."

He smirks against my lips and I know what's coming. "I've always loved you and football. I took all the pain and hurt in my life, and put it into the game. So yeah, I'm pretty damn good."

"I don't want to bring you down."

"Then don't and let me in, Baylor."

"Time. Give me time."

"Only if you promise not to run away from me."

I smile and feel his lips smile right back on mine. "I hate that word."

"Weird."

"Every time I heard it, it broke my heart because you were gone."

"I want to hate, be bitter, go back to King's and knock some heads, but I know it wouldn't fix a thing. It all happened for a reason."

He never gives me a chance to ask why or even take a blind guess.

"Because of us, Baylor. We're survivors and reunited."

Chapter 12

"How are you not fat?" I poke at his abs, thankful he hasn't put his shirt back on.

"Skills, babe, mad ass skills."

He brought me a tub of bubble gum ice cream from a creamery near his dorm. I've only managed a few spoonfuls, while he's licked the inside of the tub clean.

"Do you have to run like two hundred miles to burn that off?"

We're sitting cross-legged on my bed facing each other. We decided the couch wasn't the most appropriate place for us tonight when Miss Tami walked in on us a few hours into our make-out session. His lips are more talented than I remember his catching skills to be, and that's saying a lot.

"I have a question for you, Baylor." The light tone of our conversation has disappeared.

"Eh?"

"I have a team barbecue tomorrow at my coach's house and I want you to go."

"Oh, hell no." I don't even think about my response.

"Why?" He places the container on the floor.

"There's at least one thousand reasons."

"Hit me with the first one."

"I don't belong there."

"Bullshit. The next reason." He covers my kneecaps, stilling the slight shivers taking over.

"I might be doing okay right now, in my home, and it's because of you, but I put the capital A in awkward. It's something I've never overcome."

"Bullshit, I watched you dance in the middle of a bar."

"Miss Tami knows the owner and…"

"Next."

"Homework. I have homework and Rowe, and homework."

"So, you're saying it's a yes."

"State."

"My parents will be there and all my teammates. I want and need you there."

I bite on my fingernails that are already way too short and my teeth border chewing live flesh. "I want to, but…"

"Perfect, I'll pick you up at six."

"State."

"Nope, you just promised."

"I did not!"

"Did not, what?"

"Promise."

"You just did now." State climbs over me, pulling me into his hard chest until we are face to face.

I roll my eyes and feel the ache in my lips that want him so damn bad. "I want to kiss you, but know we won't stop."

He growls in agreement.

"Hey, State, what have all your girlfriends thought of my name on your back."

"Don't know."

"How do you now know?"

"I've never had one."

Those four words hit my gut hard leaving me speechless.

"Never wanted one, was waiting until I found you."

"Holy shit," I whisper.

"Can I be honest, Baylor?"

I nod wrapping my arm around his side. It's addicting.

"When I saw Rowe, I thought she was your daughter and even though she kept calling you sissy, I couldn't get past it. It wasn't until Miss Tami told me all about her when you were bathing her."

"She's kind of like my daughter."

"I can tell."

"I love her so damn much."

"Any of those fuckers who hurt her better never come on my radar."

I smile and kiss him, but quickly pulling away. "Always the protector."

"I'll always protect my girls."

I let those words simmer in my mind. He's in no position to take on a relationship with me, not to mention Rowe, but I'm not one to argue.

"You have no idea how big of a deal it was for Rowe to warm up to you."

"Yeah?"

"She's been so traumatized, but has made so much progress."

"How couldn't she with you and Miss Tami."

I offer him a weak smile. "It's more Miss Tami. I tend to baby and protect her too much."

"No such thing." He kisses me quickly again. "How long have you lived here?"

I smoothly flatten a crease of worry from his forehead with my finger. "It took her nearly a year and half to officially adopt me."

"You had to stay there that long?"

His face morphs into a mixture of anger and hurt.

"No, bounced through three foster homes." I shrug. "They all thought I was creepy because I didn't talk and well, uh, I still had the nervous peeing my pants problem."

"Oh, baby." He kisses me again.

Each time his lips touch mine, I fall even harder for State. Deeper in our friendship, and the strange blossom of raw need seeded low in my stomach.

"I won't lie to you State, but I don't want you to feel guilt."

I wait for him to respond, but he doesn't.

"The foster homes were hell. I hated them and the parents were terrible, not to mention the other kids in the homes."

"Did they hurt you?"

I shake my head side-to-side making sure to brush his lips. "Nothing hurt anymore after the day I lost you."

His arms wrap around me in an unforgiving hug, until both of our breathing evens out.

Chapter 13

"Shrek. Fiona."

A sweet little voice pulls me from the best sleep of my life, but I can't move under the protective and powerful arms.

"Where are the green babies?" Rowe climbs up on me peering down.

"Morning, baby girl." I wiggle an arm out to pull her down in the hug.

"Where are the babies?"

I notice State's eyes open and take in the scene.

"Uh?" I force the sleep from my eyes.

"When Shrek and Fiona finally fall in love they have cute, green babies."

"Oh, Rowe, you're forever a romantic." I squeeze her to my chest.

"Morning, Shrek." She giggles at some face State must give her.

"Let's get ready for the day, missy. Go brush your teeth and pick some cereal."

I'm surprised when she bounces off the bed and rushes to my bathroom. Even though she has one off of her room, she keeps everything in mine and loves sneaking into the little bit of make-up I have.

After we've washed the sleep from our eyes, and brushed our teeth and hair, we make it out to the living room. My heart slumps in my chest when I see my bed and no State. Panic threatens to strike, but I try to remember to breathe.

We round the corner to see State and Miss Tami sipping on coffee. It makes me smile to see them wrapped in an easy conversation. Never in my life did I think I'd feel these emotions again. It's a vortex of love, pain, and hurt seeing them together. It's my home that I chalked up to being shattered and gone forever.

"Captain Crunch or Cinnamon Toast Crunch, Rowe?" I ask her while still staring at State.

Rowe doesn't respond and bounds over to State, jumping up in his lap. I smile so large it pains my face, because he's wearing his football shirt. I'm sure he was uneasy walking around a house with three females, shirtless like a damn Greek God.

Rowe squeezes State's cheeks with her petite hands and tries to shake his head. "I want waffles."

She growls out the last word just like Donkey does on *Shrek*. We all erupt in laughter and make our way to the kitchen. State soon learns Rowe's different quirks in the kitchen, which basically consist of her being in charge in her own little way. She's to lick every spoon that's lickable, sit on the counter bossing, and to get the first taste. She's quite the little madam.

State indulges all of her demands with ease and goes about the kitchen with Miss Tami preparing the waffles. With my legs dangling from the dining room table, I watch the trio and get chills at how natural it is. And trust me, I don't miss the little grins Miss Tami keeps sending my way and even a damn wink. I'm not sure I've ever seen her so damn happy. It's as if she was floating on air.

We are complete with State in our life. I finish the last gulp of warm coffee and hop from the table. I pull syrup, butter, and fresh milk from the fridge and then set the table. I don't feel completely ditched when Rowe jumps up in my lap to eat. I'd almost wondered if she was going to go for State's.

The crew made an abundant stack of waffles and they disappear quickly. State smothers his in butter, peanut butter, and pounds of maple syrup. Rowe's not an adventurous eater, and shocks me when she dips her fork in the peanut butter and does her best job spreading it all over her waffle. I notice she doesn't eat that waffle and grabs another one, spreading it with her favorite freezer strawberry jam.

"Good girl," I whisper into her ear.

Everyone is full, except State, who polishes off the final waffles. I help Miss Tami clear the table and fill the dishwasher while Rowe lines up all her favorite princesses explaining their importance to State. He's a good sport, listening, and nodding with each of her voice inflections.

"So," Miss Tami whispers in my ear.

I give her a questioning look.

"Going good?" She nods over to State.

With my back to the princess parade, I whisper back to her. "He wants to take me to a team party."

"A what?"

"He plays for the University of Florida Gators and wants me to go the big team party at his coach's house before the season kicks off."

She claps her hands together loudly, and I cover my lips with my pointer finger.

"I'm not sure I want to go."

"Why?"

"I don't belong there."

"Enough. You'll go."

I revert to a bratty twelve-year old. "You're not my boss."

She calls my poker hand. "I'll tell Rowe and let her dress you."

"I can't do this." I grit out between my teeth.

"Looks like you were doing just fine last night and this morning."

"It's different. There's not a crowd of peers here. I feel left out, like I don't deserve to be there."

"We'll talk later, sweetie, but I have more confidence in this than anything else." She wraps me up in a tight hug.

"Baylor." A hand covers my shoulder and I turn to see State holding Rowe. "I need to get going. I'll pick you up at six?"

"Uh, I can meet you at Alley's? Isn't that closer for you?"

"I'll be here at six."

"State," I begin.

"She'll be ready." Miss Tami claps her hands proudly.

Rowe has a devious look on her face, and I know I'll be getting ready in the car for our date.

Chapter 14

5:56 the doorbell rings, sending Miss Tami and Rowe into full-action. They both race to the door and swing it wide open. State's towering stature fills the entire doorframe. My heart threatens to pound out of my chest, cracking my sternum on the way.

State's dressed in a blue plaid button-up shirt, paired with khaki shorts and sexy flip-flops. I study him from head to toe, taking him all in from the vein in his neck flexing and his clenched jaw. His eyes bore holes into me turning me into a puddle of goo. My best friend is here, but now I have a feeling we're stepping into so much more.

"Shrek," Rowe squeals throwing her arms up.

State bends down on one knee, and hands Rowe the miniature version of the larger bouquet of flowers in his hands. "For my princess."

He gives her a wink before she turns and sprints for me. Tears dabble the corner of her eyes. "He bought me flowers."

I smile down at her and whisper in her ear. "Tell him thank you."

Rowe bounds right back to him, wiping the tears that managed to leak from her eyes. "Thank you, Shrek. I love them."

Rowe studies the yellow rose petals not making eye contact and then begins petting them with her little fingers.

"You're so welcome." He lifts her chin with his finger. "I remembered Belle was your favorite and that's why they're yellow."

"You are a real prince."

"Rowe, can I tell you a secret?"

She nods and leans in. State whispers in her ear causing her head to bob up and down. We can't hear what he's saying, but he totally has her entranced.

When she finally pulls back, she tries to whisper, which never happens. "You promise?"

He places a finger over his lips and nods back to her.

Rowe's hand slams on her heart. "I've got to get water for these things."

Her voice is overdramatized, but it doesn't affect her joyous skip into the kitchen.

"I better go help her," Miss Tami says, hugging State before she rushes into the kitchen.

Glass clatters and doors slam as I can only imagine Rowe rifling around in her own personal tornado. Miss Tami talks lightly and the sound vanishes.

"You look gorgeous." State's deep voice pulls me from my trance.

His comment makes me immediately feel self-conscious. I knew letting Miss Tami talk me into a short white jean skirt that I've never worn was a bad decision. She also convinced me to wear a tight blue tank top since it's part of his school colors.

And God bless her heart, Rowe, helped with my make-up and hair. I laugh and point to my face and then hair.

"Rowe?" He asks.

"What gave it away?"

"The crown on your head, but I like it. You're royal and my queen." He walks up to me and hands me a bouquet of yellow roses.

My heart swells when I spot the yellow UNO card nestled in it. We may have been separated for over a decade, but it's like our souls never left each other. I pluck the card from the bouquet and flash it at him with a smile.

"You still a sore loser?"

He pulls me in, clutching my hip. "I don't lose, Baylor."

The meaning of his words are not lost on me. He's not going to give up on *me*, no matter how far I'm pushed from my comfort zone. The only question is will I be brave enough, or even strong enough, to handle it? I still lose my voice when I'm out of the safety of my daily routines. I always revert back to the little girl who never talked, avoiding all social interactions. It's taken years of being pushed by Miss Tami to find what I have now.

"I'm so nervous." I place my clammy palm in his.

"I can feel your heart pounding on my chest."

"Are you sure about all this?" I ask.

A hint of anger fires up in his whiskey colored eyes. "I have your name tattooed on my back, never have had a girlfriend, and can't stand the damn game UNO because it's too painful. I loved you as a best friend in King's and now, reconnecting? Baylor, I'm beyond certain I love you more than football."

He clutches my face. "It was all meant to be. We had to endure the ugly to get here, but I'm not letting go. I don't give a shit if you're nervous."

I look down at my toes peeking through my flat sandals. "Don't cuss at me."

"I'm sorry, but I don't know how to get through to you."

"Be patient." I clutch his pinky and bring it to my lips. "Please, be patient."

"Do you trust me, Baylor?"

I nod and pause for a moment. "I just don't trust myself or life."

"It will be our adventure then."

It takes a good twenty minutes of Rowe hugging us good-bye, and Miss Tami sending me messages to take a leap, before we escape. State wasn't lying about the wealth of his parents. We're seated in his blacked out Range Rover. The leather seats swallow me in; the chrome trim insides are beyond amazing. It's a perfect fit for State and accommodates his large frame. The music booms from the speaker system. I'm no expert in the radio and speaker division, but this definitely isn't stock.

Halo, by Beyoncé, blares through the speakers and State's hand covers mine perched on my thigh. It makes me relax. The bundle of nerves threatening to blossom into a full-blown anxiety attack, simmers to a dull roar with his touch. I glance over at him every chance I get to study his relaxed jaw and the sexy-ass aviators he's wearing. I'm surprised he's not wearing a snapback, but his short hair is even sexy, and I'm thankful he's not wearing a hat.

"Like what you see?" He smirks when stopped at a red stoplight.

"Busted, eh?"

He squeezes the top of my hand and on an impulse I reach over and place a light kiss on his cheek. I want to reassure him in every way that I'm in. All in, even if my weak psyche doesn't think it will happen.

The drive is over forty-five minutes and before long we roll up to a gated community. My gut clenches in horror. It's a damn mansion, or a damn castle as Rowe would classify it.

"Is this it?" I point with my free hand.

"Yeah, nothing in this lifestyle is boring or plain."

"Everything I am." I mean it as a joke, but it came out flat and all too meaningful.

"We're made of the same cloth, Baylor. King's made us and that's something none of these people will ever understand. No one can take that away from us."

"Sometimes I miss that place. How fucked up is that?"

"I do too, but it happens less knowing you're in my life again."

"Me too," I whisper.

State parks his car, then rushes around the front of it until he's at my side and opens the door. I take his outstretched hand and leap to my feet. I'm shocked when my legs don't wobble or knees knock in nerves. It's in this moment, when I look down at our clutched hands, that I know it's because State's holding me.

It takes a good while to wind around to the back of the house. The noise soon hits us hard. Music, laughter, and chatter fill the air. State grips my hand tighter and tugs me to his side. Once in the backyard, I'm assaulted by the amount of people, the colors blue and orange adorning every single thing, and then the huge men. State doesn't stand out in this crowd.

I barely hit the top of his shoulders and feel like a dwarf among the sea of football players. It doesn't take long before we are surrounded by the men giving State slaps on the back and riddling him with crude greetings.

He growls a warning and waves them back a bit. I know he's protecting me, but in a weird way I feel okay. I don't feel like a part of the group, but in turn I also feel like part of the crowd. *Shit, this is all too confusing.* State looks down at me and I'm able to give him a genuine smile.

It's in this moment when he smiles back with force, that turns off the vicious thoughts in my mind. God, I want to yell to the whole crowd that I love State and I'm his Baylor, and nothing in this world will ever tear us apart again. A new and an authentic determination bubbles up in every single one my pores. I'm going to fight for State no matter the circumstances.

"Guys, this is Baylor. And Baylor?" He looks down at me with a delighted expression. "These are the guys, don't worry about their names. They respond pretty well to dumbass."

"State." A woman's voice squeals.

We turn to an older woman rushing over to him. It looks like she literally bathed in blue and orange, from her headband, to her jewelry, and right down to her sandals.

"Momma Pete." State drops my hand and wraps her up in hug that leaves her feet dangling from the ground.

When he sets her down, he whirls her around to face me.

"Oh my lawd, you're just as gorgeous as he told me. So nice to meet you Baylor. I'm Momma Pete, the coach's wife, and I've heard so much about you."

She has me wrapped up in hug, wiping her blue and orange collage of colors on me.

"Don't scare her off, Momma Pete." State takes my hand back in his.

"Oh heaven, I'd never do that. I'm just so happy you're here."

He squeezes my hand tighter and I realize I haven't said a word.

"Thank you."

"You're simply gorgeous, Baylor. I'm jealous of that long stunning dark brown hair."

I smooth it down making sure none of Rowe's imprints are left on it. It took a bit to get all of the blue glitter off my face on the ride over.

"I'm really honored to be here with State. Thanks for having me."

It's not a lie. Not one ounce of it. I almost feel sick with the thought I didn't want to come.

"Let me get you a drink. This humidity and heat is horrible. Over near the pool is a blue cooler with cold drinks in it. You two make yourself comfortable." Momma Pete scurries off to get our drinks, even though she just invited us to get our own.

One man is left standing with us. I recognize him from Alley's. He's one of the men who was a little bit too excited to eat there.

"I'm Ryder." He reaches out his hand. "I'm really the star of the team. Don't believe anything this fool tells you."

State grunts and elbows him in the side. "Bullshit, I'm always picking up your slack."

"Whatever, pretty boy."

The men pick up in conversation and I'm off the hook. I like standing by State's side and not having to speak. It's feels good. I quickly learn Ryder is the other leader on defense with State, and they've been ranked the number one defense the last three years in the nation. Both men started as Freshman and have broken all records that could be crushed.

I notice a girl sitting by herself on a chaise lounge. She has long brown hair and plain features. She seems so relatable, except for her perfectly sculpted body. She has to be an athlete.

"Quit staring."

State's voice causes me to jump, but when I look up at him, he's not talking to me. Ryder is magnified to the same girl I am.

"You know she's off limits."

"Fuck off. I was looking at the decorations."

State rolls in a fit of laughter. "Busted, bitch."

Ryder shakes his head and then wipes his brow. This girl seems to really have him tied up in knots. My curious mind wants to know.,.but I'll file that question for later.

"Coach will kill you. It's his daughter, Ryder."

Curious mind, fulfilled!

"I'm not doing anything with Shayne."

"Your eyes tell another story, man." State slaps him on the back. "Focus on football and not pissing off the head coach."

"Did I hear my name?" An older man, wearing a blue and orange visor with grey poking up from the top, joins us. Momma Pete is by his side holding his hand.

"Sure did," State quickly recovers.

My vision darts back to the bored girl, then to the coach, State, and Ryder. An awkward feeling drifts between everyone and I feel like I have a flashing sign on my forehead explaining why the men were talking about him.

"Just telling Ryder how I'm your favorite, Coach Pete."

The man lets out a hearty laugh with a sparkle of love shining in his dark brown eyes. "You know you're all like my own kids. I can't pick a favorite."

"Yeah, good cover-up story." State beams widely.

There's a bond between these men that's contagious. They're not just a team, but a family. I've picked up on it in just a matter of thirty minutes or so.

"I'm going to the gym, if I've spent enough time here." The girl, Shayne, has joined the conversation and doesn't seemed impressed at all. She's shorter than me and definitely an athlete with her toned body. I suck in my gut feeling fat around her.

State grips my hand firmly and I suck in even harder. Shayne's hand remains on her hip and her death stare aimed directly at her parents.

"Have you met Baylor?" Her mom claps her hands together.

Talk about oblivious.

Shayne looks my way and softens her glare. Her warm blue eyes meet mine and she even offers up a friendly smile.

"Hi. I've heard lots about you. Nice to meet you." She extends a hand.

"You too," I manage to get out and shake her hand.

"Won't kill you to hang around," her dad barks out.

"Wouldn't kill you to show up…"

Her mom cuts her off. "Go ahead, honey. Text if you need anything."

I feel like a soldier on a battlefield, dodging bullets. They're streaming from every direction without warning.

"Ryder." Shayne smiles and nods before walking off.

He's not very discreet watching her sashay away in her white eyelet dress. The battlefield is distracted when other players join us, and the conversation goes right back into talk about the first upcoming game.

"Let's go sit down." State guides me to an empty table.

He receives a few jabs from his teammates about being a pussy, but he ignores them. We settle into a couple of chairs that are perched at the corner of the pool under a shade tent, with a large fan blowing. The aroma of food is overwhelming as servers in white jackets bring food out.

"Doing okay?" State asks, placing his hand on the top of my leg.

I nod to him still taking everything in. A group of girls dance on the opposite side of the bowl. Their moves are ridiculous and it seems they're gaining the attention they want.

"Girlfriends of players," State answers my unasked question.

"Wow," it slips off my tongue.

"Pathetic, I know."

"Please slap me if I ever become that." I look up at him and smile.

His large hands cup my face and he smiles right back down at me. "Will do."

"Kiss me," I whisper.

His lips brush mine before he kisses me. It's quick and just what I needed.

He pulls back. "What was that about?"

"Just felt the need to claim you."

"Really?" He raises an eyebrow.

"You're, by far, the best looking guy here."

"Want me to take my shirt off?"

I choke in embarrassment. "Your beauty doesn't need to be expanded by being shirtless."

The rumble of his laugh vibrates off his chest. "My tattoo says it all."

"Right." I giggle.

"Thank you for coming here. I know it's hard on you." He brushes away a stray hair.

I close my eyes and fight not to moan out loud. "Thank you for pushing me."

The table is soon filled with other players and few women. State's irritation is clear.

"It's okay." I lean over and whisper in his ear. "Enjoy."

He laces his fingers in mine and relaxes back a bit. It becomes evident I have no idea about football while listening to the players. The extent of my knowledge is it hurts your fingers when you catch the ball.

I grab my phone out of my small purse and check it. There's several texts from Miss Tami checking in on me and even a few selfies of her and Rowe. I give a State a quick understanding look, untangle our fingers, and send a quick text to them, then one to State.

Me: Remember when you'd force me to play catch and nearly break my digits off?

He picks up his phone and smiles when he sees my name on it.

State: You're over dramatic.

Me: It's all I know about football.

State: I know a great teacher.

Me: I'm never playing catch with you again.

State: I'm more into tackling people now.

Me: I could handle being tackled by you.

"Jesus, get a damn room," Ryder blurts out.

And we're busted in action.

"Fuck off," State growls, placing his phone on the table.

"You don't talk much." Ryder pulls a chair up behind us.

I shrug. Shrug like a motherfucking champion.

"Did State here make you mute?"

State slaps him hard in the back of the head. "Don't be a dick."

"I talk."

"She has a voice," Ryder replies.

"I do. Just a bit shy," I offer.

"No need to be shy around here, sweetie, this is your new family."

"Call her sweetie one more time and I'll break your fucking legs."

I shake my head at State's over protective nature.

"Thanks, Ryder." I grab State's hand again.

"This tough guy here has it bad for you."

"Yeah?" I ask.

"Been his roommate since our Freshman year. I was starting to think you were his imaginary crush."

"We were imaginary to each other for several long years," I offer.

"Never again." State lightly kisses me on the lips.

The action makes me blush and feel out of place. It's scary to be cared for so publically. I chalk it up to a new sensation and chose to not run from it.

"Who is that?"

We all look up to the new voice. It's the girl from sports bar that was all over State. My guts twist with fear. She's not impressed, and I have a feeling that a determination within her has just surfaced to ruin my life. Call it a woman's intuition.

"Who you banging now to get in here, Bridget?" Ryder asks.

He doesn't hold back any distain. Ryder just became a good friend of mine.

"Fuck off, Ryder."

"No, really who you banging? They'll need to be vaccinated stat."

State lets out a chuckle.

"Really, State, seems you've never minded."

And there's the first blow from the monster bitch.

"You wish," he fires back.

"And we don't care for rotten trout. Do us a favor and get your nasty box away from us."

Ryder for the touchdown. Bridget whirls around to leave us.

State's up on his feet. "Oh, Bridget this is Baylor, by the way. My girlfriend."

Girlfriend. Penalty for State, or is it the winning touchdown?

"Baylor." My name rolls off of her tongue coated in venom. "The name on your back?"

"My one and only," State says back with a gleam in his eyes.

"What's going on?" A guy wraps Bridget up, joining the conversation.

"Hey, Dylan," she purrs.

"Better get into the fucking clinic, man." Ryder laughs and stands to his feet.

"He's the fucking third string QB, he'll be fine," another gentle giant adds.

The men at the table all enjoy a good laugh. I had no idea they were even part of this conversation.

"Yeah, Burnett, careful your tiny dick might fall off."

It's the final comment that sends the pair away from out table. Studying their backs when they walk away, his number and last name strike me hard in the face. I'm barely able to breathe as it all sinks in. My blood runs cold and fear paralyzes me.

"Baylor?"

I hear State's voice, but can't quit staring at the back of the man. How did I not recognize him? My jaw clenches and face pales at the realization. It's the brother. The brother of the man who abused and raped Rowe. We've never crossed the family since the final court proceedings. His brother was tried as an adult and put away.

"Baylor." State's voice tickles my ear. "Are you okay?"

I place my shaky hand on the tabletop and know I have to lie. He'll go fucking ballistic. Football is his life and this will be the end of it. This is his family and team. I can't tell him.

I nod. "Sorry, just forgot about a paper I have due."

I die on the inside with my weak ass lie.

"Are you sure, Baylor?"

I nod again and welcome the conversation singing around us. We enjoy food, music, and talk about football the rest of the evening. A part of me has grown ice-cold knowing that a Burnett plays with State.

I learn Burnett is merely a third string quarterback, while State runs the other side of the football team on defense, but in the end they're on the same team. Coach Pete gives a short speech about the purpose behind the barbecue. The theme is team bonding for a victorious season. I can't tear that apart.

Chapter 15

"We're here." My shoulder shakes.

I hadn't even realized I'd dozed off on the way home. State is out and rounding the front of the car. He has my door open with an outstretched hand.

"Sorry, guess I'm crappy company."

"Never. I love watching you sleep."

"Will you stay the night?"

"Thought you'd never ask." He grabs me by the waist, pulling me up to his chest. "This is where you wrap your legs around the prince."

I chuckle into his neck and follow the instructions.

"My legs barely fit around you."

"You fit perfectly, Baylor."

Our lips connect. My stomach flutters as he works over my lips with his. The simple graze lights me up. I press my lips harder into his. When his tongue lazily grazes my bottom lip, I open up for him. He presses into my mouth with need and want. His taste is intoxicating. His tongue teases me with delicate brushes.

He pulls back. "I have to stop myself now or I won't be able to."

I drop my forehead to his and smile. "It feels so good to be with you again."

"I know, baby."

My heart bursts wide open with no hope of ever being the same. I shiver with the night chill. State puts me down on my feet and hand in hand we walk into my home. Rowe is passed out on the couch with her roses by her side. Miss Tami is busy working on a new blanket with the *Golden Girls* blaring in the background. It's her favorite show. I'm pretty sure she's seen every episode, but it never stops her from watching them over and over.

"Hi." I wave, keeping my voice low not wanting to wake Rowe.

"Kids." Tami beams up at us. "How was your day?"

"Good." I nod. "Really good."

Miss Tami doesn't need any extra stress or worry. She's spent a life time absorbing the stress of others while saving kids. So, for a second time today I'll be lying to a person whom I love.

"Have a seat and tell me all about it."

I wave to my open recliner. State takes a seat.

"I'm going to change into something more comfortable." I point down to the damn skirt.

"I like it." State smiles.

"Looks good on you, sweetie," Miss Tami adds.

"You two are too damn much."

I turn and go to my bedroom to find Rowe has covered my bed in drawings. She always, always, makes my day brighter no matter what I'm facing. I collect them into a pile and tuck them in my notebook with all of her other drawings.

I grab a pair of tight yoga pants and an oversized, off the shoulder, dance sweatshirt. I wash off the make-up and moisturize my face before changing into the comfortable clothing. Before I go back into the living room, I grab two bottles of water from the fridge, then join State and Miss Tami.

I clutch the hem of my soft sweatshirt and smile at the scene before me. State's kicked back in my recliner, relaxed as relaxed can get, intent on the television. He laughs at Blanche and doesn't even notice me standing watching him.

In this light, I see my childhood friend. The crazy nine-year-old boy with a big heart, protecting soul, and love of life. It's all there wrapped up in his new large frame. He still loves football and he still loves me.

"Baylor, I didn't see you."

"I noticed. I see you found some new chicks."

"Dude, they're freaking hilarious."

"Dude?" I raise an eyebrow and hand him a bottle of water.

He smiles at me, catches my wrist and pulls me down into the recliner with him. It's a bold move and I feel uncomfortable. Miss Tami starts up talking, acting like I'm not cuddled in State's lap. It doesn't bother her at all, but my stiff frame isn't so comfortable. State, too, doesn't seem effected by it all as he pulls me in closer to him, and runs his palm up and down the side of my curled up legs.

"What's your sweatshirt say?" He asks.

I blush.

"Oh, that's the studio where Baylor teaches dance," Tami offers.

"You dance?" He asks sounding shocked.

I nod.

"I tried to get her to dance competitively for years, but you know how darn stubborn that girl can be."

"I like teaching it. It, uh…makes me feel good," I reply.

"You're a star and should be dancing competitively," Miss Tami urges.

"Ugh, I know, I know."

"When did you start dancing?" State asks.

"Sometime in high school." I shrug. "It started out as a way to communicate."

I pause for a second and no one comments.

"That sounds dumb. I just like it."

"Not dumb at all, Baylor," State whispers.

"It was easier to dance and not talk. Bossy pants, over there, insisted in enrolling me into lessons and I found that I love it."

"Can't wait to see some moves," State jokes.

"Oh, just wait until her and Rowe face off in a twerking challenge."

That garners a hearty chuckle from State.

"I always lose. Go figure."

"Well, kids I'm going to bed." She stands up and goes to Rowe.

"I'll get her. Go on."

She comes over to me and kisses my forehead. "Night, Baylor. Love you."

"Love you, more."

"Night, State."

"Night." He stands up, carefully placing me to the side, and wraps her up in a hug. "Thank you for taking care of my girl."

"You have no idea how big of an honor it was. I knew you'd come back one day."

I stand listening to them while fiddling with my fingers. I already have a hard time with words and then when a conversation is being held about me, right in front of me, it makes everything even more odd.

"I'm going to take Rowe to bed. I'll be right back." I leave the two and scoop Rowe up in my arms.

"I promised her I'd take her flowers to bed with her."

"Okay, I'll come back for them."

I know State would love to help, but is so smart about walking the line of not spooking Rowe. He stays in the living room while I tuck her in and bring her flowers to her night stand.

"She still out?" He asks, running his hand over the back of his head.

"Like a princess." I hold my arms out. "What do you want to do?"

"That's a dangerous question, Baylor."

God, the way my name rolls off his tongue melts me.

"Are you ready for bed or a movie?"

"Bed?" He arches an eyebrow.

"Stop." I jump into his lap. "You know what I'm trying to get at."

He kisses my cheek. "Pick a movie."

"Any movie?"

"Your pick," he challenges.

"I don't think you'd like my pick."

"Hit me with it." He hands me the remote control to the TV.

I power up Netflix on the TV and find my all-time favorite movie. I've shed so many tears watching this. It never gets old.

The first scene of Ghost appears on the television. Patrick Swayze and Demi Moore make my breathing hitch. Their love story tears me apart every single time. It's a reminder of my past. And this may have been a mistake.

I peek up to State. "Have you seen this?"

"No, but I'm curious to why it's my girl's favorite."

"It will be obvious. Trust me." I snuggle down into him, letting my arm wrap around his middle.

State has the ability to just hold me with one strong arm, but he winds both around me and rests his chin on the top of my head. We watch in silence. The gripping scene of losing the love of your life appears, and the tears roll down my face on cue. I feel State pull me closer to him. We don't talk.

I finally speak up when Demi's character believes in the ghost of the love of her life.

"That's how I've felt for years, until now."

I don't give State a chance before turning in his lap to face him. Tears stream down my face. He tries to wipe each one away, but they fall too fast. I cry for our past, for right now, and our future.

"Kiss me," he whispers.

I take the lead, leaning forward and brushing my lips up against his before I indulge in all things State. He drags the pad of his thumb down my jawline, opening up to me. I sweep my tongue in his mouth, letting everything pour into him. State grips the back of my head, pulling me in tighter as we explore each other.

"Bedroom," I pant into his mouth.

He stands and walks us into my bedroom. We're careful not to make any noise as he lightly shuts the door and lays me back on the bed. My cheeks are flushed.

State remains standing, he slowly unbuttons his shirt until it falls off of him, leaving an impeccable portrait of his perfect sculpted chest and abs. His woodsy scent mixed with a hint of citrus hypnotizes me. My lips part as I take in all of the man standing before me.

He eyes me up and down before making a move and when he lowers his body on mine, he completely covers me from the top of my head to the tips of my toes. He keeps most of his weight centered on his elbows.

I kiss him quickly before I let my deepest and darkest secret flow from me. "I'm not a virgin."

State tilts his head.

"I've never had sex." I close my eyes regretting this. "It happened in Kings."

"Sssshhhh." He presses his fingers to my lips. "I know."

"I'm scared, State. I want you, but I don't know if I can."

He again presses his finger down into my lips. "It's okay."

Our lips crash together, my hands roam up and down his strong back. The desire to give him all of me tortures me.

"Tell me to stop if you need to." He kneels up and pulls the sweatshirt from my body and tosses it to the floor. "We're not going to have sex, so relax, baby."

His palms skim down my sides and then back up until he's cupping my breasts.

"You're fucking gorgeous," he growls.

I writhe up into him pleading for more. My gesture is not lost on him. The straps of my bra are pulled down my shoulder. He follows their path with light kisses on my skin. He sneaks his hands behind my back and unsnaps the bra, then sits back up on his knees.

I finish shedding the bra for him, then lay back down, bared to him. His pupils flare and lips part before he dips his head. His lips graze both peaked buds before he swirls his tongue around one. I moan loudly with the sensation.

He covers my mouth again with one finger. I bite down on my bottom lip to control my voice. He pays the same attention to the other nipple before looking up at me.

"So perfect." State rolls to my side and slides his large hand down the front of my stomach until it disappears under my pants. My legs part welcoming his touch.

"Tell me when to stop."

I put my hand over his, leading him down. His fingers snap the top of my panty line before he goes any further. He brushes my sensitive parts, forcing me to bite back another moan. I buck up into his touch, enjoying the sensation coursing through me.

He circles a piece of me rhythmically until it hurts so good it breaks a piece of my newly open heart. Wave after wave of sensation slam into me until I'm falling over a hopeless cliff. I slam a palm over my mouth to muffle the pleasure.

I melt back into the bed with State holding me close to his chest.

"I'm going to show you how good it feels, before we have sex."

"State."

"Yeah?" He mumbles into the crook of my neck.

"That was a first."

His smile spreads across my skin. "We have so many more firsts ahead of us."

Chapter 16

"I have an early practice."

"No," I protest.

I want nothing more than to spend the rest of the day with him.

"Shitty timing, I know, but the next few months will be packed with football."

I grin up at him as he pulls on his shorts, and I pull the covers up to my chin.

"Still not a morning person, I see," he smiles at me.

"Nope. Some things never do change."

"I remember having to run to your house and drag you out of bed for school on more than occasion."

"And now you're dragging me into bed."

My own words make me flush with embarrassment.

"You're cute." He kneels down on the bed and tugs back my covers.

"I'll text you later." He kisses me lightly on the lips.

"You'll answer." He kisses me again.

"God, I'm going to miss you." He kisses me again.

"This hurts." I wrap my hands around his neck. "I don't want you to go, and I don't want to make you feel bad for having to go, but it hurts."

"I know, baby." He grabs my forearm and clutches my pinky. "This will be forever, I promise."

I squeeze his finger in mine knowing it's the truth and our destiny. He showers me with several more kisses before leaving. Not even five minutes pass before my phone vibrates on the nightstand.

State: Tell my princess I'll be back soon to see her.

Me: Okay (heart emoticon)

State: And remind my queen she's mine forever.

Me: She knows. XOXO

It takes a few minutes for me to drift off to sleep. Right when slumber takes over, Rowe bounds into my bed and begins tapping my forehead.

"Are you sleeping?"

"Grrrrr."

"Want to get cereal?"

I pry an eye open to see her toothy grin flash at me. I roll over and tickle her until she squeals uncle.

"Why are you so happy and hyper in the morning?"

She cups her hands around her mouth. "It's magic."

"Get out of here, silly goose."

I crawl from the bed and join her in the kitchen, picking out our cereal. We both pour heaping bowls. Rowe digs in while I slice some fresh fruit for us.

"Dance day," she sings out.

"Yes, today is dance."

"Are you teaching my class?"

"I'm not sure. I'll find out when we get there."

"Mmmmm, can you invite Shrek?"

I nearly choke on a gulp of milk when she refers to State as Shrek.

"No, he has football practice."

Her eyes grow in size. "Remember, he plays football and brings you flowers."

"I hate football. It's bad."

"It's okay to not like football because you may think it's boring, but it's not bad, sweetie."

"You gonna make me mad."

I cover her little hand on the top of the table deciding on how to deliver my message. "Not everyone in life are good people. Sports, like football, have lots of good people in them. Miss Tami and I will always be here to guide you. Okay?"

"You piss me off a little."

I bite the smile on my face.

"I know it's scary, but you like State, right?"

She nods her little head.

"He brought you and me flowers. He's a nice guy and loves football."

"Can you just shut up?"

I squeeze her hand and do what she asks, not wanting to send her into an angry state. We will be forever working her through the process of vocalizing her frustration. I typically don't let the words "pissing me off" fly, but I was hoping to connect the bigger picture for her.

I turn on the shower and wait for it to warm up, but the buzzing of my phone distracts me. State's name scrolls across the screen. I slide over the green button to see his text.

State: I miss you.

Me: You just saw me.

State: That was hours ago.

Me: Like 2 (smile emoticon)

State: Two hours too long

Me: Don't you have practice or something?

State: Getting ready to go to cardio.

I think on my next text, but decide to do it. My heart zings with excitement. I've never felt the way he makes me feel. It was different when we were kids and just best friends, but this is so much more.

Me: I'm getting into the shower

State: Jesus, Baylor

Another text from him comes through before I can respond. It's a picture text of him. A whole body selfie. His sly grin is in the frame and then his chiseled chest right down to his perfectly sculpted abs. I notice the slight bulge in his black gym shorts. The man is fucking gorgeous.

State: See what you do to me.

I smile and tap out a text.

Me: I like it.

State: My turn, send me a picture.

Me: I WILL NOT.

I can practically hear his deep chuckle.

State: Please?

I snap a picture of my toes pressed against the white tile of the bathroom floor and send it.

Me: Text me later

State: You're going to pay for that. Talk later, xoxo

I let the hot water run over my skin, regretting the decision to take one. The last wafts of State's scent flow down the drain, making me instantly crave him all over again.

Chapter 17

Rowe spun off into quite the fit when she realized she wasn't in my dance group today. She's going through a lot right now, adjusting to State being in our lives. She's used to being the center of our worlds.

Miss Tami had to sit with her for over twenty minutes before she calmed down and finally agreed to join her group. I blow her a kiss through the clear glass window, while keeping my students dancing.

It's been a month of State taking over my life. He controls my every thought, action, and beautiful dreams. It's something I never thought I'd experience, but I love it. He's coming over tonight for dinner and a princess movie of Rowe's choice. My loathing of football only grows knowing it keeps us apart. However, the light in his eyes and pride in his voice when he talks about it, soothes the ache a bit.

"One more time through. Watch your toes and make sure to nail your spins." I hit play on the One Direction song one more time before leading the girls through the dance.

Parents trickle into the studio and grab their children until I'm left standing in front of the mirror staring back at myself. I feel alive for the first time in my life. I can't help the smile that grows across my face.

"Baylor." Rowe runs in and hugs my waist. All signs of her sour attitude have vanished.

"Can we dance?" She asks with a hopeful smile playing on her face.

"Of course."

"I pick the song." She proudly points to her chest and waltzes over to my iPod.

Can't Stop The Feeling by Justin Timberlake begins playing and Rowe claps her little hands together. She takes the position as the teacher and nods to me to follow her. Dance has been so good for her coordination skills. The girl doesn't let her disability stop her.

Her hips begin to sway and her feet smoothly glide on the floor, dancing her little booty off to the song. I follow her steps while pride swells in my chest. It's a dance we taught the kids a while back and she's nailing every step.

I flip my hair down and shake it in her direction, letting my feet glide across the floor, feeling the song drum through me. With her hands on her hips, she nods her head, and kicks her leg out finishing off the song. A round of applause fills the dance studio. We both look over to our audience standing and clapping. Miss Tami and State smile widely, clapping like lunatics. They're our champions in this world.

"Nice, girls." State nods. I don't miss the underlying message, but I'm thankful he keeps it rated G right now.

"State." Rowe slaps her hands over her mouth and closes her eyes.

I know it's the football shirt he's wearing. Miss Tami and I both agreed it was time to push her a bit more towards the idea of it. She adores her Shrek. It hurts like hell to see her work through this, but it's a coping skill she needs to develop. Nothing in life should ever hold her back.

"Open your eyes, Rowe." State steps closer to her keeping his voice low.

She shakes her head side-to-side.

"Please, it's me, Shrek," he whispers.

I catch Rowe peeking between her fingers, gaining a healthy smile from State.

"Look what I found." He holds out a brand new Rapunzel doll still in the package.

She squeals still peeking through her little fingers. "For me?"

"Only for you."

My heart melts listening to him talk so gently to her. I've watched footage online of him crushing men his size on the field. He's a freaking beast that dominates. Grown men are afraid of him on the field. It takes me back to our time in the King's, he was always my protector.

Lily, a little girl from dance, races back into the studio.

"Baylor." She tugs on the hem of my shirt.

"Yeah, sweetie?"

"I can't find my pink jacket."

"Let's go look in the cubbies." I point to the cubicles arranged symmetrically on the wall.

"Thanks it's new and I'll be in hot water." She wrings out her hands.

We look for only a few moments before digging it out of the cubby on the very top.

"Here, sweetie." I hand her the jacket and she bolts over to State who is still kneeling in front of Rowe.

"That's pretty." Lily's blue eyes look up to State with a twinkle in them.

"It's mine." Rowe drops her hands from her eyes and pats her little chest. She wraps an arm loosely around State's neck. "And he's mine, too."

I'm forced to bite back a giggle. Miss Tami is stepping in to run interference, seeing the fire light up in Rowe. She's tends to get a bit territorial when it comes to things she loves.

"Glad you found your jacket," State nods then whispers something into Rowe's ear. Her nose turns up for a second.

"Thank you, Lily, for telling me my doll is pretty, but don't touch it again. It's mine."

My bottom lip hurts from biting down on it, stifling my laughter. State stands to his feet, pulling Rowe up with him tucked to his side. She keeps her arm wrapped around his neck and her doll clutched to his chest. She seems to have no problem with the football on his team shirt right now.

When he turns around to walk out, I notice his number for the first time. Number seven and I know it's no coincidence. It's from an UNO game when we were younger. He was pissed I'd won when he laid down that yellow seven. It makes my footsteps light as I walk out behind him. I'm in awe realizing how he never let go of anything, even though I'd thought he had.

Rowe insists on riding in State's car on the way home. Miss Tami waves us off, letting us know she was going to stop by the grocery store to pick up a salad for dinner.

"We're having basagna for dinner." Rowe rubs her hands over her belly while I fasten her seatbelt.

The huff of disappointment when I put her in the backseat was evident, so she scooted to the center where she could stare at State in the mirror.

"I love lasagna," he sings back to her.

He waits until I'm settled in the front seat and buckled before starting the engine. A rap song blares about hoes and other foul concepts before he can turn it off. I give him a sideways look and he only shrugs.

"I was a bit fired up after practice."

"Everything okay?" I ask, placing my hand on the top of his leg.

"Yeah, it is now." He leans over and kisses me on the cheek.

"You guys are in love," Rowe sings out the last word.

State peers at her in the rearview mirror, waggling his eyebrows.

"I've always loved Baylor."

"Do you have music with good words?" She asks, brushing off his comment.

The statement hits me harder. *He's always loved me.* My name inked across his back and his heart mine. My heart swells to a near bursting state.

"I love you, too," I whisper, leaning forward to adjust the radio to a song Rowe approved. It only takes a minute for me to crank up *Party In the USA.*

State shakes his head at the music. Over the last few weeks, I've learned he's into more intense music because it helps him amp up for games. However, I've also come to find out he'd let Rowe get away with anything.

"Homework while I set the table, Rowe." I turn around to her. She sticks her tongue out at me.

"I have homework, too, Rowe. We can do it together," State offers.

She beams back at him and nods his head.

"Not fair." I protest.

"I have homework with you later," he winks pulling into our drive.

"Five days away from you really is too long. FaceTime doesn't cut it."

"I know," he growls.

Rowe hops from the backseat of the car and bounds up the stairs. I've never seen her so enthusiastic to start homework. She keeps good on her promise, working on her math problems, while I set the table and pop the pan of cooked lasagna in the oven to heat up.

I keep feeling stares my direction and when I peek over my shoulder I catch State staring.

"How's that homework coming?" I ask.

"It's not."

"Bad boy. Work!" Rowe slaps the open textbook.

I laugh hard and turn back to prep the garlic bread. State's planning on going into the social worker field. He'd be perfect with his gentle soul and kind heart. He's opened up to me that his parents are less than impressed with his choice. His dad is a high power attorney and his mom is a surgeon. They had higher hopes for their son. I personally think it's an asshole thought and they should be ashamed of it.

State talks highly of them, but there seems to be something off. He claims they only love football because he's the best at it.

"I'm home," Miss Tami sings out carrying in a few grocery bags into the kitchen.

I take them from her and finish getting dinner ready. Rowe squeals out that she's finished, right when I'm ready to set the food out. Miss Tami has a hand on State's shoulder peering over to his textbook. Her eyes beam with pride.

"So much has changed since I was in school."

"Yeah, they have cars now and not horses and buggies," State manages to get out with a straight face.

She pops him in the back of the head. "I've had to whip you once and I could do it again."

I set down Rowe's plate of food and look up at them. "You whipped State?"

State's eyes grow wide with a twinge of embarrassment on his face. "You weren't supposed to tell anyone."

"I haven't." Miss Tami shrugs.

"When?" I ask not letting this topic go.

"She really didn't whip or spank me, but took a ruler to me."

"Oh my God." I cover my mouth. "Miss Tami."

"He pissed me off and wouldn't listen to me."

"You can't hit kids," I reply.

"I always thought of you two as mine and his temper was getting the best of him at school."

State looks up to me with a smile. "It's fine. It's the year they threatened to separate us. I got into a really bad fight that day on the playground. No one could talk any common sense into me. Well, that's until Hulk Hogan here snapped me to attention with a ruler."

I begin chucking. I've rarely seen Miss Tami's temper get the best of her.

"Only did it because I love you." Miss Tami takes a seat. I place her plate down in front of her.

State refuses to let me make his plate.

"Sit." He grabs my shoulders ushering me over to the table. He grazes my neck with his lips before gently pushing me down into the seat.

"Hey, I want food." I protest.

He only turns his back to me, making his way over to the counter. He returns in a few seconds with two plates.

"Thank you," I whisper.

We eat in silence until Rowe pipes up, taking her last bite. "Baylor, Mr. Moore asked where you've been."

I choke on the swallow of lettuce that is now lodged in my throat. I pound my chest, sputter, and reach out for my bottle of water.

"Who is Mr. Moore?" State asks.

I don't have a chance to soften any blows, courtesy of Rowe.

"My principal. He gets googly eyes around her and wants to date her."

"He what?" The veins in his thick neck pulse.

"State." I cover his forearm. "I used to chat with him when I'd drop Rowe off. He came in for a massage and asked me out on a date."

Okay, that was dumb. Honesty is not always the answer. I fear for the fork's life in his hand as his knuckles turn white.

"You gave him a massage?"

"It's my job, State." My irritation level rises.

"It was good for Baylor." Miss Tami sets her fork on her empty plate. "I was proud of her for talking to someone out of her environment. It was harmless."

"Thank you," I whisper, dropping my head and feeling ashamed.

"Rowe, let's do dishes since Baylor set the table and prepared the food." They both jump up, clearing the table and then running a hot soapy sink of water.

"I'm sorry, Baylor."

I finally look up to State who's staring down at me. Tears prick at the corner of my eyes.

"It's not you and I was just a dick," he whispers. "I want to be the man in your life."

I fumble with my fingers in my lap, feeling shitty. "I've never had a boyfriend or gone out on a date, until your team party. It's always been you, State."

He cups my cheek in his large palm. "Listen to me. I'm sorry. I'm so sorry."

I nod at him. "I don't like the way you just made me feel. Please don't do it again."

I'm shocked by the brutal honestly as it flows out of me.

"Never. Promise." He wraps his pinky in mine.

State texts me all through the movie. Rowe claimed his lap, so I cuddled up with Miss Tami on the couch. I know she's reading the messages over my shoulder and I'm okay with it. It may possibly happen that she'll be talking me off a cliff later.

"He didn't mean to hurt your feelings," she whispers down to me.

I nod knowing that fact. But it was just a tiny teaser of what heartbreak could feel like it. It's an unsettling feeling I never want to experience. Fear begins to take over showing me just how fast everything can spiral out of control.

State: Quit biting your bottom lip, baby.

I peer down at my phone, but don't reply.

State: I want to show you how damn sorry I am. You can't blame me for being a jealous man. You're my love.

State: Forever

Me: Watch the movie (smiley face emoticon)

State: Harsh

Me: You're distracting.

And it goes on just like that right through *Shrek*. It's not like I don't have the movie memorized, but it does happen to be my favorite out of Rowe's collection. I even love it now that Rowe calls State her Shrek.

State scoops Rowe up in his arms and packs her off to bed. Miss Tami tucks her in tonight while I go get in my pajamas. I hear State near and turn to see him in the frame of the door with his arms propped up over his head. The way the muscles strain in his arms, destroys me. He's pure sex.

"You staying the night?" I ask feeling my tummy flip.

"Do you want me to?"

I close the distance between us, wrapping my arms around his middle, and look up at him.

"Yes." I reach up to kiss his lips. "I freaked out for a second. I'm sorry that I overreacted."

"No, it was me."

He drops his hands, wrapping them around my waist, I'm up in his arms. My ankles lock around his back while my hands lace around his neck. When our skin connects my flesh tingles. He steals my breath when he presses his lips against mine. I let him kiss the hell out of me while backing us up to the bed.

We've done our fair share of making out during his visits. State has sent me into a fire of pleasure plenty of times, but that's as far as it's gone. He's determined to make sure I'm ready and that I understand how good sex between two people who love each other can be.

He covers my body when he lays me on the bed never breaking our kiss. He pulls back, leaving my lips swollen and satisfied.

"I'm fucking going mad being away from you, Baylor." He brushes his hand down my face.

"Me too."

"I want to do something different tonight."

My body stiffens. I'm not ready, but I also know that I can't deny this man anything.

"Relax, baby, I know you're not ready yet."

"That obvious?" I ask with a smile.

"Like an open book, baby."

He moves down my body raising my shirt to expose my abdomen. He lays kisses all over my skin. He drags down the lace panties under the over-sized sleep shirt. He never stops kissing me the lower he moves.

"State," I moan out bucking up into him.

"I'm going to taste you."

He dips his head again, pressing his lips into me. His movements are gentle feeding my hunger for him. I feel his tongue sweep through me and I'm forced to slap my palm over my mouth. The sensation is too much. It's all too much as he swirls his tongue lapping me up and down.

He never adds a finger, only making love to me with his mouth. When he swirls my sensitive bud one last time, I fall over the edge screaming his name into my hand. He rises up with a smile on his face placing his finger over his lips. I giggle at his action.

He's covering me again and we're nose to nose when he places his lips on mine. I'm not ashamed to kiss him, soaking my taste from his lips.

"That's sexy as hell, baby. God, I love you."

"I love you, too."

I place my hands on his shoulders to roll him off of me. A spark of courage lights up deep inside me when I crawl down his body. God bless gym shorts. They slide down his wide hips easily. The man is a giant compared to my petite frame.

I free him from his boxers and love the gasp that escapes him.

"Baylor." He looks down at me. "You don't have to."

"I want to," I offer before leaning over, grabbing the base of his thick cock.

I swirl my tongue over the head feeling empowered when he growls his approval. His hands lace into my hair. He doesn't force me to do anything, just holds me. I take him in my mouth loving the feel of his silky, rock hard dick.

"Baylor," he warns.

Driving him crazy like this has just become my favorite past time. I begin moving up and down him. I never reach the base not wanting an embarrassing moment of gagging. I add teeth and suck harder when he begins to buck up into my mouth.

"Enough. Enough, baby, stop."

My nails dig into the flesh of his thighs, telling him I have no plans of stopping. I suck him harder and even take him deeper when his growls continue. I feel him pulse once before he's trying to pry me from him, but I don't budge a bit welcoming his release into my mouth. I don't let go until I have him licked clean.

Once satisfied and my appetite for State is curbed, I climb back up his body, and collapse into his chest. His strong arms wrap around me pulling me in closer.

"Baylor." He strokes my hair down my back.

"Yeah?"

"I want you to come to my opening home game."

I raise my head to look up at him. My gut twists. I knew this was coming and it was going to be a point of contention. I don't want to go. The team party was my limit. Will the Burnett family be there? Will I have an anxiety attack? I'll be sitting alone the whole game. The same thoughts and questions have attacked me for the last month. I want to be there, but will I be able to?

"My parents will be there and I want you to meet them."

I want to puke.

"Please." He continues to brush my hair.

I bite my bottom lip and realize love is going to have to outweigh my fears. It's the way life works. I have to quit being the victim of life and free myself.

I stroke his chest with pointer finger. "I'll go."

"You will?" He holds me up from his chest.

I laugh at his bated excitement. "Yes, State. I'm nervous, but I'll go because I love you. You love football and I guess I want to see you kick ass in real time."

"Real time? Have you been Googling me?"

"Maybe?" I shrug.

"Nice." He smiles brightly.

"You're vicious out on the field."

"Yeah," he nods. "It's going to be even worse knowing my girl will be there."

I shake my head at his King Titan attitude. The man has always devoured the game. Deep down, buried way under all my insecurities, I'm excited to watch him.

Chapter 18

"Do you have your charger?"

"Yes."

"Did you check the spare for your car?"

"Yes." I pull up my thick curly hair into a messy bun and then secure it with an orange headband.

"Pepper spray?"

"Miss Tami, I'm going to a football game not into combat."

Rowe and Tami stand in the doorway watching me get ready. You'd think she was sending her little girl off into the big wide world. Well, in a way I guess she is. This is a huge step for me. I'm busting out of my environment throwing all care to the wind. I thought I'd be sick from nerves when I woke up this morning, but they've never come.

Rowe chews on her little nails. I know she's nervous. I've been very open about going to a football game since State asked a week and a half ago. I haven't seen him since that night, other than FaceTime.

"Baylor." I turn to see Rowe's nervous face.

"Yes." I kneel down in front of her.

"I made this for you, and one for State."

She opens her palm to show me a two handmade braided bracelets. She used orange, white, and blue thread.

"I wanted to make them pink, but Miss Tami helped me."

"They're gorgeous." I pull her into a tight hug.

I immediately tie the delicate bracelet on my wrist. Tears swell up in my eyes.

"I love you, Rowe. I love you so darn much. I'll always be here for you. I'll never leave you. Do you hear me?"

She nods her head, beaming brightly back at me.

"State is going to love this."

"Do you think he can wear it during the game. Miss Tami said he might be on TV."

"I'll try to get it to him. I'm sure he'll wear it to the next game for sure. Are you going to watch the game?"

She shrugs. "Maybe."

"You are the strongest, bravest, and very prettiest princess ever."

"With Pop Tarts on top?"

"With cherry-berry Pop Tarts on top."

It's harder to leave the house than I thought it would be. I want to cuddle with Rowe in my chair and hold her as she watches her first football game. I am so in love with that little girl. I crank Sam Smith on the drive and focus on the game. State let me know he wouldn't be able to text me on game day. He focuses on the game with the team.

Picturing him in full game mode brooding in all of his sexiness makes me squirm in the seat. I have to focus on that and not everything else that might happen today.

Finding parking at the stadium is rocket science. There are signs everywhere with people in orange vests waving parking wands everywhere. I follow instructions having no clue where to go. State sent me a parking pass, reassuring me it was a prime spot. I flash one of the parking attendants the pass and he waves me on. I roll past the large parking spot creeping closer to the stadium. I find the spot numbered one hundred twenty-seven with his last name "Blake" under it.

He was right about the parking spot. I'm only left with a short walk until I'm in a long line of a sea of blue and orange. I tug on the jersey that was also tucked in the box with the parking pass. He sent three jerseys with his name and number on them. Rowe was wearing hers when I left.

I fiddle with the bracelet on my wrist while shifting from foot to foot. I have no clue if I'm sitting with his parents or all by myself. I really hope I can enjoy the game solo without having the pressure of meeting the parents.

I get through security and use the restroom. I opt for a soda and pass on the aroma of the stadium food wafting through the air. It nearly killed me to pass on the hand-dipped corn dogs. My favorite.

My jaw drops when I step down the first step into the stadium. It's huge and powerful just like State Blake. It's an electric sea of Kelly green turf. I've never been a fan of green, but I'm instantly in love. I study the intricate white painted lines on the field and also the blue and orange mascot in the center.

I step down the stairs carefully following the alphabet as I go, in search of row D. Considering I started up at Z it was a long jot. I'm heading smack dab for the fifty-yard line behind the hometown bench.

"Baylor." A feminine voice hollers out my name.

Shading my eyes with my hand, I look up to see Shayne waving at me. I relax seeing a familiar face.

"Your seat is over here." She points next to her.

"Hey." I wave awkwardly when I approach her.

"You're sitting with me."

"Excellent." I run my palm down the front of my shorts drying off the nerves. "I'm glad to see you here."

"Right back at you," she beams at me. "I'm forced to be at every home game, and not being forced to sit with my mother surrounded by the teammates family and women is a treat. I could kiss State."

My spine stiffens with her last words, but know it's just an expression.

"I was worried I'd be sitting with State's parents."

Shayne lets out a loud laugh. "Oh honey, they're up in the box with my mom. They are too good for these seats."

"Oh."

"Hear you get to meet them tonight."

I nod wondering just how close her and State are. She picks up on my confusion and growing anxiety.

"Ryder and I are...well, I don't know what we are."

"Nice." And everything just went awkward.

"My dad would flip his lid. Nothing has happened between us, but it's complicated."

"I'm sorry."

Her voice is sad and her shoulders slump in defeat. I feel for the girl. There's definite tension between her and her parents.

"What do you study?" I finally ask her as the fans pour into the stadium.

"Sports medicine."

"Nice. Are you an athlete?"

"I am." She sits up a little taller. Her pride radiates off of her. "I'm on the gymnastics team."

"Really? I teach dance for extra money."

"Sweet. I've always loved gymnastics. I've spent more time in the gym than at my own home. My dad always wanted me to be in a more jock-ish sport."

"Are you kidding? Gymnastics takes tons of strength and dedication."

"Try telling my meat head father," she rolls her eyes. "Do you go to college?"

I start telling her about my collage of jobs and my online schooling. Speaking about my three jobs makes me realize that I do work too much. The booming sound of a fast-paced song fills the stadium. Everyone jumps to their feet, so I follow looking around to see what's happening.

Shayne nudges me in the ribs and points to a tunnel where smoke rolls out of it. "State leads the team out. He'll be the first one you see."

A bundle of nerves coil low in my belly. I've never seen him on the field and I couldn't be any more excited. My hips begin swaying to the song *Shots* as the smoke continues to bellow. Shayne squeals, beginning to move with me, and before I know it we are both in a full-blown dance.

Everyone surrounding me seems to be just as into the music and environment. It makes me feel comfortable. The anticipation of seeing State run out of the tunnel leading his team, multiplies.

The song switches to a thumping song with hard beats of hip-hop. It sends chills up my skin. The crowd grows louder until only the sound of the bass of the song can be heard. My whole body hums with excitement. Then there he is with a sledgehammer raised above his head sprinting out onto the field. The crowd increases their cheering.

I join along, hopping up and down on my toes, screaming for State. It's not like he can hear me, but it's years of missing him and now watching him live out his own dreams on the field. He leads his team to the center of the field. They circle around him, bend over, and begin swaying side-to-side before they jolt from the circle.

All the players have their hands raised pumping to the crowd while jogging over to the sideline. State takes off his helmet showcasing the smile that covers his face. His vision darts right to me and I wave like a maniac. His smile grows even wider before he winks and waves at me.

I melt on the damn spot. I'm so madly in love with the man, it's insane. I blow him a kiss and then cringe at how cheesy the gesture was. He throws his head back and laughs.

"He's so in love with you," Shayne whispers in my ear.

I nearly forgot she was sitting next to me. I was so wrapped up in the moment.

"Uh?" I turn to face her.

"We've heard nothing but things about Baylor since the day he stepped on the field as a freshman. So many women have flocked to him, but not one of them ever won him over."

Now my smile matches the one State flashed me. I turn back to the field watching State and two teammates go to the center of the field. They win the coin toss, deferring the choice. I clap even though I'm confused as hell.

"We are strong on defense, that's why he deferred. Do you know anything about football, Baylor?"

I shrug and then sheepishly shake my head no.

"Okay, all you need to know is this. State Blake is a badass on the field. One of the best defensive ends college football has ever seen. His job is to break up all the plays. Go for the quarterback, read the ball, bat the ball down, and crush other players."

I nod soaking it all in, noting the things I need to remember.

"Oh shit." I reach down into my pocket. "I need a favor and this may seem silly."

"What?"

"I need to get this bracelet to State. Any chance of that?"

She grabs me by the wrist and ushers me past the spectators in our row and marches us right down to the sideline.

"Yo, Brutus." A towering bodyguard turns to us. He's scarier than fuck.

"Baby Girl," he coos to her.

"Hey, tough guy."

"You joining us on the sidelines today? It's been years."

She shakes her head no. "I need State for a few seconds."

He gives her a hard glare.

"Please."

"Jesus, kid, I've never been able to tell you no." He walks off.

"He used to watch me on the sidelines when I was kid. He'd do anything for me," she offers.

In a matter of seconds, State is jogging over to us with his helmet dangling from his fingertips. Between his pads and cleats he's easily another four inches taller. He grins at me.

"Couldn't wait until after the game?" He pulls his face to mine and kisses me hard. His tongue swipes across my lips, and I open up for him to explore for a second before cutting him off.

"No, it's not that." I laugh at his defeated expression. "Well, okay that was nice too. But, hey, Rowe is going to try and watch the game. She's wearing your jersey and everything. She made this for you to wear."

I open my palm to show him the bracelet. It's so delicate in my hand, and compared to him. He smiles wider.

"Tie it on, baby."

My fingers fumble tying the string around his wrist. He tucks the knot under his glove, but the bracelet remains on top of his glove. I admire the black stripes under his eyes for a moment too long.

"You're so sexy like this," I finally admit.

"You looking fucking incredible in my jersey, baby." He turns and rushes back to his team.

Once back in our seats, I open up to Shayne about Rowe and my upbringing. I leave King's out of it because that's mine and State's. She's a good listener and seems genuinely interested in my story. It makes me feel uneasy about meeting State's parents, but that fades when the game starts.

State is all over the field. His long legs make him faster than anyone else. He's smart and precise about every single play. I cringe with his second tackle and even hold the air in my lungs waiting for him to get up. He hops up with ease each time, even more determined to break up the offenses plays. It's third and three, whatever the hell that means.

"They have to stop them. It will give us huge momentum to shut them down on their first drive."

I look over to Shayne confused.

"State has to shut down the offense."

I nod getting that. Shayne is catching on that she needs to feed me the information in the simplest of terms. The quarterback catches the ball when it's hiked to him. It reminds me of the hundred times I had to do that for State when we were kids.

He dances back and forth, looking down the field to throw the ball. I'm too absorbed in his actions to follow State. When I do catch a glimpse of number seven, he's flying toward the quarterback. State's busted through the line and is closing in on the scrambling quarterback.

I scream louder with the rest of the cheering crowd. State collides into the quarterback, sending him to the turf. He hits hard with his helmet bouncing up off the ground. In a flash, the ball is loose. One of State's teammates swoops in, picking it up and runs it in for a touchdown.

The rest of the game goes much like this. State's defense is out on the field most of the time. He rules the field. It's insane how crazy he is out there. His speed never dies, or the hard hits on the other team.

It's late in the fourth quarter. That I've learned — there's four quarters in a football game. Shayne was very informative at half-time, giving me some simple run downs on the game.

The quarterback on the other team learns quickly, and once he gets the ball he's been releasing it fast. He gets off in the air, but my eyes are glued to State who jumps up in the air and grabs the ball.

"Holy shit, interception, run big guy," a man behind hollers loudly.

I begin screaming and chanting *run, run, run* out loud. When his feet land in the end zone the stadium erupts. He stands with one hand on his hip and the other thrust up in the air. He runs his hand in the air until he's pointing in my direction. I fall even harder for State, not knowing that was even possible.

The remaining minutes of the game fade away too quickly. As much as I thought I hated football, I'm now madly in love with it only because of State on the field.

"State wants me to walk you to the outside of the locker room." Shayne grabs my wrist winding me through throngs of people.

"You don't have to hold my hand." I laugh and point to her hand around my wrist.

"State was very clear about me not losing you."

I shake my head and laugh. "I'm not a two-year old."

"He'll kill me if anything happens to you."

"Fine."

I follow her until we're in a tunnel where it's quiet.

"They'll come out of that door after the press conference."

There's a few other people pacing back and forth. It's obvious they're waiting for players of their own. I check my phone, watching the minute's tick by painfully slowly. The door flies open and several players take turns exiting. Some have family waiting, while others have girls jumping into their chest.

It makes my heart hurt to see the players who walk out and nobody looks their way. I make a vow to make every single home game of State's from this point on. I grow impatient when I'm pretty sure nearly all of the team have exited.

"Don't worry. State and Ryder will be in the press conference with my dad."

I nod and cross my arms, clutching my phone tight to me. Barnett waltzes out of the locker room. I'm thankful he doesn't spot me and neither does the bitchface blonde who tucks herself under his arm. He's freshly showered even though he didn't play one minute of the game.

Puke-Ass loser

I'm distracted from mentally slaughtering the man when the door flies open again and State's large frame fills the entire opening. I smile and walk toward him. He takes large steps toward me. I'm sprinting at him and fly into his arms. He grunts when I crash into his wide chest.

"Sorry," I mumble into his neck.

"Feels good."

"Are you hurt?" I ask.

"Just bruised up a bit."

I pull back and spot the cut under his eye. It's sexy as hell. His lips brush against mine before I have the chance to ask any questions. I open up to him, letting him thank me for coming to his game. My hands roam up the back of his head and tuck in under the hat sitting backwards on his head.

His smell is rich and soapy. It's the best smell I've ever smelled. I playfully bite down on his bottom lip and raise my eyebrows. He smiles back against my lips.

A throat behind us clears loudly, breaking us apart followed by a harsh voice.

"State."

He sets me down on my feet, tucks me to his side, and I come face to face with a very well-manicured woman. She's standing next to a man dressed in a sharp outfit. They reek of money and class.

"Mom, Dad," he nods.

I stiffen next to State then try to pull away from him. He keeps me pressed to his side and runs his thumb along my back.

"Really?" His mom scoffs.

"Really." He beams back, not skipping a beat.

"Nice game, son." His dad steps up and pats him on the shoulder, breaking the damn tension between the four us.

"Thanks, Dad." He reaches out and gives him a one armed hug. "Dad, this is Baylor."

He nods offering an outstretched hand and takes his place next to his wife.

"The little girl from the orphanage?" She blurts out.

It just so happens her question gains the attention of Ryder, Shayne, and Shayne's parents.

"Sure is. Have a problem, mother?" He spits out the word with venom.

She goes to open her mouth, but State's dad cuts her off. "Not now."

If she looked pissed off before, then looks could kill right now. She runs her blood red painted fingernails through her hair.

"Let's go eat," his dad offers.

We follow in silence. The only thing holding me up is the strong arm around my back. I want to run. Every excuse of leaving flows through my mind, but I don't want to leave State yet.

"I'll meet you guys there." State clicks the button on his car remote.

He opens the car door for me and I climb in. I melt back into the leather seats and feel like that girl from the orphanage.

"I'm sorry." He leans over and kisses my cheek. State drops his head to my temple. "My mom means well, she's just difficult."

"She hates me."

"No, she's just a tough one."

"She thinks I'm trash."

"I'll talk to her. She's just way overprotective and has always wanted the best for me."

"And I'm not the best."

His finger stretches out, goes to under my chin swiveling my face to him. "Stop."

I try to shake my head no, but he keeps it from moving.

"You're the best and we're forever. My mom has two choices. She can either get the fuck over it or get out of my life."

"State, you can't…"

He presses his lips to mine, stopping the words from flowing from my mouth. He catches all of the fear and insecurities in his own mouth. When he pulls away he whispers, "I love you, Baylor."

We drive the rest of the way in silence. State calmed my nerves for the time being. Our fingers tangled together soothe my soul.

"Head on in with Shayne and Ryder. I'm going to wait for my parents."

I don't argue and hop from the car. I have no urge to come face to face with his mother again. Shayne wraps her arm around my shoulders when I'm at her side. Her touch is welcoming and warm.

"She's a dick."

I giggle at the term she uses for State's mom.

"Don't let that shit get to you. This world can be fucking tough as hell. You have to grow a thick skin and fight for what you want. It's what I do every day in the gym."

"Thanks Shayne."

I settle in by her in the large booth. I keep my palm planted on the empty space next to me, hoping like hell State will sit there. The conversation is light over the table with talk of football.

Shayne taps my shoulder. "Smile."

She holds out her phone and snaps a picture, then posts it to her SnapChat story. She titles the picture "State's Girl" and lines it with colorful heart emoticons.

"Do you have this app?"

"Yeah, I do."

"What's your username?"

I pull out my phone and look it up. I dismiss Shayne's puzzled look.

"Um, it's Princess B."

She giggles.

"Rowe," I offer.

Chapter 19

State joins us nearly thirty minutes later. He slides right in next to me and places a kiss to my temple.

"Love you," he whispers.

I turn to him with a leap of courage and kiss him on the lips. "I love you, too, number seven."

Eventually, I look up glancing in Martha's direction. Her eyes are puffy and most of her make-up has vanished. His dad greets me with a warm smile, yet Martha makes no eye contact.

We order our food. I wanted to order a ham and cheese sandwich off the menu, but after hearing the others all order steak and lobster, I feel dumb.

State squeezes the top of my thigh. "Want do you want?"

I look up to him and then point to the menu. He sends me a slight grin. State orders the largest steak with extra potatoes and a large salad. The waitress then glances at me waiting for me to place my order.

"She'll have the ham and cheese sandwich with fries, and a side salad with Italian dressing please."

I place my hand on top of his, squeezing it to thank him. I remain silent next to State staring down at the table most of the time while the football talk entertains the rest of the group. Momma Pete is the perfect combination to lighten the mood. She brings up Shayne's next competition and how she's in contention for Nationals this year.

State's mom beams proudly, going on and on about how proud of Shayne she is, and what an honorable young lady she is. I don't miss the jabs my way.

"What do you do, Baylor?" I look up at State's dad.

I clear my throat and try to speak, but nothing comes out. "She's enrolled at a community college majoring in pharmaceuticals, teaches dance, is a licensed masseuse, and works as a server."

"Wow, ambitious girl." He smiles back at me. "Martha's a surgeon. Both women in the medical field."

"Most students never finish schooling in the medical field." She shrugs coldly.

"Martha," State warns.

There's more meaning behind the use of her name coming from State. Tears begin to well up in my eyes. I don't think I can do this.

My phone lights up on the tabletop. It's a FaceTime call from Miss Tami.

"Answer it." State pulls his arm from my leg and wraps his arm around me.

"Are you sure?" I nod toward the rest of the party at our booth.

"Go ahead, sweetie," Momma Pete encourages me.

I slide the green button across and wait for faces to appear. Shayne leans in looking at the screen. Pretty soon one large eyeball fills the screen. It's Rowe.

"Baylor? Shrek?" She yells into the screen.

"Hold the phone back, Rowe." I hear Miss Tami's voice.

"Hey princess," State says loudly.

He holds his wrist up showing her the bracelet.

"I saw you on TV, and the bracelet."

"Brought me good luck, princess. I even scored a touchdown."

"I know," she squeals. "Miss Tami was screaming so loud."

Rowe continues to move the phone closer to her face, giving us the perfect view of both of her eyeballs and even a clear shot up her nose.

"Want to meet my coach and teammates?"

"Yes!" She squeals.

We both exchange shocked looks. It's football, and her heart is open and happy.

State leans the phone over to his coach. He takes it in his hands, with Momma Pete leaning over and waving.

"Hi." The coach offers her a weak smile.

"Do you like princesses?" I hear her ask.

"Sure do, and football even more."

I can imagine her wrinkling her nose back at him.

"Who else is there?"

We all share a muffled laugh when Rowe so easily loses interest in one of the most high-powered coaches in the nation. He passes the phone over to Ryder who holds Rowe's attention. I'm sure it's his good looks and can only imagine her adjusting her invisible crown on the top of her head.

"I'm the one who throws the football," he offers mid-conversation.

"I only like number seven."

State doesn't stifle his loud laugh at that comment. "That's my girl."

Ryder waves bye and offers the phone to State's mom.

"No." She shakes her head.

State pulls the phone from Ryder's hand. His pissed off glare instantly morphs into a genuine smile when he stares back at Rowe and a part of Miss Tami's shoulder.

"When are you guys coming home?" She asks with a hopeful tone to her voice.

He answers immediately. "Late tonight. You'll be tucked in and in sweet dreams, but we will share waffles in the morning."

"Pop Tarts promise."

"Pop Tarts promise, sweetie."

"Love you, Rowe."

"Love you, too."

We end the call and intertwine our hands again.

"You had to be what sixteen?" State's mom asks.

I finally find my voice. No one ever fucks with Rowe. "Excuse me, Martha?"

"You had to be what, maybe, fifteen when you had her?"

State begins to cut her off, but I squeeze his hand to stop her.

"No, actually. Rowe is one of *THOSE* orphan girls. Miss Tami and I took her in after she suffered unimaginable abuse." I don't break my stare with her. "Any other questions?"

Our food arrives and I've never devoured a meal so intently. Momma Pete brings the conversation back to football between her bites of lobster. Everyone seems to be professionals at diverting the real conversations of life and standing up for what's right. It's the first time I realize State being adopted may not have been all it seemed.

He devours his meal while keeping his hands all over me. He feeds me bites of his steak every once a while between quick kisses to my cheek. State fits with me, not his family.

His dad wraps me up in a hug before I climb into the car. Martha remains in the background. State doesn't offer her a hug or even a good-bye, even though they're catching the redeye in the morning.

"I'm sorry." He slams the door and picks up his phone. He doesn't offer anymore explanation to me. His knuckles go white around the steering wheel.

His voice is harsh and clipped. "I told you to respect her, that you didn't have to understand it, but I demand nothing but respect for Baylor. You were a heartless bitch, mother. I hate saying it, but you forced it. I don't want to hear from you until you have an apology."

I hear her voice scramble on the other end of the phone.

State only replies with. "I don't give a shit. Apology or nothing. I don't want to hear from you until then. Got it?"

He throws the phone down on his console, slams the middle of the steering wheel, and then tosses his hat into the backseat.

"State, you didn't have to."

"Bull fucking shit," he growls.

"Don't do this. You'll ruin everything with your family."

"You're my family and all I need. End of story."

I know I should reply with something, but there are no words. He's defending me. The only way for me to fix it would be to walk away, but I'm selfish and will never do that.

Chapter 20

The house is dark and silent when we walk in. We're careful not to make any noise getting to my bedroom. I'm thankful for my personal bathroom off my bedroom. I flick the lights on and lock my bedroom door.

"I'm going to get ready for bed," I offer.

State sits on the side of my bed with his face buried in his hands. My heart hurts for him right now and I want to take away his pain. It's a tough thing to do when pain brought us together in the beginning. I shed my game day clothes and slip into a white cami, then go about washing my face and applying moisturizer.

There's a light knock on the bathroom door. "Can I come in?"

I reach over and twist the knob, smoothing in the last of the lotion. Our eyes connect and there's a fire in his. His hands are on my waist, tangling in my panty line before he lifts me up to sit on the counter. He stares down into my eyes, not taking advantage of my mouth.

"I'll fucking protect you from anything."

"It's hurting you." I brush my finger down his jawline.

"It's fucking hurting me that someone had the nerve to talk to you like that."

"I'm a big girl." I smile up at him.

He places both hands on either side of my hips, palms down. "Nobody will disrespect my queen."

I cup his jaw in my hands. "Thank you."

Our lips connect, and we kiss hard and fast. It's been way too long since we've been alone. I float back to him on the field, ruling it. I edge toward him. scooting my butt to the end of the countertop.

"You were so damn sexy out on that field, State."

"That was the best game of my life. It was like my world finally came full-circle."

"Mine too." I smile. "I actually learned a little bit about football."

He pulls back, still clutching to my hips. "Tell me."

I scrunch my lips to the side and think for a second. "There's four quarters, it's your job to shut down the plays, the offense has four tries, and it's good when you hit the quarterback."

"Four tries to do what?"

I nibble on my bottom lip. "Honestly, you never let me see that part."

He chuckles deep. "That's good. Real good, Queen."

I drop my forehead to his, close my eyes tightly, and whisper to him. "I'm ready for you."

"Baylor." My name rolls off his lips in a sexy-ass tone.

"I'm sure. I need you."

My words send him into action. My heart skitters and my body aches with need as he roams his hands up my sides. He pulls the cami over my head leaving me bare to him. State roams his eyes down my chest to the only thing separating us — my lacey panties. I throb for his touch.

I reach forward, grabbing both of his hands and bringing them to my body, then lean forward and brush my lips across his. I dart my tongue out, running it over his. I leave his hands on my sides with his thumb grazing the underside of each of my breasts.

My hands trail down his sides, peeling his shirt over his head then to his gym shorts. They tug down, easily dropping to the floor. His tight boxers offer up more of a challenge to pull down. He's exposed to me. I can't control my hands as I grab the base of him and begin stroking him to the tip. He remains frozen under my touch.

The feel of hypnotizing him with my touch makes me powerful. I never want to stop touching, kissing, and being with him. His breath catches in his throat as heat pools in my core. State gently lifts me from the countertop, taking me to the bed.

He lays me down gently on the top of my duvet. My skin flushes with heat when his stare devours my skin. I reach up a hand to him and he takes it without a word. His other hand drags my panties slowly down my thighs. The feel of the material scraping my skin is erotic. My insides coil and I need him so badly. I've never needed anything like this before.

State sets everything inside of me on fire. He breaks our connection and runs his palms underneath each of my thighs, bringing my legs up over his shoulders. He clutches my ass in his hands, bringing me closer to the edge of the bed. State sinks to his knees. His beautiful face disappears between my legs and I feel his tongue dart out. I shiver with pleasure and ache even more for him.

He takes me in his mouth, licking and tasting me with his tongue. My hips move up into him, needing more. The bundle of pleasure builds rapidly, deeper inside me. I'm going to reach my goal in a matter of no time. It only takes one harsh swirl around my clit to send me over. I grip onto his hair and buck up even harder, riding out the last wave.

"You're so wet," he hisses.

He climbs up my body easing me comfortably back in the center of the bed. He keeps one hand cupping me while covering his mouth with mine. I devour his lips letting him know how much I need him. He sinks one finger into me.

"State," I whimper.

"You have to be ready, Queen." He licks his lips while working me over with his fingers.

I find my hips bucking up into his touch. I'm all sorts of worked-up, falling again into pleasure. I open my legs wider for him, letting him settle between them. He brings his hand to his mouth, seductively licking off each finger. I take his mouth with mine helping him soak up the rest of the taste he elicited from me.

I feel the tip of him lined up perfectly where I want him.

"I got on birth control after the first night you came here for me."

"You did?" He's shocked and it's simply adorable.

I nod to him. "Make love to me, State."

I see the question on his bottom lip that's clutched with his teeth.

"I've always used condoms, Baylor."

"Something I don't want to think about right now, baby." I brush his cheek.

He clenches his eyes shut, reaches down between us, grabbing the base of his throbbing need, he lines up the tip until he's pushing into me.

"If it hurts, I'll…"

"Shut up, State." I pull his face down closer to mine.

My hips thrust up into him, helping him. He slips in inch by inch stretching me to the limit. I'm not well-diversed in this area of life, but like every other aspect of State, he's a giant. I focus, taking oxygen in and out of my nose while never breaking our stare. *Breathe in, breath out, Baylor.* He squeezes his eyes shut when he's all the way in me.

"Fuck, fuck, holy shit, Queen."

"Oh my God, baby," I whimper. "Feels so good to have you in me."

He slowly begins to move in and out of me. My hands roam down his strong back until I have my fingertips grazing the top of his ass cheeks. Tears begin to roll down the side of my face. His hands catch each one.

"Okay?"

It takes me a few moments to finally respond and it's only with a nod of my head. There are no words to describe the feeling of what's happening right now. It's surreal, all mind numbing, and making me whole in the same aspect. My world is complete.

Gently, I lift my face to his and take his lips with mine. I mimic his action with my lips and cry into him when he hits the spot that sends me over the edge. I feel his body begin to tremble, and then his growls vibrate against my chest when I feel him release in me. He shudders and then collapses down, keeping most of his weight balanced on his shoulders.

"Jesus, Baylor."

"I love you so much, State."

"It's more than love, Queen."

After several long moments of silence, he stands from the bed leaving me naked and feeling open to the world. I hear the running of the water in the bathroom and then see him appear with a warm wash cloth. He spreads my legs and runs it over me, cleaning me.

When he returns once again from the bathroom, he scoops me up like a baby cradling me to his chest. I brush back the hair matted to the sides of my face and look up into his eyes.

"Thank you for coming back to me, always saving me, and giving me all of you, State."

Chapter 21

Our limbs are tangled underneath the sheets. I'm not sure where I begin and end when pressed against State's chest. He's still breathing heavily, deep in sleep. The rhythm of his chest rising and falling against me lulls me back to sleep.

I wake to a little squeaking voice out in the living room. I can barely make out Miss Tami's voice trying to convince her to put in a movie until we wake up. It warms my heart knowing she assumes State is with me. *My family forever.*

I try to weave from State's body without waking him. He has to be sore and exhausted from yesterday. I can't imagine how his muscles feel. I sneak into the bathroom to brush my teeth and check my hair, and also make sure my all my clothes are covering the right parts.

Slowly and very quietly, I shut the door. Rowe is bounding into me, wrapping her arms around my legs, and squealing my name.

"Baylor."

I lean over and pick her up. "Oh, I missed you little one."

I shower her with kisses and then place my nose in the crook of her neck sniffing around. It's her crazy ticklish spot, always guaranteed to get a hearty laugh out of her. She's already dressed in a petal pink princess dress, tutu, and a pair of my high heels.

"Is Shrek here?" She brushes her bangs away. "Wait, I know he is. His car is here."

"Sssshhhh." I place my finger over my lips. "Let's let him sleep. He's tired from his game."

"Oh, is that all he's tired from?" Miss Tami asks from her chair.

I look up to her and she sends me a wink.

"Ha ha, very funny." I wrinkle my nose and then automatically replay last night. We were silent. I turn from her to hide the blush of embarrassment painting my face.

"Let's start those waffles."

"Waffles," she growls out, imitating Donkey from Shrek.

By some sort of miracle we quietly get the bowls out and the batter started with no sign of waking State. I decide on cutting up some fresh fruit to pair with the waffles. Rowe is distracted with her Rapunzel doll on the floor. She's threatening to cut her hair off, making me smile. She gets into character so easily with the biggest imagination to top it all off.

My stomach growls and the sugar shakes kick in quickly, so I plug in the waffle iron to get breakfast going. I set the table with all the toppings, waiting for it to warm up. On my last trip to the table I nearly get caught up in the Rapunzel scene playing out on the floor.

Strong arms catch me before tumbling face first, smearing the front of me with butter. The plate trembles in my hand while State stands me back up.

"Well, good morning to you too, my Queen."

I look up at him and smile. Last night bonded us together forever. His touch feels different, sending chills all over my skin. I don't have a chance to analyze it before Rowe is up on her feet throwing her hands up to State.

"Shreeeeekkkkk." She squeezes her arms around his neck as he hoists her up to him.

"Princess," he sings right back out to her.

"I made you waffles," she fires right back.

"Oh, you did?" I quirk an eyebrow, pouring the batter onto the greased iron.

"Yep." She claps her hands together.

Miss Tami joins us. "One day you won't be able to be held like that Rowe."

She taps her nose as she walks by her. Miss Tami is always scolding me when I pick her up. It will be a sad day when she is too big for that. I bring the first plate of waffles to the table as State places Rowe down in her chair.

"I'll get the drinks," he offers.

He opens the refrigerator, pulling out the milk and orange juice. He comes to me before going to the table. He blows air down on the crook of my neck. His front pressed to my back.

"You look so amazing this morning."

"It's your glow." I turn my head enough to kiss him.

Rowe and State devour their breakfast. He coaxes her into helping me wash the dishes while he takes a hot shower. She's like a puppet on strings with State. As soon as he's out of the shower in a clean pair of gym shorts and a workout tank, Rowe bounds to him in the living room. Hell, I didn't even notice him bring in a bag last night.

"Your car?" Miss Tami's voice interrupts my thoughts.

"Uh?"

"Your car?"

"Oh, it's at the stadium. State is going to drive me back to it later this evening. We wanted to spend a lazy Sunday with you guys."

"How was it?" She asks stepping closer.

"You have no idea. It was amazing. State is phenomenal. He was the star. It was so fun."

I chose to leave out his mother and the fact Burnett was there. She doesn't push any harder and only smiles. We join State and Rowe on the couch. He has his hat on backwards with the mandatory tiara sitting crooked on top. He has Rowe and a whiteboard on his lap explaining football plays to her.

"See when they're lined up like this you have to watch for the screen. It's like a trick play."

"Ohhhhh, like the villain in the castle."

"Yes, and it's my job to take the dragon."

"The guy throwing the ball?" She asks.

"Yes."

"And you can't get burned by the fire." Rowe plucks the marker from his hand. "What if you did this."

She draws lines all over the board with X's just like State had. He scratches his head for a few moments trying to decipher the play she's drawn out.

"I see." He rubs his chin. "I'll try that next game."

"It will work. I promise you." she looks up at him. "Do you think I'd like to go to a game?"

His eyes soften and I can practically see his heart swell with pride.

"I think you'd love a game, but let's check in with the fun police, okay?"

"Okay?" She nods her head and then looks up at us. "He called you the fun police."

Rowe giggles and points at us. I roll my eyes at State letting him know he's not playing fair. We settle in for a movie, but end up wrestling around on the ground and playing a game with Rowe. Miss Tami heads out to her weekly girl group. They knit and mainly gossip. It's good for her to get out.

"I'm hungry."

I look over to State. "There's no way you can be hungry."

"I'm starving. Let's go get pizza."

"Pizza," Rowe sings out rubbing her belly.

The two of them are up and waiting for me at the door. I'm still lying on my back studying their excited faces. State shifts his cap so it sits backwards on his head.

"Let's roll," he offers.

"Yeah, let's get our pizza on." Rowe wiggles her waist.

I groan pulling myself up to my feet. As usual Rowe is not impressed with the backseat, but State whispers something into her ear as he buckles her into her spare booster seat. I give him the stink eye, knowing he's just promised her ice cream. It's his signature move and he knows all too well, that I won't complain.

"Bubblegum," he winks at me and clutches my hand as he drives.

Chapter 22

"Want to see my dorm?" State asks, tucking his hands in his pocket.

I fell asleep on the drive over and I'm feeling sheepish again. Rowe ran us around like crazy, from pizza, to ice cream and the park. I have no idea where State and Rowe mustered up the energy to not stop once today. Me? I crashed in the car on the drive.

"Yeah, I'll follow you." I reach up to kiss him quickly. "Can't stay the night though."

"Ball buster." He pulls me in closer to him.

"I have to drop off Rowe at school in the morning and have some early massage appointments."

"Mr. Moore?" He raises his eyebrows.

"Shut-up."

I follow the back of State's sexy car until we pull into a parking lot. It's full and buzzing with college students. So this is dorm life, I think to myself. There's four large brick towers that I pass and before I can turn off the engine, State is at my door.

"Is this okay?" I gesture to my parking spot.

"Perfect. It's Ryder's and he's not here tonight."

"Oh?" It comes out as a question.

"Shayne. They meet up every Sunday night. I have no clue where they go. It's all a damn secret. The boy is going to get his balls busted."

"Oh." This time it's a statement.

He clutches my hand, leading me into the middle tower on our right. We pass a guard station and the man sitting behind the desk beams up at State. It's clear he's a hero, even here. We ride the elevator with some drunk, giggly girls who don't seem to care State has me at his side and we're hand in hand.

"State," one of them purrs.

He squeezes my hand tighter and he nods, acknowledging her.

"We missed you at the after party," she says.

"Lindsey was really looking forward to riding you after that victory."

I try to let go of his hand, but State refuses. My stomach drops with the rise of the elevator. I'm going to be sick.

"Excuse me?" He snarls. "That never happens."

The girl who has giggled the whole time pipes up. "We thought it was worth a try."

"I'm taken and not into that shit."

We step off the elevator and I gasp for air.

"You okay?" He looks down at me.

"I'm good as I can be."

"It's all bullshit. I hope you know."

"I do. You told them."

He unlocks his door and we step in. He has me whirled around and backed up against the door. His palms plant against the wood, trapping me in. His stare is even more determined than last night with his parents. It hurts to see how hard he's fighting for us. Before he can get a word out, I run my finger down his jawline.

"State, I believe you. It was hard to hear, but that's life."

"I'm sorry."

"Don't be!" I grin wide.

"Don't be? That was fucking horrible."

"Not that bad, I guess now that I think about it."

"Have you lost your damn mind, Queen?"

"Nope." I cup his face in my palms. The light stubble peppering his face tickles my skin. "Look at it this way, I have the hottest, most talented football player in the nation, and none of those skanks can do a damn thing about it."

He processes my words for a minute and then offers up a half smile. "You are so right."

His stomach growls and I roll my eyes. "No damn way you can be hungry again, State."

"I'm a growing boy," he smirks pressing his hips into mine.

"In more than one way," I laugh at the corny-ass joke.

But the raging erection pushing into my abdomen is anything but a joke. He wants me. I press his chest back. He entertains me and moves. I eye the two beds and wait for him to answer me. He nods to the left, and I back him up all the way to it until the backs of his legs hit the mattress. State goes down easily onto his ass, spreading his legs wide for me to stand between.

He glides my shirt off and then pulls down my shorts. His lips trail kisses underneath my bra while his fingers fumble with the straps of it. The lacy material tumbles to the ground effortlessly. He pays very close attention to each perked up bud of need.

My head goes back when whimpers escape me. His fingers dip low into my panties. I adjust my legs wider, giving him better access.

"God, I need you right fucking now," he moans into my flesh.

I push my panties to the floor and then shove his chest until he's laying back on the bed. He tries to protest, but the sound of his zipper shuts him right up. I much prefer the gym shorts he was in earlier. Easy access. But in a matter of moments, some tugging, and hip shakes from State, he's bared to me.

I waste no time wrapping my hand around his thick cock. We keep eye contact while I work him from base to tip, only stopping to massage the head. I lick my lips and then take him in my mouth with no warning.

"Baylor, Jesus Christ." He thrusts up into my mouth.

I smile around him, loving the sensation coursing through me, knowing I'm driving the man mad. I'm more adventurous this time, taking long strokes and working him at the base with my hand.

"Ahhh, fuck," he groans and then pulls me off him.

Our connection is lost with one loud pop. He pulls me up to his chest and attacks my mouth. It's passionate and raw. His teeth sink into my bottom lip until I whimper out in pain. He catches the sound and then massages the same area with his tongue.

"God, I want you," he whispers.

I roll off him onto my back and hold my arms open.

"What's this?" He asks.

"Take me."

He turns his head to the side in question.

"I feel safe when you're on me."

State rolls on top of me, settling between my spread legs.

"I like your dorm room," I grin up at him remembering why we came here.

"You haven't even got the grand tour yet."

"Don't need one. I came for you."

He slowly enters me. I keep my eyes open the entire time. His face contorts through a rainbow of emotions making my knees go weak. Watching him enjoy the feeling, nearly brings me to climax. It's the sexiest thing I've ever seen.

He begins moving slowly at first, but then something breaks between us. My hands race up and down his back. My hips buck for him. State picks up on the urgency and begins pounding into me. A strange combination of pain and desire pool inside me.

"I'm close." He drops his elbow to the mattress, relaxing his forehead on mine.

"Me too."

"Let go, Queen. Fall into me."

With his last words, my insides clench and I tumble. The free-falling sensation low in my belly bursts until my head spins. When the sensation is about to vanish State grunts low once, then thrusts three more times before he releases in me. He coaxes the tail end of my orgasm sending me straight into another one. I flex up into him riding out the final sensation.

"Hell of a tour." I brush my lips against his.

His stomach responds with a loud growl that vibrates to the back of my spine. We both erupt in laughter.

"You're a pig!"

He leans around and smiles at me.

"A very hot, sexy, and talented pig," I correct.

State leans up, beaming with pride, and rubbing his belly. He ushers me to the bathroom in his room and goes to order, what I'm presuming, is pizza. The man really needs to invest in a large chain with as much as he eats.

When I finally make my way back into his room. I take it all in. Ryder's side of the room is plain, actually bare. No pictures or posters on his side. It's a mess, too. Papers, dirty clothes, and wrappers are the only decorations strewn around.

State catches me eyeing Ryder's side and points to the ceiling above his bed. I crane my neck to look where he's pointing. There's a so not classy nude picture of a blonde straddling a motorcycle. She has one finger dangling from her lips and the other hand cupping her private parts.

"Gross." I cover my eyes. "Did you really have to?"

State's deep chuckle is contagious and I finally join in. His side of the bedroom is stark contrast from Ryder's. It's tidy and organized. His desk matches the chair. He also has a cork board plastered with notes and pictures. I step up to it and cover my mouth.

"Printed them off from my phone. They get me through the week."

There are pictures of me, Rowe, and Miss Tami. In some, I'm sleeping or staring off, while others I'm staring shocked at the camera. There are several selfies of Rowe and him, and even one of him and Miss Tami.

I turn to look at a shelf with several trophies and plaques. But it's the few family pictures that catch my attention. State through the years with his two proud parents by his side. Martha looks kind, caring, and proud of her son. It makes me feel like shit.

"Stop," he warns.

I stick my tongue out at him while running my fingers along the edge of his desk. He's written a quote on the top in a thick black sharpie maker. I trace the outline of each letter. *"I will love you, even if I never see you again."*

He responds, even though I don't ask a question. "That got me through the endless years without you."

My eyes water and I don't stop the tears. They're happy and thankful ones that I kindly embrace. My eyes catch an unopened box of UNO cards next to the retro lamp on his desk. I look over at him and raise my eyebrows.

"Those were for our rematch, if I ever found you. No rigging the deck this time."

I laugh through the tears, then pluck them up and plop down on his bed.

"May I? Or are you too chicken number seven?" I raise an eyebrow.

"I've waited years to kick your ass."

I rip the box trying to pry open the fresh pack of cards and take several moments shuffling them. I don't want to hear any moaning about this epic rematch of proportion, so I shuffle the cards a few extra times.. I fling a few cards out of my shuffling hands every few times just to give me an excuse to reach over into his lap to grab them. I'm a bad girl and let my fingers graze him a little too long.

By the time I have all the cards shuffled, the pizza has arrived. I'm thankful to see he ordered a salad and wings as well. He warns me that I better grab what I want before it's gone, so I tuck a package of buffalo wings under my knee.

"I'd suggest strip UNO, but then I'd have you naked and under me again. I need to focus on this shit."

"Chicken," I taunt him.

"Chelsea Cheater Pants."

I roll my eyes at him, deal the seven cards, and then review our rules. He agrees to everything and the match begins. He devours his pizza while playing, making some of the cards greasy. It doesn't bother me.

We take turns almost going out with one card left, but then the inevitable Draw Four shows up. I'll hand it to the man, he never lets me get away with shouting UNO first for a long time. His phone buzzes several times, but he chooses to ignore it.

When he finally looks down at the screen filled with text message notifications, I strike.

"UNO," I scream.

The word comes out so loud I scare myself. He quirks an eyebrow up at me and shakes his head.

"That's cheating."

"Whatever, you chose to look down at your phone."

"Cheating," he repeats.

He fans his cards deciding what to play. It's hard to keep a poker face, so I nervously bite down on the end of my finger to throw him off his game. He eyes me carefully before laying down a Wild Draw Four card. He relaxes back down on his elbow and gives me A *Gotcha Sucker* look.

"State," I whine.

"Told you I've been waiting on this rematch for years."

"You're a jerk." My voice is filled with defeat.

"Some people just aren't made for cut-throat UNO."

I drop my hand to pull from the draw pile, but in a swift change of movement I lay down my Wild Draw Four on his.

"Sucka." I throw both hands up over my head.

"No fucking way." He slams his hand down on the bed.

"Way!" I brush a shoulder off and then the other. "Ain't nobody taking down the Queen of UNO."

"You little cheat."

He pounces up from his relaxed state on his side and attacks me in upright cross-legged position. We both fall back onto the bed. He peeks down my shirt, then runs his hands up my shirt cupping my bra. He squeezes my boobs and even dips a finger down low, running it along the cups.

"What are you doing?"

"Finding where you hid all the good cards, Chelsea Cheater."

"State," I giggle and squirm under him.

He runs his hands down the front of my panties and then rolls me over. He does the same, running his palms over my bare ass.

"Did you kiester them?"

"Stop." I giggle even harder.

He finally settles down next to me.

"The best out of five?" He asks with a hopeful expression.

"I'd love to, but I have to get going."

"I hate this part."

"Me, too." I wiggle my nose on his cheek. "When will I see you again?"

He nibbles on my jawline. "It will be a while, Baylor. Our next game is away. I won't have any time to come see you this week."

I deflate next to him. "Okay."

"We'll fly home Sunday. We usually get in super late. The game is going to be intense, we're playing our conference rivals. They're out for blood this year."

"So, like two weeks?" I ask.

"Fuck, I hope not. I'll do my best."

I'm being selfish and I know it. I prop up on one elbow to look down at him. "It's okay. You're a busy man with lots on your shoulders. I know you'll come to me when you can."

"I am busy and have tons of responsibility with football, but Baylor you're number one in my life. Do you get that? Number one. Day or night."

I nod. "Okay, but seriously State, my name on your back is all I need."

"What do you think of Rowe coming to my next home game?"

"Honestly?"

He nods.

"I really don't think she's ready. I mean football aside, she's really sensitive to loud noises."

"Down the road?" He looks hopeful.

"I'll talk to Miss Tami and we can make a plan."

"I really want her at a game. Hell, I'd love to bring her down on the field."

"I know. She adores you, Shrek."

He brushes off a shoulder throwing my own move in my face. "I'm pretty damn loveable."

"That you are."

Chapter 23

"You're crazy. It's still light outside."

"I'm walking your fine ass to your car and sending you off with a proper farewell."

We walk hand in hand past the security guard and avoid another elevator soap opera. State gets stopped by a group of men. I recognize some from the team party, but step back while they talk.

I send out a quick text to Miss Tami while I wait. State holds up a finger to me and jogs off with the men. I can still see him, even though he's like the size of ant in the distance.

"I know you from somewhere."

I turn to see Dylan Burnett behind me. He's alone and eyeing me up and down. My skin fucking crawls. No way he recognizes me. Hell, I didn't even put a name to the face until it was announced at the party.

"Nope, sorry." I turn my body to face the direction that State went in, hoping the fuckface walks off.

"I'm pretty sure I do." He steps in front of me tapping his lips. "You star in any porns?"

"Excuse me?"

"I never forget a face."

"Leave me alone. State's going to be right back. Get away from me. I have nothing to say to you."

He's just trying to upset you. Stay calm. He's one of State's team members. State needs to have a good season. Stay calm.

His hand wraps around my wrist and he tugs me to him.

"Let go of me."

His grip tightens and he jerks down hard. I feel a pop in my shoulder and then shooting pain strike down my arm.

"Rowe, the little retarded girl. You guys ruined my brother. He's serving time."

I react, ignoring the pain. I spit in his face and then knee him in the groin as hard as I can. I connect hard, sending him backward. I'm not finished though. When he hunches over, I send my knee up into the air connecting with his nose.

My kneecap aches with pain because of the brutal connection. Blood spews from his nose, and I bring back my fist to take a swing at his perfect lined jaw.

"Baylor, Jesus." Someone pulls me back by the shoulders.

They're stronger than me, but the anger and rage in me fuels my adrenaline.

"Let go of me." I swing my arms and try to kick whoever has me in their grasp.

I'm spun around and come face to face with State.

"Let me go."

"No." He looks over my shoulder. "Get that fucker out of here."

Campus security shows up and escorts him off.

"I'm not talking to them. Let me go."

"Baby, what's going on?"

"I want to go home. Please."

One of his teammate bends over and picks up my phone. "State, I think it was all caught on video."

I look down at the phone and go for it, but the man holds it up over his head. I begin to tremble and feel my legs go weak. The world spins, I see stars for the second time tonight, but not the good ones.

"Jesus, baby." State scoops me up in his arms. "Do you trust me?"

Sobs wrack me.

"Follow us in her car."

I feel State reach around in my purse for the keys. The sound of them jangling together fills my ears when he tosses him.

"Green, drive my car."

He has me clutched to his chest in the back of the car. "Are you taking me home?"

"No," he whispers into my ear. "You have to talk to me and trust me."

I close my eyes willing everything to disappear. I want to be back home and the Baylor I was before reconnecting with State. I don't want him in my life. This is going to ruin everything.

I'm not sure what happens or even how much time passes before I come to my senses. I'm sitting on a couch in Coach Pete's house. He's sitting across from me with a concerned look on his face. Momma Pete is on one side of me with State on the other.

"Whenever you're ready, sweetie. You need to tell us what happened," she reassures me.

"It's them or the cops," State whispers, clutching my hand.

"Where's my phone?"

"Right here." State hands it to me.

I swipe it open and pull up the camera roll. There's a new video that's three minutes long. It starts out with a view looking up on my face. I push the triangle button to play and feel the sensation of losing State. I won't make it through this.

The whole nasty conversation plays out. I cringe when I hear the top of my kneecap collide with his nose.

"Rowe," State whispers.

"I didn't want to tell you. It would ruin your football season."

"How long have you known?" The hurt is evident in his voice.

"The team party."

"Mind filling the rest of us in?" The coach asks.

I can't look at State. He's pissed. I can feel the anger radiating off of him.

"I was taken in by a woman named Miss Tami. She was a social worker at my elementary school. It was after State was adopted. I had a great life growing up. Long story short, a few years ago she also took in a little girl named. Rowe. She has down syndrome and was severely abused by the high school football team. Dylan Burnett's brother was one of the boys."

"What did they do to her?" State viciously growls.

I swallow hard. "State, I don't want this to affect you. You have so much going for you."

He slams his fist down onto the coffee table in front of us. The corners containing glass shatter.

"It's okay. Go ahead." Momma Pete gently squeezes my hand.

"They did horrible things, State." Tears begin to fall from my eyes. "Her parents didn't even know. Her brother was on the team and they were terrorizing him through Rowe."

"Miss Tami told me that part. I need to know what they did to her."

I choke back a sob. "They molested her, State. The school nurse found her in pain one day at school. She was taken to the hospital and objects were removed from her rectum. That's why she hates football."

I bury my face in the palms of my hands. Each word slices my tongue as I'm forced to speak it. The long and brutal hours in the courtroom come back to me, along with the testimony and pictures. I break on the inside just like I did when we experienced it.

"This will be handled." Coach Pete stands. "State, my office now."

I don't look at him. I know he's gone when I hear a door slam.

"Sweet, baby." Momma Pete wraps me up in her arms and holds me while I cry. Her hands run down my back. After several minutes she speaks again.

"I must say I'm impressed with your self-defense skills. Good girl."

"The product of being raised on the streets." I manage to get out through my sobs.

State's booming voice echoes throughout the house, then the Coach's, and then State's, again. It goes back and forth for a long time until I can't stand it any longer.

"I'm going home." I raise up on shaky legs.

"I don't think that's a good idea."

"Please." I look down to her with a pleading stare. "I want to go."

She nods her head and ushers me outside. Momma Pete takes my phone from me and types in a number.

"Please call or text when you get home." She places her hands on top of my shoulders squaring me to her. "We care about you."

I nod toward her and then get into my car. I twirl the phone over and over in my hand debating whether to text State or not. There's nothing left to say. I fire up the engine and push shuffle on my iPod linked up to my stereo. The drive back goes quickly and I'm pulling into the driveway. All my tears have dried up and I'm thankful the house is dark.

When I enter the house and see all of Rowe's princess dolls strewn around the house, the sadness slams back into me. I refuse to cry any longer, but I just don't know how I'll handle losing State. The look on his face killed me.

I'm thankful he has his coach there for him. He'll be the one person to keep State's head square on his shoulder. I recognized the rage State flew into. It was a glimpse of him when we were young and he was protecting us, but now it's intensified.

I scrub my face in the bed and let a few tears flow. It's grieving. The loss of him. I drift off into sleep when my phone buzzes on the nightstand. It takes me several minutes to even roll over to see it, but it buzzes again. I finally reach over and grab it. There's several text notifications from State.

"Shit, I forgot to text Momma Pete," I whisper.

I send her a quick text and then read the others.

State: I'm coming to your house.
State: I'm here.

State: I don't want to wake Rowe and Miss Tami

State: Please let me in.

State: PLEASE

The three dots at the bottom of the screen jump around. He's not going to give up, so I crawl out of bed. When I open the front door, State is standing there with his head dropped down typing furiously away on his phone. He looks up at me shattering me with the desperate look on his face.

"Thank you," he whispers.

I'm greedy, so I grab his hand and lead him to my bedroom. Once in the room with the door shut, there's only the dim lighting of my bedside lamp lighting up the room. Neither of us talk. I'm not sure why he drove all the way here to just let me go. Football is his future and I won't stand in the middle of it.

"State, you didn't need to come out here to end things. I get it."

He looks up to me with a dark and wicked stare. "Fucking really, Baylor? Read your fucking texts."

The angry tone in his voice scares me. He's never talked to me like that. I look down to my phone lying on the bed and noticed he managed to send three more texts while I went to let him in.

State: I'm hurt.

My fingers tremble around the phone.

State: Why didn't you tell me?

State: I fucking love you more than anything. Even football. I love Miss Tami and Rowe. I'll do anything to protect you guys. Are you really going to shut me out that easy?

"I'm sorry, State," I whisper.

He looks back down at his large unlaced sneakers he'd slipped on to walk me out to the car.

"I didn't want to interfere with football and your career. It's your future."

He stands to his feet, putting his hands on the top of his hat in frustration. "I really don't know what else I can do, Baylor. I've tried showing you everything that you are to me. It's like you have no desire to fight for us."

He walks out of my bedroom. I crumple to the bed and, like usual, I lose my voice. I'm streamlined right back into my ball of fear where my voice is lost. I fade away in the darkness of a life I'm so damn used to.

I wake up hours later with a kinked neck and a very dry mouth. My face is plastered with dry tears. I go out to the kitchen not turning on any lights to fetch a bottle of water from the fridge. The cold water coats my dry throat. I gulp more of it until my head hurts from a brain freeze.

There's two cupcakes on the counter decorated with way too many pink sprinkles and note lying by it in Rowe's writing. *To my sissy and Shrek. I love you. XOXO Rowe.*

How can I break anymore? Shattered tiny pieces of glass can't break any further, but I feel it crack. The tiny shards pierce my already broken heart. Tears spill down my face when I walk back to my bedroom.

I notice State's large frame sleeping on the couch. His legs dangle over the end and his head at that angle that looks painful. Without thinking, I go to the basket in the corner of the room and grab him a few blankets.

It takes two to cover his large frame. Once he's covered up, I lean over and kiss his forehead leaving my lips there for a long time. I pull back a little bit and whisper to his sleeping frame.

"I love you, State. I'm sorry. I thought I was protecting you. I'll always love you."

I stand up to walk away when he clutches my wrist in his enormous hand.

"It's my job to protect you. It always has been, Baylor."

He drops my hand and I walk back to my bedroom. My alarm sounds way too early. The throbbing pain in my head makes me dizzy, but like so many other times in my life when I didn't want to live another day…I get up.

I shower quickly, knowing I'm already fifteen minutes late to get the morning started. I know I should be buzzing around getting ready, but the lead weights on my soul slow my every move.

A loud ruckus in the living room causes my head to ache even more. When I open my door, Rowe and State come into view. He's sitting in front of her tying her tennis shoes.

"Sissy," she squeals.

"Hey." I blow her a kiss.

"Look." She pops up on her feet. "State brought me this."

She twirls around in her blue and orange tutu and new football shirt.

"Wow, you look beautiful."

"There was one in the box for you, too." She pulls it out and hands it to me.

"Thanks." I look over to State.

He shrugs. "I was going to mail them to you guys this week, but brought the package in from car this morning."

"Oh." I look down at my bare feet. "Okay, Rowe, you need to eat breakfast."

"Already did. State made me waffles this morning and he's taking me to school." Her toothy grin is contagious.

"Exciting, sweetie," I offer, still feeling hollow on the inside.

She runs for her backpack and grabs State's hand. "I'm ready, Shrek."

"Would you like to go with us?" He asks.

I look up at him and realize he's talking to me. I'm scared. I don't want to hear how much I've hurt him.

"Baylor looks sad," Rowe says.

"She does," State adds.

He steps up to me, grabs the back of my neck, and pulls me into him. He kisses me hard and then pulls back.

"I'd do anything to make her happy." He brushes his lips against mine.

Rowe squeals. State takes my hand in his and we walk out to his car. My nerves are on high alert, but State acts like last night never happened. When we pull into the school parking lot, Rowe buzzes with excitement.

"Will you walk me in, State?" Rowe asks from the backseat as she frantically undoes her seat belt.

"Yes, sweetie. I'm dying to meet this Mr. Moore." He jumps out of the car, helps Rowe out, and then makes his way to my side of the car.

I'm shocked when he extends his hand to me. I take it without second thought, jumping down and colliding with his hard chest.

"I love you, Baylor."

"I hurt you," I whisper back.

"You did."

His acknowledgment of the statement devastates me.

"I understand though. You've protected Rowe, and I get it. You don't have to protect me the same way."

He kisses me lightly and then succumbs to the tugging of Rowe. She guides us up the sidewalk like shiny new toys. The three of us never let go of each other's hands while winding through swarms of excited children.

Rowe rushes right up to her favorite principal.

"Mr. Moore." She tugs on the bottom of his suit jacket.

He looks down to her, smiling widely.

"Good morning, Rowe."

"Morning." She beams with excitement.

I follow Mr. Moore's sight to my linked hands with State. I feel sheepish for a few seconds until State begins to talk.

"I'm State." He extends his hand out.

Mr. Moore shakes his hand. "Nice to meet you."

"I'm Baylor's boyfriend."

"And my prince," Rowe squeals.

Between the two of them, I'm pretty sure Mr. Moore gets the hint loud and clear. He's professional at all times, even though I sense the air of disappointment flashing on his features.

"Mine," State growls when we leave Mr. Moore. I squeeze his hand reassuring him that I am, in fact, his.

It's an even bigger production when we hand her over to her teacher. We walk back to his car hand in hand right past Mr. Moore. I don't miss the nod State sends his direction.

"Enough, State."

"What?" He asks, opening my door.

"I think you've pissed on me enough."

"Good."

When he gets in the car he doesn't start the engine, but turns to me in his seat.

"I need to say sorry, Baylor. I overreacted."

"State, do we have to do this?"

He slaps his palms on his chest. "Is this worth fighting for?"

"Of course," I shout at him.

"Then I need to say sorry for blowing up last night. I understand you were protecting me. You knew I'd blow my fucking top and kill Burnett, especially after he put his hands on you. Coach had to talk me down, so I get it. You were protecting me. But that's not how this works."

I swallow hard.

"We need to talk and trust each other. I promise to you, right now, that I'll fight to keep my temper tamped down."

"Okay," I nod. "State, I still need to tell Miss Tami."

"What?"

"She doesn't know I ran into a member of the Burnett family."

"Yes, you do need to tell her."

State drives in silence to a coffee shop. I hop from the car and let out a breath when he grabs my hand guiding us in. We settle in a little corner of the shop. I clutch my coffee and feel hopeful.

"I'm sorry, State. I was just trying to protect you. It seems dumb now because I know that you're all in."

"I am." He grips his coffee cup.

"I am, too. I promise."

"I know you're scared. I get it, Baylor."

"Yeah, some things never change." I sit back in my seat and roll my eyes.

"That's not what I'm saying here." He reaches out to cover my hand near my coffee cup. "I'm telling you one more time that I am your safety net. I'll always catch you."

I don't respond.

"You could tell me that my coach was Satan and I'd be on your side, Baylor. I love football. Hell, I've eaten, breathed, and slept football my whole life, but my world is nothing without you in it."

A single tear rolls down my face, but I refuse to cry. "I know, State and I love you for that. I'll always love you."

"Good. That's past us. Want me to make time this week to be with you when you tell Miss Tami?"

"No." I shake my head. "You have football."

He interrupts me with a warning tone. "Baylor."

"Let me finish," I say leaning forward. "I can do this on my own and I want you to focus on football. I mean, if I'm going to date then I need to be dating the number one defensive end in the nation. I expect no less."

He lets out a light chuckle lightening the mood. "I'm serious, Baylor. Not even my parents will get between us. They can see it my way or kick rocks."

"State, you can't give everything up for me."

"I will," he growls. "Watch me. I'm not fucking around."

I feel pieces of the open wound on my heart begin to heal. He's always been the one standing by my side no matter what. The man is opening up to me and telling me he'd sacrifice everything for me. Love doesn't even begin to define what's going on between us.

"Thank you. I love you, State." I swallow hard and stare into his deep chocolate brown eyes. "I'm all in. I deserve it and no there's no way I can live without you again. Last night scared the shit out of me."

"It sounds all sappy and shit, but I can't function without you Baylor."

"I get you, man cub." I stand and walk over to him nestling down into his lap. We finish our coffee in silence.

Chapter 24

Life sucks without State in it. He's been booked solid with football and classwork. We FaceTime daily and he even snuck by a couple of times during the week. I'm quickly learning what college football entails. Your whole damn life!

The last two weeks he's had away games. The man is exhausted from the grueling game, but always makes time for me and most certainly Rowe. He has sent several packages chalked full with princess dolls and new game day shirts. We're going on week three of him being super busy. Thank God, it's a home game this week. Saturday can't get here soon enough. Fuck Wednesdays.

My phone chirps lighting up the quirky selfie of me and State. I have baby carrots hanging out of my nose and he has celery sticking out of his ears. All Rowe conspired of course, State insisted on a selfie.

State: God, I can't wait to see you Friday night.

Me: 45 Hours and 13 minutes…but really who is counting!

State: Jesus, I'm going to devour you when I see you.

Me: I'm not thinking a family dinner would be the place to devour.

My stomach rolls in disgust just thinking about another encounter with his mother. Thank God, Shayne will be there to distract me. We've grown closer over the last few weeks via texting. I know all about her gymnastic career and how badass she is. I've also discovered that the tension between her and her father is well and alive, and that she's hopelessly in love with Ryder.

State: I don't give a fuck.

I smile down at the new message, knowing all too well he truly doesn't give a fuck. I smile at the five words.

Me: Aren't you in class?

State: Fucking economics are boring as hell. I keep thinking about you naked on me.

Me: Pay attention, man cub!

State: Oh, I'm paying attention. Your creamy skin pressed against mine. Those perked up nipples begging to be sucked on.

Me: You're impossible. I have a massage appointment. Have to run. My nipples will be impatiently waiting.

State: Love you, Queen.

Me: Love you even more, lover boy.

And that's how most of our conversations flow. It eventually leads to something sexually initiated by State and it leaves me wanting him more than I ever thought possible. It sucked, but I quit my job at Alley's. The sole purpose of working there was to push me out of my comfort zone. Miss Tami agreed it was too much on my plate and that I was doing a fine job of trying new things.

I blushed when she'd told me those exact words. She had no idea how many new things I'd been trying, tasting, and licking. I'm pretty sure the expression on my face told her everything she needed to know.

I'm focusing on finishing up my few online courses, my massage clientele, dance, and State. If I'm being honest, I focus on State more than a healthy mind should be allowed to.

Rowe is more than eager to attend her first home game. Miss Tami broke down in tears when I shared the whole story with her. We all agreed that I'd test out the waters of the next home game and then make a decision. It hasn't stopped State from buying her headphones with his team logo on them, along with the rest of the gear. She'll look like a Momma Pete Junior when she finally attends a game.

The afternoon flows by in a mindless state, as do the rest of the days. It's Friday afternoon and I feel like a kid on Christmas morning. Not that I'd ever know that true feeling. Just have to get through dance and my little ass will be blazing down the interstate to State.

"Rowe, grab your backpack."

"Baylor, I am," she sings back with sass.

She's decked out in blue and orange, and ready to tackle the dance lessons, quite literally. She's taken her spin on princess glam and football, creating a new look for herself. She has her favorite Rapunzel doll tucked under her arm and a toothy grin plastered on her face. I cringe when I spot her front tooth dangling from her gums. She refuses to pull it and has adapted to a way of eating that doesn't knock it out. I've begged and begged.

"Why do they wear these things anyway?" She plays with the thick black stickers under her eyes while we drive to lessons.

"I'm not sure. You'll have to ask State."

"Yeah, right." She rolls her eyes.

"What's that supposed to mean."

"I never get to see him anymore."

"I know, baby, he misses you."

"Can you record a bit of my dance to send him?"

"Of course."

I mentally try to figure out the game plan since I'll be teaching my own class, but this I'll give her. We walk hand in hand into the studio and it's abnormally quiet. Usually there are girls of all ages, running around in their dance outfits, giddy with excitement.

"Baylor, darn, I was going to call you," Shelia, the owner announces. "We're really short today. I guess some stomach flu floating around. I was going to tell you that I didn't need you today."

"Oh, it's fine." I wave her off and then dart for the hand sanitizer dangling from Rowe's backpack. I lather her and myself in it. I know it won't be of any good, but it's one of those things that makes me feel better.

Then a slight pang of anger sets in. I could've been driving to State already. Shit! I'm half tempted to call Miss Tami in, but I'll just swallow the pain and wait a few more hours. Time makes the heart grow fonder, or the ovaries explode in anticipation. I'm not sure which.

"Hey, I'll record you for a bit, then I'm going to hit a private studio to dance for a bit. Okay?"

"Yes." Rowe claps her little hands together in excitement.

No freak out this time. I was waiting for her to pitch a fit for me to teach her class. She amazes me every single day with her resilience. I'm watching a shattered child bloom into a beautiful young lady. There's truly no great honor than that.

I record her hopping around to her first song and then send her a quick good-bye wave.

Me: Rowe wanted me to send you this video. I'll be hitting the road in a few short hours, big guy.

I wait for a response, but get none. I don't worry because the man is either in the gym or running through new plays with his team. I tuck my phone in my duffle bag and make my way to one of the small private dance studios. The room has mirrors lining two walls, a ballet bar, and a smooth dance floor.

I pull my hair up into a messy bun on the top of my head, press shuffle on my iPod, and then begin stretching out. Dance has always been an escape for me since Miss Tami introduced me to it. It's a place where I'm not forced to talk or interact with anyone. It's just me, my body, and music.

Beads of sweat begin to roll off my forehead as I dance to each song. Most of them are choreographed and I know the moves by heart, while other songs I make up new moves and just let my body go. Dancing has to be best form of mental and physical exercise.

One of my all-time favorites begin to play. The song absorbs every single part of me. It eats at my soul and speaks to me in every way possible. *Skinny Love's* sweet melody floats around me, hugging me tight. I float across the dance floor in long powerful strides, twirling, and losing myself into the song.

Sadness strikes me like it does every single time, but in the end I'm winning. I'm defeating the sad parts of my life and finding myself. I'm winning at this. So, I pronounce each move with more conviction and power than ever before.

It starts out as a pirouette and then I spin until I nearly become to dizzy to land on both feet. I let everything go as I twirl around. The final chords of a piano playing, ends the song. Two large hands slam together clapping. I turn to see State sitting on a bench with his team hat on backwards. A smile covers his entire face.

"State."

I barely manage to get his name out between my pants.

"Fucking amazing, baby. Miss Tami is right. You need to be dancing professionally."

I shake my head at him. "You're crazy."

Drums and a hypnotic beat light up the small studio. Janet Jackson's *What Have You Done for Me Lately* begins to play. My hips begin to sway to the beat. I do some fancy foot work knowing the choreography to this song by heart. I slide from side-to-side hip popping along the way. The song and my dance moves have ended our conversation abruptly.

Improvising, I add a few moves of mine own like dragging the hem of my shirt up to expose my stomach and even facing my ass to him while shaking it. During the whole song I close the distance between us. I'm mere inches from him, gyrating my whole body and even untying my hair letting it whip around.

If he came for a show, I'm sure in the hell not going to disappoint. It's been too many long nights without my man in my bed. I slow my hips near the end of the song making my moves long and languid, and right in his damn face. State bites down on his bottom lip showing his appreciation.

I hop in his lap, straddling his thick thighs and finishing off my last dance moves. My chest grinds up and down his long torso while I keep one hand planted on top of his shoulder, waving the other over my head.

When the song ends I giggle and stare him in the eyes.

"That's for me and no one else. Do you hear me?" His voice is thick with want.

"What about men's night here. I get my best tips then." I bite down on my finger.

"What in the hell?"

I slap both of my palms down on his shoulders. Our skin to skin connection ignites me. Thank you God for inventing tank tops.

"I'm kidding." I manage to get out between giggles.

"Well, look at my girl." He brushes my hair away from my face. "She's confident, glowing, and fucking gorgeous."

H.O.L.Y by Florida Georgia Line begins to play in the background setting the mood.

"Because of you."

State grips the back of my head, twining his fingers into my hair, and brings our faces together. We don't speak anymore. Our lips connect and we kiss each other hard. Like, being separated for too long, hard. I open up when his tongue licks across my lips. He takes his time exploring the inside of my mouth, meanwhile I melt into him, letting him devour me.

A piercing alarm goes off on my phone. I pull away feeling my lips pulse from the hard kiss. *Best feeling ever.*

"Rowe's class is about to end. She'll shit herself seeing you."

"Well, let's hope she doesn't shit herself."

I slap his cheek playfully. "You know what I mean."

"I don't. Maybe another kiss?"

"Get your ass up." I slip on my tennis shoes and gather my stuff.

State's on his feet with the door held wide open for me to step through. I lead him to Rowe's studio and we slip in as quietly as possible. When holding hands with a towering six and half foot man whose shoulders barely fit through the door jam, it's quite the task.

I don't miss the stares the damn dance moms give him. In an over-exaggerated move, I throw a leg up on his lap and clutch his hand. He smiles down at me not missing the obvious move.

He leans forward, gives the women a wink, and nods. "Afternoon, ladies."

I elbow him in the chest causing him to chuckle down into my hair.

"I like jealous Baylor."

I wrinkle my nose up at him. He kisses me quickly on my lips before I turn around to see Rowe staring at us. I send her a quick wave. She shocks me when she goes right back to dancing. Each one of her moves are overly done with a dramatic flare. Between songs she points to her game day shirt and winks at State. It makes me giggle. Rowe remains focused on her dance teacher, showing off for State.

He bends down and whispers in my ear, "God, I love that little girl so much."

I squeeze his hand letting him know that I know. His phone flashes in his lap. "Mom" scrolls across his screen. I don't let the name upset me. Instead, I focus on his screensaver. It's one of him and Rowe. It makes me happy to see her on his phone. This man is so much more than love. He's my shelter.

He doesn't even flinch or reach for his phone. I'm not sure he even recognized the text because his vision is on Rowe. Her dance teacher must pick up on Rowe's excitement and lets them dance a little longer than usual.

"Shrek," Rowe squeals, racing toward him with her arms wide open.

He stands up on his feet, letting me slide to the side. She's the only person on the face of this Earth that would make me smile being pushed aside for.

"You're here." He cups her cheeks, pinching them.

"I had to see you dance, princess."

She dramatically flings her hair back.

"Yeah, why did you come?" I ask, stepping up to them carrying all the duffle bags.

"To watch Rowe dance, duh," he responds.

"Duh!" She mimics State.

I shake my head at both of them as we walk out hand in hand. State never puts Rowe down and she waves to all her friends as we go.

"I don't want you driving down to the campus. I wanted to surprise you," he finally whispers down to me.

"Did you get the video?"

"Duh." He raises his eyebrows. "That's how I knew you'd be here."

"Can you buckle me in your car?" Rowe asks.

"Sure can, princess."

"Rowe, how about you just ride in my car since your booster is there."

"No, thanks."

Well, at least she added thanks.

"I've got you covered, sister." He opens the back door to his sexy car.

There's a brand new princess booster settled right in the middle.

"Oh my Pop Tarts." Rowe scrambles from his arms and buckles herself in.

"That's a miracle," I whisper. She never buckles herself in.

"What can I say? I bring out the best in beautiful women." He winks at me and then turns to Rowe.

"Where shall we dine, my lovely lady?"

"McDonalds," she sings out.

I groan. It's her go-to restaurant and I hate it.

"Deal." He turns to me, pulling me in a hug. "Want to call Miss Tami to join us."

"Oh, I'm sure she'll be jumping with freaking joy."

"Not a fan of McDonalds?"

"Hell no. How about you work that magic and convince her she wants Subway or something."

He lets out a hearty chuckle. "I'll do my best."

We exchange a few quick kisses, which are not nearly enough, but will have to do. I send Miss Tami a quick text, once I'm in my own car and before I have my phone sat down in the passenger seat it chimes.

State: Subway on Broadway Avenue it is.
Me: THANK YOU!!!!!!!!!

I follow the taillights of his car as he weaves his way through traffic. At one stoplight I can hear the bass of a Taylor Swift song pumping through his car windows. I can only imagine both of them belting at the top of their lungs together. And I smile.

"No Miss Tami?" He asks walking into Subway.

"No. She said she'd just meet us at home."

State's still carrying Rowe, and she's still beaming from ear to ear.

"Just so you know, we only chose this place so we can have pizza." She smiles down at me.

"Of course, you two would go for the pizza."

State orders five pizzas and only shrugs when he hears me clear my throat. Rowe goes for the kid meal with a pepperoni pizza.

"I hope I get the pink toy in mine." She closes her eyes.

I don't miss the glare State sends the young boy behind the counter.

"Stop," I whisper.

"What?"

"You're scaring him."

"He's going to be more than scared if she gets one of those creepy yellow or green toys."

"Stop." I can't help the giggle that escapes.

"I'll break his legs."

"Enough," I hiss, but it's hard to hide the laughter.

I order a six-inch ham and cheese.

"What veggies would like on it?" The poor boy asks.

"None."

"Mayo or mustard."

"No thanks."

"Salt and pepper?" He asks.

"No."

He goes to open his mouth again, but State not-so-politely interrupts.

"Wrap up the damn sandwich."

"Wait," I squeak. "Could I get it toasted please?"

"Toast it and wrap it up," he growls.

"Jesus." I turn to State. "Cool it."

"The kid is pissing me off."

"Are you han-gry?"

"Yes, I want food, and you, now."

I laugh and pat his shoulder. "I'll get the drinks."

I fill mine up with Diet Coke, Rowe's with lemonade, and State's all the way to the top with ice and then water.

It seems the man only binges on pizza, but besides that he eats pretty damn clean. We settle into a booth with no bodily harm to the employees. Rowe lets out an ear piercing squeal when she pulls her pink trinket from her kid's meal.

"Look!" She holds it up like she's just won a gold medal.

I laugh at the pure joy radiating off of her. State's three pizzas in and not slowing down, while Rowe picks off the pepperoni nibbling on each piece, and I nibble on the ham and cheese sandwich. I love that State has never asked questions about my weird eating habits. I'm convinced he remembers how I use to hoard food back in King's. I was always weird about it.

After Rowe finishes her apple slices, State gathers all of our wrappers on our tray, and then tosses it in the trashcan.

Chapter 25

"Mom and dad are meeting us for dinner tonight."

I look over to State and study his side profile. His eyes are covered with aviators and I'd wish like no other to peel them off his face and climb into his lap, but that would probably cause a twenty-car pile-up on the interstate. It's twisted that I give it even a second thought.

"That's fine, babe." I squeeze his hand.

"I've talked to my mom a few times."

"State." I twist in my seat to face him. "I know you'll protect me. I'm not worried."

On the inside, my gut twists. I'm not that sick of a human being to want to be treated like a dirty hood rat, but knowing it's for State and he'll be my side makes the sting less painful.

He pulls into his parking spot at the dorms and I'm thankful for the time needed to freshen up. I don't even flinch when he grabs my bag and then my hand. I walk in the dorms this time with my head held high. I even gain a bit more confidence when the horny-ass women stare at our connected hands.

State leans down, kissing the top of my head several times as we walk in. He's doing everything to show me I'm his and I fucking love it. I've never felt so bold in my life. With each kiss, I squeeze his hand tighter in my grip.

"I'm impressed," he says when he shuts the door to his dorm room.

"About?" I pull my shirt over my head and then turn to him.

"Holy hell, Baylor."

"What are you impressed about, man cub?" I slide my shorts down my thighs stepping out of them and then kick off my flip-flops.

"You."

It's a one-word response that means the fucking world to me.

"I've heard there is this prince," I step closer to him. "That has magic to bring out the best in women."

He steps closer.

"Beautiful. Beautiful women," he repeats, emphasizing the word beautiful.

"And he's all mine." I grin.

His lips brush in the crook of my neck. "Too bad you undressed yourself. I was going to ask for a dance."

"I'll file that information for later." I bite down on his neck.

"Mmmmm. We don't have that long."

"Then I suggest you make love to me now."

He gently pushes me back onto the bed until I'm lying flat. I feel him tug off my panties and then hear his jeans drop to the ground. When he covers my body, I slip his shirt over his head and pepper kisses all over his chest. I lick and nip at his skin.

State's hand trails down my belly until he's rubbing my folds. I buck up into the sensation, yearning for more of it. He smiles on my skin, then moves his lips to my breasts. I feel each one being removed from my bra and then his tongue races over them. I fall faster and harder than I ever thought possible.

"State. Oh my, State," I sing out, clenching around his fingers.

"That's my girl."

I grip the sides of his face while writhing out the sensation of my release. My hips roll back and forth, begging for more.

"I need you." It comes out as a throaty whisper.

He climbs back up my body, my legs widen letting him settle between me.

"Guide me in, Queen."

I follow his simple instruction and grab the base of his throbbing cock. I stroke it from base to tip watching his face turn into pure pleasure. It's so fucking sexy on him. I could stare at it all the life long days.

"Now," he hisses between gritted teeth.

I run the tip up and down my folds wetting him with me. The action sends chills through my body and I find my hips bucking on their own, hungry for him. He growls a few more times, but I continue to tease him. State loses all self-control and slowly pushes into me.

"Baylor," he moans out. "God, I need you every single day. I need to hear your laugh and see your smile. Fuck, I need all of it."

I wrap my arms around his thick back and hold tight to him. "You have me, baby."
He drives in and out of me. I push up into him, driving each sensation to my core. He has me all wound up again and ready to see stars.

He begins to growl and I know he's close. I bite down on his bottom lip the same time my vision goes black. Every single known emotion overtakes me as we both release at the same time.

State collapses down on me causing a slight *umph* from me. He's quick to roll off to my side, but takes me with him.

"You're going to kill me, Queen."

"Right back at you." I reach up to kiss him.

We lay in silence until our breathing matches each other's. It's my favorite part of the entire day; laying in his arms letting him absorb all my worries in his strong chest.

"As much as I hate to say this... we better shower and get dressed."

"No, let's skip dinner."

"And go straight to dessert?" He asks with a raised eyebrow.

"Yes." I smile up to him.

"I fucking wish, Baylor, I wish."

I'm the first one to push up off the bed and head for the shower. I take his fleece blanket with me to wrap up in it. I don't miss State's amused look. He's on my heels.

"I'll join you."

"No, you won't."

He pouts for a second. "We'll never make it on time, dumbass."

"Dumbass?" He grabs his chest and pretends to be hurt.

I step in the shower giggling and not long after State joins.

"Another first and I'll be a good boy." He holds both hands up.

"I wasn't worried about you being the bad boy." I wink.

"Enough." He warns me with a warm smile. His message and body language contradict each other.

State takes his time washing my back, ass, and boobs. I don't think they've ever been so clean in my life. I brush up against his hardened cock a few times before stepping out. He pouts like a little boy with his bottom lip sticking out.

I only laugh at his ridiculous gesture.

I leave State in the shower while I dry my body. I figure it's a good idea to be fully clothed, or at least halfway, by the time he gets out. I did not miss his need for me while in the shower. But if I'm being honest, it left a huge grin on my face.

By the time he turns off the shower, I have my panties and bra back on. I dig around in my bag to find my favorite coconut flavored body butter to slather up all of my skin.

"Jesus Christ, Baylor my balls are going to grow to the size coconuts if you don't quit that shit."

I laugh at his silly remark and continue rubbing the body butter up and down my legs, giving him a little show.

We drive in silence to the restaurant where we are meeting his parents. I'm sad that I will not see Shayne until tomorrow at the game, I was hoping for her distraction over dinner. But tonight it's just us and his parents. State has reassured me several times that he's told his mom to be on her best behavior.

It saddens me that he even has to do that, but on the other hand it makes me a very proud woman. Just like last time we ate dinner with his parents, we pull into a very fancy restaurant.

I already feel the hives climb up the back of my neck thinking about what to order. State jumps out and rushes around to the front of his car and opens the door for me. He holds a hand out and I place mine into his as I hop down. He tugs me close to him and places a quick kiss on the top of my head.

"Baylor, I'm honest, if my mom pulls anything, this is our last dinner."

I breathe a sigh of relief into his chest and begin walking by his side. I begin to second-guess myself on the outfit I chose to wear tonight. It's a simple white maxi skirt with a dark tank top. I pick at the hem of my top until State takes my fingers in his.

"Stop."

"Stop what?"

"Your fidgeting with your dress, you look just fine."

"I was playing with the hem of my top, not my dress. Actually, I'm not in a dress. I'm wearing a maxi skirt paired with this perfectly dark tank top," I say in a fun and flirty voice trying to tamp down all the unease threatening to spring out of me.

"Whatever. You look beautiful."

I lean in and whisper so no one else can hear me. "If you think this is beautiful you should see what I'm wearing under it."

His eyebrows shoot up into his hairline and dreamy look covers his eyes.

"I changed into something underneath while you were dressing."

I send him a flirty wink. As soon as we enter the restaurant the host ushers us over to a table where his parents are already waiting. Defeated, when I see that we are seated at a table set up and not a booth. I was hoping to be able to slide in as close to State as possible and let him act as my shield for the night.

His father rises to shake his hand and State offers his, then wraps his dad up in a one-arm hug. His mom finally stands to her feet and wraps her arms around State's neck. He's the giant of a man, so it takes her to rock up on her tiptoes even though she's wearing spiked high heels.

She's elegant and gorgeous. Regal and beautiful. Everything I'm not and everything she wants for her son. I don't have long to dwell on that fact because I'm pulled into a hug by State's dad, which surprises me.

When he pulls back he says, "Thank you for joining us. It's so good to see you again, Baylor."

I'm a little taken aback by his welcome as I move away, and I'm even more surprised by my words. "Thank you for inviting me."

State's mom makes no attempt to walk around the table to hug me or even acknowledge my appearance tonight. I figure being ignored is better than being treated like trash, so I'll take it.

My mouth feels like I've swallowed one-hundred cotton balls, so I focus on my water glass and drink as much of it down as possible. State places his hand on top of my thigh throughout the conversation that flows easily between the three of them.

I'm not sure what his mom is thinking. It feels like she's relented a bit on terrorizing me and maybe, just maybe, she has come to terms with the fact that I'm with State. When it's time to order, State gives me a sideways glance and I look at the menu. There's no ham and cheese insight, so I go with the next thing that I know I would like. I point to the pasta. State gives me a nod and then looks forward, continuing with his conversation.

It's all about football and the big game tomorrow, and the two away games where he totally annihilated the competition. His dad talks about a Heisman award that he'll be up for, and his mom drools over the fact that her son will one day be playing in the big leagues. Nice to hear him in such easy conversation this time with his parents, it's like I'm getting a glimpse of what life was like when he was growing up.

It's obvious that they were good to him, very good to him. You can see the love and admiration in their eyes as they stare at their son. For the first time, I'm not jealous, resentful, or even hateful for the fact that the State was taken to such a lovely home. Actually, it's a beautiful sight that makes my heart swell. They took my State from me, but only to turn him into a strong man. And that strong man came for me once again.

Who knows what would happen if people stayed in foster care? Or, who knows what would happen if I was the first one to be adopted? I'm not so certain that I would have ever been strong enough to go back for him or find him. If roles were reversed and I spotted him waiting on my table at Alley's, I probably would've run like a scared little chicken.

I owe this man so much. Tears prick at the corner of my eyes just thinking about what he's done for me in the short time he's been with me. Then dread overtakes me. What if I ever lose him? Answer, I would simply not exist.

"How's school going, Baylor?"

I feel State's squeeze on my thigh before I realize the question was directed toward me.

"Oh, good." I nod. "Really good. I'm just about to finish two courses and then on to the next."

"Do you only take two courses at a time?" His dad asks while taking a sip of his fancy wine.

"No, Sir. I'm actually taking five, but with my schedule and online courses, they all finish up at different times. It has to be flexible with my schedule."

"Nice."

"Your schedule?" His mom spats my direction. Oh, she's still full of venom.

State goes to open his mouth, but I stop him. She will not control this. It's my time to stand up for myself.

"Yes, my schedule. I work two jobs and help raise my sister. It's quite time consuming, but I'm very dedicated to my studies. It's always been my one goal in life and nothing will get in the way. Oh, and State has taken up a bit more of my time as well."

I look up at him. The smile radiating off of his face melts my soul. He bends down and kisses me.

He mumbles into my lips, "I'm so damn proud of you."

"I've raised you better, State," his mom scolds him.

"You're lucky I didn't slip her the tongue," he fires back.

His dad clears his throat and gently guides the conversation in another direction. "Are you going to the game tomorrow, Baylor?"

"Yes, I am!" My voice booms out with a little more excitement than I meant. "I wouldn't miss a home game for anything."

"Good to hear. You're always welcome up in the sky box with us."

"Thank you, but I'm sitting with Shayne again. I need to show off all my new football knowledge."

"You picked a girl with no football knowledge?" His mom arches a perfectly sculpted eyebrow.

"Mother," State grits out.

Game on, bitch. I wave off her statement like it's a punch line to a damn funny joke. "Oh no, trust me, I had plenty of knowledge before the last home game. See, State use to *forrrcce* me to play football when we were little. So, I know it hurts like hell when he threw me the ball and all the *x*'s and *o*'s he'd sketch out on a piece of trash, were just damn boring.

State and his dad share a hearty chuckle with my take on football.

"Mmmmm." His mom strokes a napkin near her. "He's never shared stuff from his childhood."

"Good. It's mine." I stare her down and flash her a genuine smile.

Our food arrives as the words evaporate between us. State has a death grip on my thigh, which I can't tell if that's a good sign or bad one. My phone chirps in my purse and without thinking to excuse myself to check it, I just pull it out. State's name flashes on the screen. I slide open the green button to read his text.

State: I've never been so in love with you. Fuck, you're hot when you're all defensive and shit.

I feel the red flush creep up into my face from his words. I turn and smile at him and then enjoy the rest of my meal. The rest of the dinner goes by quietly, with only his dad making conversation. His mom excuses herself early from the meal to take a so-called phone call. Just like he greeted me, State's dad tells me good-bye with a warm and welcoming hug.

"Are you going to drop me off at Shayne's?"

"Nope."

"What?" I turn to study his profile while he drives. I'm finding it's my favorite pastime.

"I'm staying at the hotel with you? I'm staying in the dorm by myself?"

He roars in laughter.

"Knock it off." I slap his forearm. "Spill."

"I made a deal with the defensive coach. If I got three sacks in my last game I could stay in my dorm room."

"And why would you make a deal like that?" I ask biting my bottom lip.

"Because I want to sleep with you."

"State, you need to be with your team."

"I'm with those stinky fuckers enough. I need you in my bed tonight."

"I don't want you to get into trouble."

"I'll go fucking mad if I'm not with you tonight and then I'll be in trouble."

"Thank you," I whisper.

The dorm tower is unusually quiet as we make our way to the elevator. I never think like a college student, but since it's a Friday night then I assume they're all out doing keg stands or playing beer pong. I welcome the silence. No prying eyes on us or obnoxious twats.

The book nerds huddled on the couches and over-stuffed chairs couldn't care less about us. I tug on State's arm as we wait for the elevator.

"That would be me."

He grunts. "Yes, it would be."

Then he shocks me with a question. "Do you think you'd ever live in the dorms?"

"Nope."

It comes out fast, requiring no thought at all.

"Do you ever imagine yourself here as a student?"

"Nope. But I've imagined other stuff here."

"Like?"

I blush a bit, but then spill covering my eyes. "You know late at night when I'm missing you. I picture you sprawled out in your bed, thinking of me."

"Then?" He urges me to go on. The ding of the elevator sounds off in the far distance.

"I touch myself."

The door glides open. I breathe out relief when no one is on it. He tugs me into the elevator and I nearly lose my footing as my back is pressed up against the wall. State's palms slap down on either side of my head. He presses his want into my center. I feel every single inch of him.

He bites down on my bottom lip until it hurts, then sweeps his tongue over it making the pain fade away. His hands slide down the elevator wall until he's clutching my ass.

"I'm going to take you in so many different ways tonight."

"You have to rest before the game. I will not be held responsible for you being slow tomorrow."

"I won't blame you. I'll blame your magical vagina."

"State," I squeal and burry my head in his neck.

"What? Just being honest."

"Stop, it's embarrassing."

"Okay, Queen."

He chuckles the rest of the way to his room with me in his arms.

Chapter 26

I'm straddling him, moving up and down finding the perfect pace. It's all so overwhelming. State insisted I be on top this time. I finally relented, but only in the pitch dark.

"Don't quit touching me," I whimper out.

State rolls my clit around with his thumb while keeping a tight grip on my hip. He helps guide me up and down him. It's all too much. My nerves are tattered and ready to explode any minute.

State sits up until we are face to face. He continues to coax my hips to move. It's a new angle, deeper, and even more delicious. My lips brush his and then I lick my own.

"State, I can't hold it off any longer."

He thrusts up into me. "Go, God, Go. Queeeeeen."

We both fall into our cyclone of pleasure. State shivers, pulling me closer to him until nothing is between us.

"I made a wish," he says.

"Eh?"

"I made a wish and then found you."

I cup his face. "Ahhh, baby, I love you so damn much."

State falls back into the bed with me on his chest. We don't bother to clean up before sleep takes over. It's the best night's sleep ever. My body is completely relaxed, my thoughts light, and my heart full for the very first damn time in my life.

When a sliver of sunlight drips into the room I feel light kisses up my arm.

"Baby."

I open one eye, refusing to fully wake up from the best night of my life.

"I'm heading to the field. I have coffee on for you."

I make a show of sniffing the air with one eye open. "Ahhh, you're a keeper, number seven."

"Shayne will pick you up in two hours. I'm also having breakfast delivered here for you."

I groan and finally roll over on my back. "Ahhh, a double keeper. How did I get so lucky?"

"God made me for you."

I slap his bicep. "Aren't you supposed to be in tear em' up destroy them mode, and not sappy man mode?"

He lets out a hearty chuckle and kisses my lips.

"Eeeeewww. I probably have morning breath."

"It's worse than anything I could imagine."

"Asshole." I throw a pillow at him and then push him away.

He dips lower and kisses me harder. "But I love it."

"State, I can't wait to see you play again."

"You have no idea how much adrenaline it gives me when I know your ass is in those stands wearing my number."

"Go!" I push his chest. "Before I drag you back into bed."

"Okay, only answer the door for breakfast and Shayne."

"Yes, daddy." I bat my eyelashes at him.

"I'll give you daddy tonight."

"God, you're gross, but I love you."

State sends me a wink before he shuts the door. I hear the lock turn on the outside and then his heavy footsteps trail down the hall. I sigh loudly and melt back into the bed. I inhale his scent and then cover my face with his pillow. It doesn't take long before I'm fast asleep in the comfort of forever.

***

Shayne may as well be a damn NASCAR driver. You'd never know she was a champion gymnast with her lead foot. I've lost count of the number of yellow lights she's blown through. My knuckles are white, gripped around my seatbelt.

"You can slow down. We have plenty of time," I offer.

"Uh?"

"Slow the hell down," I finally scream when she blows through another yellow light.

"Nobody can stand riding with me."

"I can see why."

"Did you know that all the stop signs with a white border around them are optional to stop at?"

I give her a sideways look and let it process. "So, you just chose whether you want to stop or not?"

"Yeah, but only the ones with a white border around them."

Four blocks later, and I call her out on her bullshit. "They all have white borders, jerk."

"Did you really believe me?" She laughs until she's gasping for air.

I raise my eyebrows. "Yes, like a dumbass, I did."

She laughs the rest of the way to her parking spot. Just like State's it's a lot closer than where others have to park. I'm all turned around and couldn't even tell you where State's parking spot is. I'm curious to see if it's open or filled.

I don't recognize anything on our way through security.

"I don't remember any of this?"

"Yeah, you probably came in the wrong entrance last time. This side is used less often and is about the same distance to our seats from the recommended entrance."

"I'm not sure I'm going to believe anything that comes from your mouth again."

She sends me a grin while continuing to wind us through the crowds. We stop in front of the food stands.

"I'm starving. You hungry?" She asks.

My stomach takes the invitation, growling loudly. State's breakfast didn't settle well with me and I gave up after the second bite of the egg sandwich.

"What do you want?" She asks.

"I don't care." I shrug. "I'll get what you get."

She rushes over to a pita booth. It's a long line, but flows quickly. I just slip Shayne my money and have her order me what she's ordering. I pray that there's no fish or pineapple in it. Anything else I can pick through easy enough.

"Don't tell State I did that." She turns and hands me a huge wrapped pita.

"What?" I ask.

"That I ordered for you." She takes a huge bite out of her chicken pita and begins speaking around it. "He said to make you decide and order."

"Really?" I quirk a smile.

"Yeah, call it bitch code."

"Bitch code," I repeat. "I like it."

"It's not to be taken lightly. It's like fight club, but with bitches and codes."

"Got it." I laugh and follow her.

I'm jealous how she so easily scarfs down her pita while walking to our seats. It's definitely not her first rodeo. Me, I wait until we are at our seats with napkins spread across my lap.

Shayne lets me eat in peace while she attacks her phone. Whoever she's texting is really getting a piece of her mind. I love hanging out with her. She's plain like me. Not like the other college girls I've run into who have layers of make-up plastered on and slutty clothes hanging from them.

Today she's not wearing Ryder's jersey, but rather a gymnastic school colored t-shirt. I admire her dedication and deep down I'm a bit jealous of it. I could totally see myself on the college dance team kicking ass, or at least trying to. It just wasn't in the stars for me and in a sick and twisted way I wouldn't change a thing. God, I'm confusing my damn self.

"Baylor."

I hear my name right when I take an un-lady-like bite of the pita. Way too much food goes into my mouth. When I look up, I'm face to face with State's parents. I mentally curse damn end seats in this moment. His mom seems just as happy to see me.

I wave and fight to choke down the food in my mouth. Shayne hands me her Coke and I'm thankful, taking long swallows of the fizzy liquid. My body is thrown into a coughing spell before I can stand to talk.

"Hungry much?" His mom asks. "And look it's not little kiddy food."

I ignore her bitch-asshole-jerk comment and hug State's dad. "Hey."

"Hey, just making our way up to our box. State wanted me to make sure you made it to your seat okay."

"Oh, I'm here and stuffing my face." I run my sweaty palms down the front of my torn, denim capris.

"Good deal. Stadium food is the damn best."

"You'll have a heart attack and get fat," his mom sneers.

Jesus Christ, this woman needs the corncob that is shoved up her ass surgically removed.

I go to open my mouth and just lay everything out between us, but she beats me to the goddamn punch.

"Baylor, I want you to meet Tia." A gorgeous woman near my age steps out from behind her.

She has long dark hair that waves perfectly down her back, olive skin, and delicate features. Tia is also wearing a number seven-football jersey.

"Hi." I send her a warm wave, praying like a damn fool that's she's just a cousin.

"Tia and State use to date back in high school. They were homecoming king and queen two years in a row."

"Nice." I go on autopilot and reach out my hand to shake hers. "Nice to meet you. I'm Baylor. State's girlfriend."

I roar the last two words like a powerful lioness and I'm damn proud of it.

"Funny, he's never mentioned it," she purrs right back.

Shayne is up on her feet, and I can feel her hot breath on my neck. "Funny? How long have you known State, Tia?"

"Since middle school."

"Then you're full of shit. He's had Baylor's name inked on his back for years now. So, I'm calling your bluff, bitch."

I stifle back a giggle when both of the women's jaws drop. State's dad clears his throat.

Just call me a predator who has found her new fangs. "I'm his forever, but it was so nice to meet you."

"Baylor."

I hear someone bark my name and swing around to see State leaning over the guardrail separating the field from the stands. I rush down to him not worrying to excuse myself.

"Queen."

"Number seven."

He peers over my shoulder for a brief second and I know exactly who he is looking at.

"Seems your mother is upping her game."

His lips crash on mine. His gloved hand twines in my hair pulling me closer to him. I feel my feet lift from the concrete and fly into the air. I giggle into his mouth, not stopping his tongue from claiming me. He pulls back for a second and places another quick peck to my lips.

"Fuck them," he growls. "I love you."

He adjusts the bracelet on his wrist that hasn't left since the day he put it on and backs away while, not so discreetly, adjusting his jock strap. There couldn't have been a more perfect response to meeting one of his exes.

I prance, yes prance, right back up those stairs and square back up to Tia and his mother while I brush away the lose curls framing my face.

"Where were we?" I ask, smiling.

"We are just off to our seats. Had to make sure you made it here okay."

"Thanks." I wrap his dad up in a hug again before they leave.

Shayne grabs me by the shoulders. "Jesus, Baylor, I'm afraid of you in the bitch code. That was badass."

"Holy shit, Shayne." I let out a long breath of air. "I have no idea where that came from."

"Your inner bitch and I like it. I like it a lot." She nods.

I focus back at the field and sigh in disappointment. I wanted to see State take it for warm-ups. I make up for missing and watch his every move. Out there he looks tiny and the way he moves is so stealthy and natural. Oh, and very damn sexy.

Shayne and I are up on our feet shaking our shit when the team rushes out of the smoking tunnel. I don't think I'll ever get tired of seeing State lead his team out. Just like last home game the stadium is wild with excitement. It's a contagious feeling.

"Oh hey." I slap Shayne's shoulder.

"What? Don't tell me you're pregnant that will just kill bitch code."

"No." My eyeballs pop wide open. "Hell no. Listen to this."

I turn to her, place my palms on my hips and begin. "This team has a solid offensive line which will make State's job harder breaking through. He's going to have to watch for lots of screens and rush like hell. Ryder needs to throw the ball in the air because their ground defense is tough on the other side."

"Damn, someone has been doing their homework."

"It's easy when the number one player is yours." I shoot her a wink.

"I might argue on the number one player. I think I have him."

I want to ask her more questions, but the ball is up in the air and the crowd goes wild. State's on point during the first set of downs, not allowing the other team to get a first down. He has two sacks back to back. I almost feel for the quarterback as he gets up slowly from the ground during the first quarter.

My voice is nearly non-existent by the fourth quarter. The score is tied and Ryder's game is off. He's thrown three interceptions and can't get anything going on offense. Our defense has been out there most of the game and by the way they move they're exhausted. Their bodies have been through hell and back.

There's only thirty seconds left in the game and the other team is only ten yards out from scoring. We can't stop their running game. Shayne and I are standing in our seats, screaming at the top of our lungs, when State raises his arms to get his fans to scream louder.

I can't even hear my own voice or know if any sound is coming out. The center hikes the ball; quarterback goes back for a pass. I catch Coach Pete jumping up and down screaming something, but everything happens so damn fast.

I spot number seven, my man, jumping up into the air. He extends his fingers as far as they'll go, and comes back down with the ball. Everyone on the field is stunned. State is sprinting down the field towards his team's end zone before anyone knows what's happening.

His long legs stride effortlessly. There are three opponents threatening to catch up, but he never slows down. He's at the ten yard, then the five-yard line, when a player from the other team snags his shoulder. State doesn't let it stop him, and drags the guy right along with him into the end zone.

I leap into the air, screaming even louder with the rest of the joyous fans. Shayne tugs on my arm and points to the time clock. Game over. We just won. I turn back toward State who is standing in the end zone swarmed by his teammates, but when he steps out of the circle. He looks in my direction and points right at me.

I know he can't see me, but the gesture makes me giddy with excitement. He's pulled me into his life effortlessly and now makes me a part of it every chance he gets.

Shayne and I hug each other like idiots. I blame it on the adrenaline coursing through me and a bit of team spirit. When I pull back I lift my index finger and waggle it.

"He's number one and mine," I shout over the roar of the crowd.

"Look." She hits my shoulder and points.

State's back at the guardrail waving me down. I sprint like a fucking track star down to him. And this time he pulls me over the rail and holds me to his chest. I wrap my legs around his sweaty and sexy body hooking my ankles right above his ass.

"It was the night with you." His lips are on mine before I can respond.

I bite down on his bottom lip, dart my tongue into his mouth, and kiss him like hell. His hands are in my hair tugging and pulling on it. We kiss like no one is watching us, even though the whole world is.

Chapter 27

"Baylor, ESPN was zoomed in right on you," Shayne repeats for the tenth time while we wait outside the locker room.

I answer with a shrug like I did all the other times.

"That was some intense mouth fucking."

"Shush it." I give a slight a head nod towards his evil mother and Tia glaring at us.

"It was. That shit was like straight from the Titanic."

I can't help, but laugh at her analogy because it was spot on. I've never felt like Rose on the front of that ship with her arms wide open ready to take on the world, but I do now. State and I have our whole future ahead of us, and nobody or nothing will stop us.

Like last time, State and Ryder are two of the last men to leave the locker room. I fly into his arms, not even caring how damn sore he is. The smell of woodsy, manly body wash hits me hard and I want to eat him alive right damn here.

He pulls back a bit. "What did you do to my girl?"

His smile is so wide I can't help but offer one right back at him.

"She's right here. Number seven taught me how to live and it feels damn good."

"Kiss me."

I follow his order sealing our lips together. He pulls back quickly.

"What's wrong, State?"

"That." He nods his head towards his mother and Tia.

"Fuck them," I say with joy.

"Jesus, what has football done to you?"

"Turned me into a tiger." I giggle feeling high on life.

"Simmer down, tiger."

He sets me down, never letting go of my hand, while we walk to his car. Shayne and Ryder pile in with us using an excuse of their cars being too far away. It seems her parents bought the story. They're quite oblivious. An astronaut on Mars could detect their chemistry from there. Lip smacking soon fills the backseat.

State cranks up his stereo booming out *C'mon Let Me Ride* by Skylar Grey. I'm not a college student like the rest of them, but in this moment I sure in the hell feel like one. The night breeze flows through the car with the catchy song. State squeezes my hand tight in his, leaning over to steal a kiss at every stoplight.

I never miss a chance to return it or tell him just how much I love him. We pull up to the same fancy-ass restaurant we dined at the first night with his parents and coach. Again, we walk hand in hand and sit at the same booth, but with one new member, Tia. State doesn't acknowledge her even when his bulldog mother is persistent as hell.

Each time she tries to get State tangled in a conversation with Tia, Shayne stomps on my foot. Jesus, I'm going to have broken toes by the end of the night.

"What do you want to eat?" State whisper to me.

"You." I send him a devilish smile.

"Behave," he growls.

"I'm not too hungry. Can I just eat off your plate?"

He nods. "I'll order an extra garden salad and I'll eat all the vegetables from it that you don't like."

"Perfect." I kiss his lips.

State orders the biggest steak, mashed potatoes, a bake potato, and two dinner salads. Once the waitress leaves I feel the evil glare from his mother.

"Not hungry for a sandwich, dear?" She asks me.

"No, I ate at the stadium," I reply with a tight smile.

"Oh, that's right we interrupted you pigging down on it."

"Mother." State slaps his palm down on the table.

I grip his flexed bicep. "No, she's right, baby. I was eating like a hog, but it was so good."

He looks down at me with a question on his face.

"That breakfast you had ordered to your dorm room was nasty. I appreciated the gesture after you left though."

Score: Baylor-one Cuntasaurus- zero

He bites down on his bottom lip recognizing my game.

"God, I wish you could stay again."

His voice is loud enough for the whole table to hear.

"Nope, my place tonight!"

If I can't kill them with kindness then sluthood will do. As per usual, the conversation goes right into football like a pissing match over State did not just ensue. Ryder and State tangle into their endless topic of who is better than the other. I've soon realized there's no way to compare their positions, but they seem to love arguing over that shit.

Our salads arrive and I wait patiently for State to pluck the olives, cucumbers, and other vile shit from it. I'm left with a perfect bed of iceberg lettuce drenched in ranch dressing.

"Wait." State stops everyone. "I was going to wait until after dinner, but just can't. My dad helped me with this."

I look over at his dad who is smiling with a huge grin on his face. State turns to me and just as my bitch code courage seems to evaporate. All eyes are on me. I'm about to step on his damn foot, hard.

He pulls a black box from his pocket and I nearly faint. I begin to shake my head from side-to-side. I know I'll marry this man someday, but a proposal like this? No. Really? No.

Yep, he pops open the black box to a ring. A fucking ring with diamonds, yellow damn diamonds.

"I love you, Baylor. You're my forever. Actually, the only person for me. It's been like that since day one of meeting your snotty little ass. I forced you to play football with me and you cheated at UNO like no other. King's brought us together and then tore us apart. Funny thing is, nothing can ever tear us apart now.

This is a promise ring. My promise to you. I promise to love you every single day for the rest of my life. You are the most important person in my life. I'd hang up that number seven jersey just to play UNO with you for the rest of my life."

I wrap my arms around his neck, not caring about our audience.

"Thank you, State. God, thank you!"

When I pull back he slides the ring on my finger. It's quite the statement with the huge yellow diamonds on it. I pull my hand to my chest clutching it. The rest of the dinner is pretty much awkward beyond belief, but the high I'm currently riding is too good to be ruined by anything or anyone.

"I have one for Rowe, too, my little princess."

I fork a piece of steak from his plate. "She'll love it."

We say our goodbyes and jump in the car.

"State, can I talk to you?" His mom asks before he folds his large frame into the car.

Oh shit! She's about to score.

He's a gentlemen and steps toward the back of the car, leaving the door open. Oh, how I wish like hell he would've shut that door. The most heartbreaking conversation takes place between a mother and son.

"Are you serious about this?" Her voice is nasty.

"Yes, mom. I've told you to accept it or move on."

"Are you fucking serious? We saved you and this is how you respect us."

I bury my head in my lap wishing like hell to not have to hear this.

"What's the God damn problem, Mom? Dad's been on board from day one. You're the only one acting like a bitch."

"She's trash, State. Fucking trash. You deserve better."

"You need to shut the hell up and think about what you're saying. I've never seen you be so nasty, mom."

"It's because I actually love you and care about your future."

"So, you try run the one good thing out of my life by being cruel."

"She's trash. You're so much better."

"We're cut from the same cloth," he growls.

"You were saved. She wasn't. Her way of life will destroy you."

"What in the fuck?" he roars.

"Oh God." I turn back to Ryder.

"Let me handle this, Baylor, stay in the car." He gets out, but their voices keep going.

"Son, you're going to lose everything you've worked for."

"You've lost me, Mother. I'm done with this."

"Don't, State. I'll fight for your future."

"I don't need you or need your shit in my life."

"She's trash."

"So help me God, if you repeat that one more time, I'm going to blow."

"Well, blow and walk away while you still can."

"You're worried about Baylor when you just fucking crushed my heart? My own mother being so cruel and heartless? I don't even recognize the monster you've become."

Ryder must get between the two of them since silence settles around us. My head spins with confusion and mostly hurt for State.

"Baylor, want to drive us back?" Ryder asks.

I scramble from the passenger seat and climb behind the wheel. I catch State slamming his fist into the metal pole before Ryder can get him into the passenger seat. The drive is quiet on the way back to the stadium. Another word isn't spoken when we go to the dorm room to gather our clothes. State doesn't refuse when I drive us back to our house.

"I'm sorry, Baylor," he finally says a few miles from my house.

"Don't be. I feel horrible that she hates me so much."

"I don't get it. I don't get it at all."

"It's okay, baby, I don't want to see you hurt."

"Me hurt?" He yells. "You think I'm fucking hurting to hear her call you that shit?"

"State, you're scaring me." My hands tremble around the steering wheel.

"Sorry, Queen, just know I'm not hurt. I'm fucking pissed. Dad said he'd talk to her."

I pull into the driveway and catch Rowe peeking out the front window with her damn-dangling tooth still in place. I turn to State and hold my ring up.

"You promised me the world and I believe it. That means we share the joy, sorrow, and pain of the world together. I'm here. I'm not leaving."

He drops his forehead to my shoulder. "Jesus, I was so afraid you were going to tell me it's over. That's why I didn't say a word on the way over."

"It's never over; until my last breath."

"I love you," he whispers.

"We better get inside. Rowe practically has the blinds off the wall. I'm betting she conned Miss Tami into letting her stay awake until we got home."

He doesn't miss a beat and morphs back into the strong, solid State I love, before hopping from the car. And just like all the other times when around Rowe, I become an observer to their crazy antics. He has her scooped up in his arms before the door fully opens.

"Shrek! I just knew you were coming home tonight."

I replay her words over and over in my mind. Home. Home. Yes, State is home.

"Hey, princess. I missed you."

"Nice tackles."

He chuckles at her compliment before settling down in my chair. I excuse myself to go wash up. I feel filthy from living it up in the stadium. I rush to the shower and quickly wash off. I hop into some spandex shorts and oversized Cinderella t-shirt. It falls off the shoulder since I have a habit of cutting the collar out of all my t-shirts.

The sparkle of the yellow diamonds on my finger catch my attention. It's simple and beautiful. I lightly kiss it before heading out into the living room. Miss Tami stares at it as I cozy in next to her.

"You like it?" She whispers.

"You knew?"

"Of course, I knew. State and I talk a lot."

That statement warms my heart.

"I'm in love."

She squeezes the top of my kneecap, kisses my temple, and says, "Watch this."

We both study Rowe and State who are deep in conversation about the princess play he was supposed to execute on the field tonight.

"The dragons were just too vicious. Maybe next game."

"You gotta get to the castle, State." She wipes her brow exasperated.

"Hey." He sets her in the over-stuffed recliner. "I may not have defeated all the dragons, but I do have this."

He gets down on his knee. "It's for the fairest princess of the land and my best football play advisor. Rowe, with Pop Tarts on top, I want to tell you something."

She claps her hands in front of her chest with a gleam of hope twinkling in her eye.

"I promise to be here with you forever." He flips open the black box to a miniature version of my ring.

"Damn," she whispers before plucking the ring from the box. She slides it on her middle finger and prances around the living room singing to the top of her lungs. She freezes in the middle of a hip pop.

"Wait." She clutches her chest. "Sissy, are you okay with this? I mean he gave me a ring."

I giggle and then lift my hand up to her.

"We're twins." She hops into my lap.

"Yes we are, always." I hug her tightly.

She whispers in my ear, or whispers as much as Rowe can, "Thank you for bringing him to us."

I look over her shoulder to see State wipe at his eyes before resting his palms on his hips.

"He's ours forever." I don't break eye contact when I tell her this.

Chapter 28

"It's just not fair." Rowe stomps her foot in frustration.

No shit, I think to myself as I stuff the skimpy Dalmatian Halloween costume in my bag.

"We'll be back on Saturday to spend the whole day with you and take you trick or treating." I tap the tip of her nose.

"Promise?"

"I promise. Keep State's Shrek outfit safe."

"Okay."

A knock at the door interrupts us. Shayne is smiling brightly on the other side with two large cups of coffee in her hands. She's been over a few times for girl's night and won over Rowe just like State has.

"Shayne." Rowe bolts to her, wrapping her arms around her waist.

"Hey, sweetie."

She manages to pass my coffee off to me and sit on the couch, before Rowe is all up in her face. She's assaults her with one-hundred questions.

"Let me grab my bag and let Miss Tami know we're heading out."

Shayne nods to me, but keeps her attention focused on Rowe and her wild story. She's explaining her costume to perfection, State's, and mine.

I hear Shayne giggle when I leave the room. "Baylor will make the perfect Donkey."

I creak open Miss Tami's door and peek my head in. "I'm getting ready to leave."

"Okay, sweetie." She groans sitting up out of bed.

"Are you okay?" I ask her.

"Just the lovely effects of old age creeping in."

"Let me help you."

"Get away." She bats me away from her.

"Hush it, old lady."

I help her up and straighten out her night dress, and smooth down her hair. I really don't want to leave her right now. I know she's been feeling under the weather, but will never ask for help. It's funny how the woman gives everything, but refuses any help.

"Get out of here, you sexy Dalmatian."

"I'll be paying you back for that one," I reply.

Her and her friends made my costume for the college Halloween party. I'm pretty sure they had a ball making the skimpy damn outfit. They created a costume for the ages with sparkles, dots, and all.

"Get on the road, girls," she announces when entering the living room. "I don't need State blowing up my phone."

"Oh you know you love being adored by a hot college guy." Shayne waggles her eyebrows.

"Hey, he's mine." Rowe clutches her chest.

I give them lots of loves and kisses before heading outside with Shayne. The autumn sun is high in the sky. The perfect amount of heat and cool breeze mingle together in the air. The trees have long changed colors. The combination of orange and yellow leaves tumbling to the ground. It's simply a beautiful afternoon. I watch the trees blow by as we drive and feel a connection with them. I've changed just as they have, except I'm never going back to the shell I use to call life.

"Did you and Ryder decide on a costume for the party?"

"He's going as a football player and I have a kitten outfit."

"I was going to backhand you if you said you were going as a gymnast."

"Nice idea!"

"Shut your damn mouth when you're talking to me, girl."

We both share a light giggle, but I sense a lingering topic bothering her.

"Are you okay, Shayne?"

She shrugs and pops a few Tic-Tac's in her mouth. "Just a bit stressed about the upcoming trials."

"You'll be fine. What else is bothering you?" I hold up my hand and flash some weird-ass sign to be funny. "Bitch code."

"Ryder," she sighs.

"And?" I push her.

"He's scared of my dad."

"Rightfully so."

"Don't you even dare take his side," she spats.

"I'm not. Open up to me. You never talk about this. We all know it's going on. Hell, I'd bet your dad even knows."

"It's pretty basic. He loves football and doesn't want to piss off my dad."

"Do you want more with him?"

"Yes, I want it all." She glances over at me. "He won't even hold my hand in public. It has to be this big top secret relationship. He knows I want more, but it all comes back to fucking football."

It's the first time, I realize how incredibly blessed I am. State has, from day one, let me know that I'm his number one priority, even over football. At times the fact has gutted me, even made me feel guilty, but now I'm thankful. It's like Shayne is the mistress to Ryder and the stepchild to her father when it comes to football.

"Maybe when the season is over you two can talk about it, and also sit down with your parents."

"Not likely. It's all about football and I'm done."

"Your mom seems to understand you."

"She does, but she's more of the peace keeper." She slams the steering wheel making me jump. "Do you realize he doesn't even come to any of my competitions, not even Nationals last year?"

"I'm sorry, Shayne." I grab her hand and squeeze it because I am really sorry.

It's seems like slow torture to have the picture perfect parents right in front you, but not have a connection with them. The stark opposite of what I experienced. I'm not envious of her situation at all.

"Hey, I have an idea." I offer after thirty minutes of silence.

"I'm not going to sing love songs to you." She rolls her eyes.

"Funny, loser. Let's get ready at your dorm."

"Really? Figured you'd want to make hot puppy love to your firefighter before the party."

"No, let's get ready at your dorm!"

It's the first smile I sport since Shayne left Rowe. She lives in the tower opposite of State. The Halloween spirit fills the campus with décor and rowdy college students. I notice her dorm tower is much less populated. More of the nerdy crowds, my people, fill the open spaces.

Shayne's room is plain. Unless you consider yoga pants and other workout clothes crumpled on the floor as decoration, then I guess it's decorated.

"Do you have a roommate?"

"Theoretically, but she's never here. She bones her boy toy twenty-four seven."

"Gotcha." I plop down my bag and then use her restroom.

By the time, I'm back out in the living space Shayne is already beginning to curl her long brown hair. She showed me a picture of her kitty cat costume on Pinterest. It's a cute combination with a sprinkle of sexy.

"Wait, until you see the damn costume Miss Tami and her friends put together for me."

"Hit me with it." Shayne looks back to me.

I pull the tight black mini skirt from the bag. They've sewn a very tight white tank top from to the top of the skirt. It has carefully placed dots all over it rimmed with rhinestones.

"Dayyyyyuuuummm," she sings.

"Oh, that's not it."

I pull out the spiked black high heels, fish net stockings, and the headband with puppy ears on it.

"Jesus, I hope there's a crotch hole in those fish nets stockings. State is going to jump your bones. Woof Woof."

I fall on the bed in a fit of laughter, imagining my fireman attacking me from behind. Shayne tosses me a light up mirror and gestures for me to start on my make-up. I dab some concealer on my trouble spots, then spread out a thin layer of foundation over my face. Next a perfect swipe of eyeliner and a thick coat of mascara.

"Here let me do your eye shadow. I'm pretty damn good at it." She licks the tip of her pointer finger and presses it to her ass.

"Not too much," I warn her.

"Shut it and close your eyes."

I think about for a second, but soon realize she's not going to give in anytime soon. I close my eyes and relax as she glides the soft pad of the eye shadow brush over my lids. I hear my phone ding off in the distance, but find myself in a hypnotic trance. The movement of the brush goes out past my eye, but I don't dare move.

"Okay, open."

I flutter my eyes open a few times before adjusting back to the normal lighting in the room. I first spot Shayne's huge grin and then I look down into the mirror.

"Holy hell!"

I move my face from side-to-side to view the whole effect of the make-up.

"You just need a bit of blush and I think it's perfect."

"How in the hell did you do that?"

"Years of dance and gymnastics." She offers. "We get pretty damn good at it."

She applied a thicker layer of eyeliner, smeared my top lid with a gorgeous shimmery silver with layers of a deeper steel color, leaving me with a gorgeous dramatic eye. There's also a spackling of black dots placed strategically around my right eye.

"Close your eyes again."

I'd let this girl paint my face any day, so I close my eyes and let the master work her magic. I feel her applying a thin line of something on my top lid along my eyelashes, then I feel her outline the black dots with something. Shortly after, a plush brush runs along my cheekbone. I try to pull back, but don't escape the eyeliner pen running a circle on the tip of my nose.

"You, my darling, are an official dog. Woof Woof."

"Don't woof at me again!"

I peer back in the mirror and squeal like a little girl. She's outlined the dots around my eye with light glitter, applied a set of fake lashes, and a perfect black dot on the tip of my nose.

"Careful with those lashes, they'll need a bit longer to dry."

"I love it! You're awesome."

I watch Shayne powder her face and begin applying her own make-up. It's clear she's going a shade lighter. Her eye shadow is a light pink with a bit of a shimmer. She makes wispy little whiskers, with petite little dots around her nose. She enhances the color of her eyebrows with a light brown.

My phone pings again.

State: Are you guys ready?
Me: Not yet.
State: I need help getting dressed.
Me: I bet you do!
State: Pleassssse

Me: No! We'll meet you at your car in twenty minutes.

I can't stand the wait, so I snap a quick selfie of my make-up. I have one finger twirled around my hair and my head titled to the side. He replies immediately.

State: You just gave me a boner…woof woof.

Me: Not you too!!!

State: Who else got a boner?

State: I'm on my way over to beat ass.

I bite my bottom lip stifling a giggle.

Me: No one, Hulk! Shayne keeps woofing at me!

State: Thank fuck. I'm at the elevator…I'll turn around and wait…hurry your cute little doggy ass up.

Me: (heart emoticon)

"What do you think?" Shayne asks.

I look up to a gorgeous kitten face. Her eyebrows are fluffed up, with white in the corner of her eyes, leading to the bridge of her nose, and her top lip is painted black with a thin layer of glitter all over her face.

"Meoooow."

"No, dumbass, you're supposed to bark at me and then I hiss back."

A garbled bark escapes me and then I giggle like a lunatic. "What are we? Ten?"

"Why not?" She shrugs.

Shayne cranks up her iPhone on the speaker dock. Taylor Swift booms out through her room. It's clear she's an athlete and has no insecurities about undressing in front of me. I, however, sneak off to the bathroom. It takes too much time and delicate hands to pull on the fishnet stockings. I have no idea how in the hell hookers operate in these things.

The netting is very delicate, so I roll them up slowly and very carefully, inch-by-inch, until they're nestled low on my waist. It was just the warm up for the damn skintight dress. I curse Miss Tami as I wiggle it up over my curvy hips. She must have measured me in my damn sleep because it fits like a glove.

My breasts nearly spill out of the top and my hips are *bam,* in your face. I smooth my palms down the sides of my hips. I fasten the thick red belt around my middle, pile up my loose curls on the top of my head, and then finally settle the doggy ear headband in the mess.

There's no doubt left what I'm supposed to be. State would go wild if I sent him a picture. I think about it for a minute, but then decide against it. His face will be priceless when I see him.

I enter the main part of the dorm woofing like a sexy Dalmatian to catch Shayne's attention. We snap several selfies in front of her floor length mirror and exchange high fives like little kids before we leave.

Shayne's athletic body is rocking in her brown leotard and tights. Her kitty tail sashays behind her as she walks, while her rhinestone kitty ears shine. We receive a few catcalls as we walk outside. Shayne silences them with a middle finger. But we receive far more odd looks.

A hipster college man stops us on the sidewalk. "Right on. Love the outfits, girls."

"Thanks." Shayne smiles brightly back at him.

"It's cool to show off your love for each other with matching costumes."

"Excuse me?" I ask.

"Lesbians are hot," he replies.

"I like sausage. Lots and lots of big and thick sausage, asshole." Shayne stomps off and I follow her.

"I think you just gave that guy a stroke."

"Good, he deserves one," she replies.

"He was just being nice."

"It doesn't help my ego. I mean I can't even get the guy that claims he's in love with me to fall for me. Jesus, take the wheel." She throws her hands up. "I'm getting tanked tonight."

"Dear lord," I whisper.

I try and focus on staying upright on these damn heels. The uneven sidewalk doesn't help matters much. Thank God, I have a bit of coordination in these legs. I look up into the sun and shade my eyes. A tall, handsome man fills up my vision in the distance. As I near, I notice his tight white tank top and suspenders hooked to olive colored canvas pants, with a yellow firefighter hat on the top of his head.

State's pearly whites shine through as we near him. Then I spot his stormy eyes taking all of me in. Yes, it was his idea to be a firefighter and Dalmatian duo for the annual Halloween party at a frat house where most of his buddies live. He claims it was a childhood fantasy. To me, it's an awkward as fuck fantasy, but I went along with it.

"Hey Captain," I purr when feet from him.

"We are not going," he growls. He grips me by my shoulders and turns us around. "Get your ass back to the dorm room and change."

"State."

"You're not wearing that," he says down into my neck.

I manage to turn around and look up at him. "Why?"

He grabs my hand pulls it to his erection. "That's why."

"Seems you have a fire in your pants to put out, captain." I catch his bottom lip at the same time Shayne grabs my wrist.

"We are going, lovebirds. You can put out that fire later."

State groans, but finally gives in. Ryder's standing by State's car dressed just like himself, a football player. I have an urge to kick him in the nuts and scream at him to get his head on straight. But, I have enough problems in my life and since it's finally on track, it's none of my business.

The sexy and now pissed off kitten climbs in the back, as does the football player. There's no lip smacking action tonight. The ride is rather uncomfortable with no conversation at all, so I turn to State.

"You really don't like my costume?" I run my hand up the fishnet stockings to drive him nuts.

"I like it too damn much. I should've suggested priest and nun outfits for us."

"I feel good in it."

"You look like fucking sin on a stick that I want to devour."

"That's the reaction I was looking for."

"If anyone looks at you, or even glances a bit too long tonight, I'll rip their throats out."

"Stop."

"I'm serious. There are going to be manwhores everywhere."

"I'm all yours." I clutch his hand. "Let's just enjoy the night."

"I will after I take you. I'm finding a room when we get there."

"Um, sorry, captain. These stockings aren't coming back off until the end of the night. I should've received a gold medal for getting into them."

He glares down at them while stopped at a stoplight. "Damn cock blockers."

State makes good on his promise, growling at everyone who looks in my direction. Shayne also dives right into the alcohol floating around and Ryder works the room with his dazzling smile and goofball personality. They've really nailed the façade of not caring for each other.

I remain nestled under State's arm, avoiding being bumped into. He's offered several drinks, but turns them all down. He's told me he doesn't drink. I know it's because of our childhood and the damage alcohol caused.

The three-story frat house is packed with bodies all dressed up in varying costumes. For the first time, I fit in with the other women in slutty outfits. The only difference is, I already have a man on my arm and not on the hunt for one. The music blares throughout the room with grinding bodies in every direction.

State catches me yawning when he glances down at me from a football conversation with three other large men. I recognize two of the faces from the pre-football party, but couldn't tell you their names even if my puppy ears were on fire.

A version of Elvis' *A Little Less Conversation* begins playing and I'm shocked when State lifts his arm from my shoulders and steps onto the dance floor. I watch him with curious eyes. He turns to me and begins to rock his hips from side to side then extends his hand, pointing at me. His moves become more exaggerated as he waves me over. I notice his little stunt catches the attention of several whores.

I walk toward him in my heels, bobbing my head to the beat of the song. When I'm mere feet from him he spins around and then goes into straight dance moves. His feet move with ease as he hooks his thumbs under his suspenders pulling them out and down his shoulder. The man has moves. It takes me a moment to take it all in as he smoothly controls the dance floor.

I place a hand on my hip and begin swaying to the beat. My feet shuffle side to side in front of him. He winks at me, continuing his performance. I run my hands to the top of my head and let him have it with my hips. My body moves evenly to the beat of the song, with quick foot work.

I roll my hips back and forth, then let my torso follow the same action. I lick my lips and it must be the undoing of State. He grabs me by the hips, moving his body up against mine. He rolls his pelvis into mine making me smile.

I step back from him and twirl around. I heat up the dance moves giving him some stripper action with my hips. A random guy bumps into me, nearly knocking me off my feet and State knocks him in the back of the head. He turns around and raises his hands mouthing *sorry*.

I figure the best spot to dance is right up next to him. We don't stop after the song ends. We dance through all kinds of hip-hop songs. I keep hoping for a slow one, but it never comes. For a girl like me, this is like my first prom. By the third song, State reaches behind him tugging his tank up and over his head.

Now, I get to grind on his sexy-ass body. The tempo of the songs may never slow down, but we do. We've made our way out into the middle of the dance floor. We're surrounded by other bodies who seem not to give a shit about us.

Gorilla by Bruno Mars begins to play. The chemistry between us combusts instantly sending us into a frenzy. His hands roam all over my ass as I press into him. I throw my head back and feel his lips connect with the front of my neck. He bites down onto the sensitive skin and then licks trials of pleasure behind my ear. I roll my hips even harder into him and he matches with each push. He sings the chorus of the song down into my ear.

I'm done for the night. Melted.

He drags me off the dance floor after the song. He snags two cold bottles of water from the fridge before walking us outside on the back patio. We both down the water and then stare at each other.

I finally break the silence. "That was so much fun, State."

"God, I've waited forever to dance with that body of yours."

I wrap my arms low around his waist and plant my cheek on his sweaty chest. "I never went to any dances in school. Don't laugh at me, promise?"

He reaches an arm around his back and finds one of my pinkies. "Promise, Queen."

"That felt like the prom to me. Better than I ever imagined, even if I'm dressed up as a damn dog."

The vibration of a deep laughter from his chest tickles my chest.

"Want to know a secret?" He asks.

"Yes." I look up at him.

I'm sure my make-up is halfway melted off, but I don't care.

"This is the song I've always wanted to dance with you to." He pushes play on his iPhone.

Lucky by Jason Mraz and Colbie Caillat begins to play.

"Really?" I ask him.

"May I have this dance?" He wraps his arms low around my waist.

I place my hands on his chest and sway to the song of us.

Chapter 28

The joke is on State today.

"Stop laughing."

I roll on the bed barely able to catch my breath. My lower abdomen aches with laughter pain. Every time I settle down, I look right back up to the tower that is State staring down at me in a spandex lime green body suit and break down all over again. Rowe busts into the room squealing. Panic flashes in State's eyes.

He hisses, "My junk."

He points down to his crotch to a perfectly outlined ding dong and set of nuts.

"Out, Rowe. We'll be out in a second."

She sticks out her bottom lip.

"You can't see your prince until he's fully dressed."

State remains panicked with his back to her. She finally gives in, sticks her tongue out at me, and shuts the door with an extra dash of vigor. He leaps onto the bed covering my body. The suit is slick causing him to slide all over.

"If you think this is funny I can't wait to see you dressed up as a jackass." He bites down on my neck.

I bust into another fit of cackles that have no promise of stopping. My core still aches from our all night love making session. We both finally collapsed at five in the morning which now, looking back, was a terrible idea since we have a day filled of pumpkin picking and trick or treating with Rowe.

"I can't even piss. I have to take the damn thing off."

"Stop." I press up on his shoulders.

"Who in the hell invents this shit?"

"Shrek lovers."

"I'm going to kick your ass," he growls down at me with a playful smile.

"You love my ass too much to kick it."

"Fuck, my weakness. You're right."

"I bought you lime green gym shorts. I didn't know how to explain to Miss Tami that you had too much junk for this outfit."

"Are you ready yet?" Rowe drums her fingers on my door.

"God, I need sleep, Shrek," I whine.

"Oh no, you don't. There's no Shrek without his cute and adorable jackass."

I'm pretty sure Miss Tami took a shot or two before venturing out for the day. Damn, I should've taken a note from that smart woman's page book. We are trotting down the third neighborhood in full force trick or treating.

"Turn around," I holler to State and Rowe.

I snapped a picture of their backsides holding hands walking down the sidewalk before I interrupted their moment.

"Say cheese," I sing out and snap a picture of Shrek and Fiona.

They stop only long enough for a quick picture before they're off again. State's plastic pumpkin has just as much candy in it as Rowe's. I'm chalking it up to all the lonely housewives ogling my ogre.

"Time for dinner," Miss Tami announces.

Rowe whines when they're at the end of the block. I'm thankful Miss Tami is taking the lead role of fun cop tonight. We end up at a local pizza parlor. Shocker, I know! State orders for us girls and even pays. I was ready for a full-blown wrestling match between him and Miss Tami. He's lucky he caught her on a night she's exhausted.

State has Rowe on his hip while they pile their salad plates high.

"You feeling okay?" I ask Miss Tami.

"I've just been so exhausted lately."

"Doctor," I ordered.

"Yes, mother." She rolls her eyes. "I have an appointment Monday."

"Good little girl." I pat her hand and laugh.

"It's just old age, you know?"

"Or a man keeping you up late at night."

"No, Tom has been away on a business trip the last month."

I stick my fingers in my ears and chant. "La, la, la, la, la, la."

"What's going on?" State sets Rowe in the booth and slides his mask over his neck.

"Nothing," I fire off a bit too quickly while getting up to get my salad.

State doesn't just stop after pizza. He orders him and Rowe an Oreo dessert pizza. I'm stuffed and can barely watch them eat. Something catches my attention and when I turn I nearly lose my dinner and grounding.

I come eye to eye with Dylan Burnett. I look around quickly to make sure his family isn't with him. I don't see any of them and more importantly his younger brother. State reaches over the table and grabs my hand. When I look up at him, I see the question all over his face. It only takes a quick nod for him to catch on.

State is up and out of the booth. Rowe bounds out, but I catch her before she follows him.

"He's using the restroom, honey." I brush her bangs back and stand up. "Sit between us for a bit."

I track State, trying not to alert the rest of the table to the new patron of the pizza place. State walks right up to Dylan, grabs his collar, and drags him right out of the restaurant. There are a few hushed murmurs that float around for a few beats. It takes everything I have to stay in my seat.

My heart thuds with fear. State will kill him. I struggle to keep up with Rowe's conversation as I wait for State to return. It feels like endless hours before he strides back to us. I can tell he's putting on a face for us.

"Did you pee outside?" Rowe asks.

"Uh?"

"I told her you went to the restroom," I offer.

"No, honey, just went and checked on our candy stash."

"Is it okay?"

"Everything is just fine, princess."

Once we're at the pumpkin patch there's enough distraction to corner State.

"Everything okay?"

"Yeah, I think he got the point."

I grab his face and force him to look down at me. "Don't let him ruin this. We're safe with you in our lives."

"I'll try."

"No, you will just leave it alone."

"They hurt her."

"I know. We have her. Don't let it ruin us."

He nods. "Okay, I'll try, but I will be tracking the fucker."

"Of course you will, and that's why I love you." I kiss him on the lips.

"I won't feel comfortable until he's gone to California."

"State," Rowe squeals and points. "I want this one."

Of course, she'd pick the biggest and brightest pumpkin in the whole damn patch. He strides over to it, snaps it from the plant, and hoists it on his shoulder. I pick a fat, round one for me and a tall, skinny one for State.

Rowe and I pull the two pumpkins in a little red wagon behind us, while Shrek packs his up to the stand to pay. We sit on the straw bales and let Miss Tami snap a few pictures. As exhilarating as State's football games are, it has nothing on this moment. I sneak in a quick kiss on State's cheek while him and Rowe smile brightly for the camera.

We spend hours gutting the pumpkins and carving them. Rowe sets her LED lit candle in the pumpkin before being tucked in bed. I perform our ritual as State sits on the other side of Rowe. She snuggles down in her blankets clutching her Rapunzel doll to her side.

Through sleepy eyes, she says, "I love you guys so much."

"We love you, too, Rowe," State whispers. "You're so beautiful, smart, and brave. Thank you for the best day of my life."

She stares him down. "Don't you dare eat my Snickers."

He wraps his pinky in hers. "I promise."

"Will you wait until I fall asleep?" She asks.

He lies down next to her with his feet hanging over the bottom of the bed. I pull another string of pumpkin innards from my hair.

"I'm going to shower," I whisper.

He winks up at me. "Take your time, Queen."

I take my time cleaning the remnants of the Halloween make-up from my face while the shower heats up, then strip off my clothes. I turn slightly so I can see the top of my back in the mirror. It's so bare. State owns all of me, yet I'm bare.

The hot water feels good after a long day of running around on fumes. Even though I wore my comfiest pair of Nikes the pads of my feet ache. I lather up my hair and let the sudsy water flow down the drain.

I shave my legs while I allow the conditioner to soak in my long locks. I feel a whoosh of cold air and look up to State stepping in the shower.

"Good girl."

I wrap my arms around his chest and let the water relax both of us. Our worries and stress all sink down the drain. State has a Monday night game. It's some celebration and is being televised on national television. The only bad news is it's on the west coast. It will be another long two weeks not seeing him.

"Hey." I look up at him and pat his chest. "No packages this time. You spoil us too much."

"Okay."

"Okay?" I ask.

"Yeah, okay."

"You never give up that easy."

"I already hid them around the house and will text you clues."

"Of course, you did."

"You'll never find them without my clues."

"Won't stop me from trying."

He smiles widely before lowering his lips to mine. We move slowly working our mouths around each other. His hands roam down to my ass and then he hoists me up to him. My ankles lock right above his ass. I trace my name on his back even though I can't see it. I let my fingerprints soak into his ink, connecting us forever. State pulls back, kissing along my jawline until he's sucking on my neck and then down to my collarbone. My back is pressed up against the wall of the shower.

The water continues to massage our skin pouring down on us. I widen my legs around him being careful not to slip from his hold. I feel his hard cock bobbing between us and need to devour it, but he has me pinned.

"Please, baby," I whine.

I flex back my hips and he follows my plea for him. His tip rubs up and down my folds. I seal our lips together to stifle my moans. It feels so good, sending greedy need through me. I want him inside me, controlling my every move, but what he's doing now is so delicious I can't find my voice to beg for more.

I'm wound tight, ready to fall over, so I move my hips as much as I can until I see stars. I moan loudly into his lips riding out the waves of the feeling. He enters me without warning. I up his game and let go of my grip on his back, so I sink all the way down on him.

I'm the only fool because it sends me straight into another orgasm. State begins pumping into me slow at first and then quick with punishing desire. He has me all worked up in a matter of no time.

"Go, State, go. Jesus, fall with me."

He works himself faster in me until I feel his whole body tense right before he melts into me. His large frame folds into me, but never eases his grip from me. I'm on my feet. State washes me, dries me, and carries me to bed. It's these memories that will get me through the next two weeks.

Chapter 29

"Holy FUUUUUCCCCKKKKK." I clench the bench I'm face down on.

Shayne's cackles fill the tattoo parlor.

"It's not fucking funny." I grit my teeth. "Are you almost done?"

"With the S," the badass tatted guy replies.

"Hold my hand. Sing to me. Fuck, fuck, fuck."

"He's not even done with the S," Shayne says between her laughter.

"Fuck," Trick huffs out. "I need a smoke break."

"Me, too." I carefully stand up.

"You smoke?" Shayne asks.

"No, but I'm about to take it up."

She doubles over in laugher with her cellphone clutched in her hands.

"Asshole, are you recording this?"

"No, not me." She raises her hands up cellphone in tow.

"I'll dice you." I grab it from her hand. "Dude, it fucking hurts."

"I couldn't tell," Shayne replies. "Here."

I look up to her. She has her hand outstretched with two white pills in it. "Take these. It will chill you the fuck out. Will make the video footage dull, but I kind of feel bad."

"What are they?"

"Valium."

"Where did you get these, Shayne?" I raise an eyebrow.

"Chill the hell out. They are my mom's. She uses them during football season."

"Will they kill me?"

"Jesus, for a kid raised on the streets you'd think you'd have more cred. Take them, Pollyanna."

"If I die…"

She interrupts me. "State would crush my spine and kill me. I'm thinking I like my body more than that. They will chill you out."

I drop the pills in my mouth and wash them down with the bottle of water. "Are you a pill popper?"

I blame the blatant question on the pain and fear of the fucking needle about to attack my back again.

"Jesus, no. I stole them from mom. I had a feeling you wouldn't be able to handle it."

The inked devil waltzes back in. The sheer sight of him put the ever-loving fear in me. I swear to God I'll never ever, as long as I live, get another damn tattoo. I was a real badass when this idea drifted in, but now I feel dumb as hell.

I lie back down on the table and have Shayne readjust my shirt. My head soon swims. Panic begins to set in until everything dissolves. I hear the singing of the tattoo gun, but feel nothing. I close my eyes and float away. Shayne must find the scene quite boring as she finally sits down in a chair next to me.

Before I know it, badass tattoo guy stands up and taps me on the shoulder.

"All done. Take a look."

I stand up and expect my legs to feel like rubber, but they don't. My entire body is relaxed with no worries in the world. I grab the hand-held mirror and peer into it. I gasp out loud when the five simple letters come into view. It's my future and worth every single bit of pain.

I'm sent out of the tattoo parlor with strict instructions and feeling fulfilled. I'm no longer a blank canvas. I'm Baylor Jones who is madly in love and ready to face the future.

Chapter 30

I glance into the rearview mirror. "It's going to be super loud, Rowe."

"I know." She rolls her eyes.

"State has a job to do on the field. You're not going to be able to talk to him much after the game."

"I know." She rolls her eyes again. "He promised he'd do the princess play and that's why I'm going."

Miss Tami places her hand on top of my leg. "She'll be okay. Quit worrying."

I chew on my bottom lip, worried about her reaction to attending a game.

"You know I wouldn't let her go if she'd freak out. I always push you girls for more, but would never force you into something that would scare you."

Her words ease me a bit, but I'm terrified for Rowe. There's no way I can prepare her for how loud this stadium will be or how everything bleeds football. I glance back to her one more time through the rearview mirror. Rowe is in her number seven jersey twirling her blue and orange hearing protection in her fingers. She has her matching bracelet on, completed with a poofy neon orange tutu.

State reserved us four seats near where I'd sit in every other home game. They're just a row down and four seats over. He made sure Shayne had one, too. I pull into his parking spot, make sure everything is safely stowed in our tote bag, and begin to weave through the maze of the stadium.

Shayne is waving from our seats. When Rowe spots her, she squeals, and begins to dart down the stairs. I'm able to snatch the corn dog from her grip before she dashes down. She leaps into Shayne's arms.

I let Miss Tami go before me, making sure she makes it down all the way. She's persistent that she's healthy as a horse and that I'm over reacting. Once all nestled in, I sink into my seat, already exhausted. Miss Tami is right; she's never shoved me into a situation that would hurt me. Of course, she's pressed me to test the limits and has allowed me to grow comfortable in those boundaries.

My damn back itches like the mother of Satan, but like all other times I try to ignore it. The crowd filtering into the stadium erupts in cheers when the home team takes the field to do their warm-ups. Rowe stands on her feet jumping up and down. Her scratchy orange tutu rubs against my face only making the need to itch more intense.

"State," Rowe shrieks.

I look up to see number seven jogging our way. He waves her down. I'm surprised when she leaps over the stadium seats to get down to him. In one quick lift, he pulls her over the guardrail.

"Sit." Miss Tami pushes me down into my seat. "Let her fly."

We watch from the stands as Rowe mimics every one of his stretches. When he goes back for passes, State sets her on the bench and hands her a white board. Rowe's little hand flies over the whiteboard with her black marker. I notice a giant of a man standing at her side, and I know for certain he's standing guard for State's princess.

State finally jogs over to the bench, takes a knee and nods while Rowe schools him on the play. He finally waves over Coach Pete who also takes a knee and studies whatever is on the whiteboard.

Once Rowe is satisfied her message has been received, State hands her a ball, and picks her up. He bends over, whispering something into her ear. State takes the field once again with her in his arms, and begins jogging towards an end zone. He jukes imaginary players. A player from the opposing team jumps in front of them playing along with their game. He falls down on his back when State rushes past him.

The whole stadium erupts in cheers. I look up to see everyone on their feet cheering the duo on. Shayne punches me in the arm and points to the jumbotron. A huge image of State and Rowe's smiling faces fills the screen. I join the crowd cheering them on.

Their feet land in the end zone and he sets her down to perform her own victory dance. The rest of the starting team surrounds them in a victory dance. Rowe finishes her moves and leaps right back up into State's arm. He's saved her, just like he saved me.

Unashamed tears roll down my face. I thought I'd experienced joy until now. It's all too surreal to experience. State trots right back over to us and I stay put, letting Rowe walk back up to us on her own two feet. She's experienced terror and has now looked it in the eye and won.

Everyone below us helps her leap up the rows over the back of the chairs. She could've taken the aisle steps, but in true Rowe fashion she blazes her own trial. Rowe stands on her chair, places her hands on her hips, and talks.

"We've got this. We just ran the winning play."

Everyone around us erupts in cheers, gifting her with high fives. I look back down to the guardrail to see my number seven smiling back at me. He mouths, *I love you* before jogging back out onto the field.

Rowe eats her corndog while waiting for the home team to come back out to their official introduction. Her personalized blue and orange headphones lie under her seat while she cheers with the rest of the crowd. Our offense takes the field first. She claps along with the rest of the fans.

It's a different story when State takes the field. Rowe hops back up onto her seat giddy with excitement. I have to fight the need to comfort and warn her about what's about to take place. Our gentle giant is about to abuse his body on the field.

I keep my hands poised in front of me. The center hikes the ball to the quarterback and State sprints from his line. It's like magic as he realizes what the play is going to be before the ball leaves the quarterback's hands. He gets through the line and is about three steps away from taking down the quarterback.

"Oh no, Shrek," Rowe yells.

I look up at her standing on her chair. I wait for her reaction. Her face twists in pain and I can only imagine State has just crushed the quarterback. A glorious smile appears on her face and she begins clapping then immediately covers her ears.

Bending down, I grab her hearing protection. I don't offer them to her when the stadium erupts in cheers. She grabs them from my hands and places them on her head. I smile up proudly at her.

Rowe proudly cheers on her State the rest of the game with her hearing protection on. She offers up high fives to the surrounding crowd and nearly leaps out of her seat when State finally completes the princess play. I truly have no idea or can even being to pinpoint the play. It's their secret and she beams with pride.

I'm not the first one scooped into his arms outside the locker-room. It's his princess and it feels even sweeter than I could even imagine. State introduces Rowe and Miss Tami to his father. His mother is nowhere to be found, and I don't ask any questions. Rowe orders her meal with vigor right along State. It's nice to have her as a distraction.

On the drive home, Miss Tami and Rowe are both asleep in the backseat. State keeps my hand in his own on the console.

"You made her day."

"No, Queen, she made *my* day."

Chapter 31

I start a hot shower for State. I know he's showered in the locker room, but I didn't miss his sore muscles when he packed Rowe to her bed snuggling her deep in her blankets. He made sure she was asleep before leaving her.

"Hey, baby." I snag his hips when he walks into my bathroom.

He kisses me before stripping bare to get in shower. "You joining me."

"No, sweetie, enjoy the hot water."

"Okay, stay awake?"

"Of course."

Once he's in the shower and the steam covers the glass, I grab the shirt he was wearing and pull it on. I let him take his time to wash away the game and all the sore muscles. The way he pushes himself on the field, I know there's no way it's possible.

I'm perched on the end of the bed, pretending to read a magazine when he steps out and dries himself off. State flicks the bathroom light off, strides towards me then eases his way onto the bed. He's body covers mine. I kiss his scented skin and roll over on top of him.

"You mean everything to me." I roll my hips on his boxers.

I feel him grow hard underneath me.

"You, too." He picks up my hand and kisses my ring.

My hands run down his chest to his abdomen. I sneak my hand underneath his boxers. I work him from base to tip and then reach over and flick on the lamp on my nightstand. State struggles when I swivel on his hips. With my back to him, I slowly drag up his shirt over my back and rub my core over his. He had no idea I was panty less.

My palms press down on his thighs, then I sit back down with him filling me entirely. I don't have his mouth to stifle my moan this time. It's sheer determination. My teeth sink down into my bottom lip until it's painful. It takes all my strength to sit up tall.

I hear the audible gasp from him and know he's absorbed the message loud and clear. My fingernails dig into his flesh. I rise up and fall down into my forever. The pace picks up. It takes long conflicting moments until I feel his fingertips dig into my flesh. He guides the pace from here on out and we fall together.

Chapter 32

His face is there and then gone. I stand by a little girl screaming his name over and over. Her knees collide hard into the cold tile below. She's scared and hopeless. Her brown eyes are familiar. When I study them a bit longer, I recognize her. It's me.

State's walking away with his new parents. The woman holding his hand peers over to me with no emotion in her eyes. I scream louder and fight to get to him, but then he's gone. Vanished into thin air.

I open my mouth to let the little girl know everything will be okay and to be brave, but no sound comes out. I try again, but no sound. I tug on her shoulder to get her attention, but my hand doesn't connect with anything. A bright flash lights up the entire hallway.

Current day; State is standing there with Rowe on his hip. They're happy and waving to me. I run to them but an invisible glass wall stops me. A woman steps up beside them, running her hand down his arm and then kissing his lips.

I lose it all. I fight to find my voice, kick, and claw at the translucent barrier, but they don't hear. I watch her hands then glide over her swollen belly. State reaches down and place his there, too. She's wearing my ring.

With the last bit of energy I can muster, I scream again as loud as I can until my vocal chords ache.

My shoulders begin to shake and then I finally hear my name roll from the deep voice I'm trying to scream out.

"Baylor, baby, wake up."

My shoulders continue to shake and his voice soothes me. The images slowly disappear when I roll over and open my eyes.

"Hey." He brushes the hair back from my face. "I'm here."

I throw my arms around State's neck and roll up on him. "Oh my God."

"It's okay, Queen." He runs his massive palms up and down my back.

"It was horrible. The day you left me and your mom sneering at me, and then you were holding Rowe with another woman. She was wearing my ring and pregnant."

I let it all out in long rush.

"It was just a nightmare." He grabs my hand and kisses my ring. "I'm here. You're okay. I'm never leaving you."

"State. It was awful." Tears stream down my face. "It felt so real."

"It wasn't. Just a damn nightmare."

"Something bad is going to happen."

"Don't go backwards, baby. Everything is okay."

His finger traces the healing tattoo on my back.

"Make love to me. Take it away."

He rolls me over, settles between my legs, and drops his head to mine. His lips lightly brush mine. We don't kiss. We absorb in all the feelings circling us. State plants his elbows on each side of my head and pushes into me. He works himself into me slow and steady.

"I can never lose you, State. I'll die."

"You'll never lose me." He continues his rhythm. "This is forever."

My fingernails dig into the top of his shoulders. I match his pace with my own hips. I arch my head back into the soft pillow, and State lowers his head and kisses my neck.

"Together," he growls.

The harsh tone in his voice sends me over the edge. I feel him pulse inside of me. He keeps his normal growls silenced.

"Together forever."

With State on top of me, I let my eyes flutter shut until sleep takes over once again. No more nightmares come, only bright light surrounds me.

We sleep late into the morning and I know it's from our lack of sleep the two nights before. I pry my eyes open when I feel the bed dip. State's sitting up and smiles back at me. He stands to his feet moving slow. I can see he's hurt and stiff from the game yesterday

He picks up my panties from the floor and slides them up my legs. I raise my hips to help him.

"You doing okay?" He asks.

I nod to him. "You don't look so hot."

"I won't lie to you. I'm hurting bad."

I sit up in the bed and lace my arms around his neck. "I'll grab my oils and set up my massage table before Rowe wakes up."

"Mmmmmmm. You always take such good care of me."

"It will be a struggle to stay in professional mode with you." I wink.

"I better be the only one you tell that to."

"You'll never know." I wink and swing my legs off the side of the bed.

I use the restroom and brush my teeth quickly. State already has the table set up and he's still in his glorious black boxers.

I lean on the door jam admiring him for a few seconds. "I'm sorry about last night."

"I'm glad I was here." He walks over and snags me by the waist pulling me to his chest.

"It was so real."

"No, this is real." He seals his lips to mine.

I enjoy the long kiss before pulling back and pushing him away. "Lay down or this is going south."

"My south likes you." He places my hand over his indeed very hard south region.

"Lay down. You need worked on, baby."

State reluctantly follows my instructions. I play some Sam Smith and begin rubbing down his shoulders. He squirms a bit every time I hit a sensitive spot, so I take my time and rub out his muscles.

"Why haven't you done this before?" He finally asks.

"Seems we're typically busy with other things."

We both share a light laugh while I continue to work him over. Rowe bounds into the room at the end of the massage.

"State," she squeals.

She plops down on the ground and peers up to him through the face hole.

"Morning, princess."

"Your face looks funny."

"Now is that anyway to treat your Shrek."

"Well, it does."

"I'm going to get you."

"You're not fast enough."

"You're probably right, princess. I'm hurting this morning."

"Geez, they don't make football players like they used to."

"That's it." State raises himself from the massage table in one swift movement, swoops Rowe up from the ground, and tosses her on the bed. They ensue in an all-out wrestling match, giggling and squealing the whole time.

Chapter 33

It's the last home game of the season. They're undefeated and only have one game left before going to the championship game. The championship game will be held in Arizona and State already has my airline ticket booked. Rowe is in her game day gear and already buzzing with excitement.

It will be her fourth game at the stadium. She's already won the heart of the entire team. They make it a point to bring her down during warm-ups for their own little coaching session from her. It makes my heart smile every time I see her tiny frame surrounded by goliaths of men on their knees circling her.

I answer my phone while Miss Tami maneuvers the crazy traffic.

"Hello."

"Hey, Queen."

"What's up?" I ask. He never calls this close to the game.

"Just calling in to check on my girls."

"We're heading to the game right now."

"Why did you answer if you're driving?"

"I'm not, father." I emphasize the last word. "Miss Tami is so I can turn in one of my online assignments."

"Good."

"Just a second, State." I turn to the back seat and glare at Rowe.

"Get back in your seat now and buckle."

"But I want to talk to Shrek." She pouts throwing herself back in her booster seat.

"Buckle up and then you can."

I place the phone back to my ear and ask State a question. "Everything okay?"

"Yeah, I just wanted to hear your voice."

"Ahhhhh, such a little sap you are."

"I've missed you, Queen."

"I've missed you, too."

"So, I hear my princess wants to talk to me."

"Yes." I turn to check on her again. She's struggling to fasten her seatbelt. "She's getting buckled again then I'll let her talk."

Miss Tami grumbles about traffic in the background.

"See you soon."

I catch it out of the corner of my eye before it happens. A large semi-truck blows through an intersection. Everything happens in slow motion. I scream.

"Baylor." State's voice floats through the phone.

The speeding semi-truck crashes into the driver's side of my car. The sound of metal colliding and crushing fills the air. Shards of glass pepper every single inch of my skin. My head bounces off the passenger door and then airbags whip me around. My head spins. Blood drips down my face. When I look over to Miss Tami she's slumped over the steering wheel with a deflated airbag between us.

"Miss Tami," I scream.

I fight to get out of the car, but I'm trapped. Rowe screams from the back. People from the outside of the car tap on the window and I hear their voices about calling for help. I try to slam open my door again, but then quickly realize it's blocked by a large tree. Rowe's screams continue making my head swim. When I turn back to her, she's covered in blood and not in her seat.

Chapter 34

State

"Baylor," I scream into the phone.

The locker room falls silent as I roar into the phone. The line finally goes dead and so does my heart.

"State?" Coach Pete steps in front of me. "Everything okay?"

I bury my face in my palms feeling sick. The bile rises up in the back of my throat.

"State, get up." I hear off in the distance.

I look up to see my coach. The one man I've never disrespected and have always put my entire faith in. I've pushed my body to the limits for him and the team. The rest of the guys stand behind him. I finally rise to my feet and look them all in the face.

"It was Baylor. The call ended. I think they were in an accident."

Coach nods. "Get undressed."

He turns, pulls his phone out of his pocket, and begins talking to someone. The problem is I can't move. I remain frozen, feeling the ground dissolve below me. Ryder steps up to me and pushes me back down on the bench, then he kneels before me and pulls off my cleats. Another teammate raises my jersey above my head and then unlaces my pads.

I let them dress me while replaying the scream over and over again in my head. She's hurt. She could be dead. I bolt from the bench barefoot and make it to a urinal just in time to lose the contents of my stomach.

"Shayne and my wife are out in the car ready to take you." Coach Pete pats my back.

"Where?"

"To the hospital."

Somehow, and I have no clue how, I make it to the car and climb in the backseat. Shayne's at the wheel and Momma Pete tries to hide her rolling tears behind her large sunglasses.

"They're at the Piedmont Hospital. It was a wreck, State."

I look up to Shayne with a blank stare. I can tell there's more she's not telling me, but I can't find the courage to ask her.

"It was fatal."

Those three words roll of her tongue and crush my world. My chest grips with fear. I open my mouth to ask more questions, but nothing comes out.

"Miss Tami didn't make it," she continues. "Rowe and Baylor were taken by ambulance to the hospital."

I stare at her, willing Shayne to tell me that they're okay and everything will be just fine. This is all just a nightmare and not real.

"That's all we know." She focuses her eyes on the road and another word isn't spoken.

We drive by the scene of the wreck. The state police are still there along with a clean-up crew. There's a semi-truck with a large trailer and then the remnants of Baylor's car. The driver's side of her car is gone. Crushed beyond belief.

Shayne has to open the door for me once we arrive at the hospital. She takes my hand, and Momma Pete takes the other. We walk down a long, sterile hallway to a desk. Shayne does all the talking for me.

"Baylor Jones."

"Are you immediate family?" The receptionist asks.

Shayne chews on her bottom lip.

"I am." Words finally escape me.

"ER room number three. I'll let them know you're heading back. You two can take a seat."

I trudge with heavy footsteps down the hall where she pointed. I count the rooms as I pass them until I hear Baylor screaming.

"Sir, you need to wait a second." A nurse presses a palm in my chest.

"Let me go. I need to get to my family. Rowe and Miss Tami need me. Let me go." Baylor's voice is frightened.

I have to get to her.

"Let me in," I growl with a new determination to be there for my girl.

"Sir, they're trying to get her stitched up."

I push past her with her petite form no barrier for me. When I step into the room, I see Baylor being held down by nurses while a man tries to get a needle into the crook of her arm.

"Baby." I rush to her side and grab her face.

She's hurt, bruised, and cut.

"I'm here."

"State." My name falls off her lips before panicked sobs kick in.

"Hey, let them help you. I'm here."

"Where is Rowe?"

"I don't know, baby. I'll go find out as soon as you get help."

She rises from the bed with anger streaming from her core. "NO!"

"Baylor, come on, baby." I peer down and notice the man has the IV in her arm while pumping meds into her.

"Where are they?" She screams.

God, how in the hell do I tell her? What in the fuck do I do?

I make eye contact with a nurse and she gently shakes her head side to side as if reading my mind.

"I'll go check as soon as you let them help you."

"FUCK you…." Her words trail off and her eyes become droopy.

Immediately, my lips are on her forehead. "I love you, Baylor. God, I love you. Please come back to me."

Her eyelids flutter shut and I'm not sure we'll ever be the same.

"Thank you," the man says to me.

"Is she going to be okay?"

He nods. "She has some severe lacerations and a possible concussion. We'll perform other testing just to be sure."

"Thank you." My whole body begins to tremble. "Do you know where the little girl that came in with her is?"

My voice cracks with fear.

"She's in surgery right now," he responds. "Why?"

"I can't divulge that information with you since she's a minor."

"She's her custodian and the other one was killed. Jesus." I run my hands over my head.

One of the nurses grabs me by the arm and pulls me outside the room. "I'll give you her patient number and you can watch the television in the waiting room for updates."

I nod.

"I'll also come let you know Baylor's room number once we get her all fixed up."

I nod again.

My parents are in the waiting room when I sit down. Neither of them says a word. My mother takes my hand in hers and gently kisses my cheek. The minutes that tick by are painfully slow, since no one wants to update us because we aren't immediate family. It makes the engagement ring in my pocket burn with hot flames. *Why didn't I marry her?*

"Do you need anything, son?"

I shake my head and then feel the rage boil up.

"Yeah, I fucking need Baylor right now. I need to know Rowe is okay and I fucking need Miss Tami to be alive again. Think you can handle that, mother?"

She cringes back with my words and I don't feel a bit bad.

"I'm sorry, son. I'm so damn sorry." She kisses my cheek. "Let me go see if I can help."

She stands from the chair and digs around in her purse. She pulls out her credentials and heads off.

"She just wants to help, State. Let her." My father pats my back.

"Maybe she shouldn't have been a bitch to Baylor."

"She has her reasons."

"What, for fuck sakes?" I roar.

"She'll tell you in her own time."

"Fuck this." I rise to my feet and send my fist through the wall.

"Sit." My dad throws me down into a chair.

I stay there with my head in my hands for the next several hours. Soon Ryder and Coach Pete are in the waiting room with us. Other teammates trickle in over time. Nobody talks as the time ticks by on the clock.

"State." A nurse walks into the room.

"Baylor would like to see you."

I shake my head side to side. "I can't do this. I can't."

Coach Pete stands before me and holds out his hand. "Stand up, son."

Like always, I listen to him. He wraps me up in a tight hug. "She needs you now. She deserves to hear it from you. Be there for her and fucking love that girl like no tomorrow."

I back away and nod. I ride the elevator three floors up with the nurse, and follow her as she guides me to Baylor's room. She's relaxed in the bed unlike last time I saw her. Both of her arms are bandaged along with one of her claves. She's shivering in the bed.

That makes me go to her in three long strides. I pull the blankets up over her body and want to yell at a nurse asking why she was lying there shivering.

"State."

"Baylor." I smile down at her.

"It's bad, uh?" Tears roll from the corner of her eyes.

"Yes, honey, it is."

"Lay with me." She pats the side of her bed.

I round the end of the bed and then fold my body next to hers. I'm careful not to bump or hurt her already damaged body.

"No, State, hold me please, before you have to tell me."

"Baby, I'll hurt you."

"Not any more than I already am. Can we just lie here for a while before my whole world is destroyed? Just hold me."

I scoop her up in my arms and hold her to my chest. She silently cries for a long time. I smooth down her hair and kiss the top of her head over a hundred times.

"Miss Tami didn't make it."

I squeeze my eyes shut and cry with Baylor. Her body wracks with sobs. It breaks my heart for so many reasons. Miss Tami saved us over and over again, and now she's gone.

"Rowe's in surgery. I'm not sure when we will be updated."

"State." She pounds my chest. "Take it away please. Just take it all away for me."

"I can't, baby. I can't. I would if I could. I'm here. Always here for you."

We lay in the bed silently for the next several hours crying for our loss. She never asks me to leave and for that I'm thankful. Floods of anger stream from her, but she keeps me close.

"Baylor." There's a slight knock at the door. I look up to see my mom.

She lets herself into the room and walks up to the side of the bed opposite of me. She grabs Baylor's hand, and I notice she's in scrubs. It's the mother I know and love.

"Rowe is out of surgery and doing well."

"What?" Baylor's confusion is all over her face.

I sit up to allow her to sit up as well, but pull her right back into my chest.

"I-uh." My mom fumbles over her words. "I was able to step in and help with her surgery. They were going to have to fly in a surgeon from Chicago. I didn't want to wait."

She takes our silence as approval to go ahead and explain details.

"Most of the time was spent reconstructing two of her fingers. They were nearly cut off."

"She was buckling," Baylor whispers.

Guilt washes over me. Did I cause the wreck? She unbuckled to talk to me. Did I distract Miss Tami, too?

"They'll heal fine. Her spleen and appendix also ruptured. It was a very traumatic crash. She's one very blessed little girl. She should be waking up soon. She'll want to see both of you."

"Thank you," Baylor whispers.

"This may not be the right time, Baylor, but I need to apologize to you." My mom wipes a tear from her face. "I was scared and reacted horribly. There's no excuse."

Baylor shakes her head side to side. "It's okay."

She reaches out and grabs my mother's other hand. "Thank you for helping Rowe when I couldn't be there."

This woman and her heart of gold never cease to amaze me. She's one of a kind and my soul.

"When I met you I saw me. State doesn't even know this. I was a foster kid, but never found a good home. I battled my way to where I am today. I've always felt like trash. It's my biggest insecurity. I wanted more for State. I have a tendency to think running from my past has been my biggest saving grace. It crushed me when I saw my son running back into his past. It's the worst mistake of my life. Your love for my son has opened my eyes and I can only hope you'll forgive me some day."

Baylor leans forward, opens her arms, and brings my mother into a hug. They cry on each other's shoulders for a long time. I can only sit back and watch.

"I need to pee." Baylor finally breaks the silence.

"Let me help you."

"No, I have her, mom." I'm up on my feet, getting ready to carry her to the bathroom.

Baylor takes her hand and lets my mother guide her to the bathroom. My mom cradles her to her side guiding her into the small bathroom.

The day my world crumbles around my feet, it also comes full circle.

Chapter 35

State hasn't left the hospital since the day of the accident. He's been by my side every second of the day. I've cycled through a range of emotions the past few days, and I have no idea how life will go on.

State grabs my hand, wraps his arm low around my back, and guides me into Rowe's room. That's exactly how I'll get through life, in the arms of State. We stand in the doorway watching his mom read a book to Rowe. Her washed Rapunzel doll is tucked under her arm.

I'll never forget the moment when we had to tell her about Miss Tami. It shredded me. Rowe was devastated and angry, just like me. She's been going through attachment issues ever since.

State's mom closes the book and kisses her cheek.

"Do you believe in heaven?" She asks State's mom.

Without skipping a beat, she answers her. "I do, Rowe. I work in a hospital and see miracles every day, but I also see things that are horrible. I know there's a God and a heaven."

"Do you think Miss Tami is there?"

"I know she is and I also know she's now your angel who watches you every day."

"Do you think she put this on my Rapunzel doll?" She points to a little Pop Tarts pin on Rapunzel's dress.

His mom looks up to us and we both shake our heads, having no clue where it came from.

"It was on her when I woke up this morning," Rowe offers.

"See, she's telling you that she'll always be with you, sweetie."

State and I step in the room and take a seat.

"Yeah, but I want her in my life instead of just this pin."

"Me too," I add.

"Me too," State says.

"But the three of you have each other forever. Miss Tami helped you all become strong and independent people. Now your job is to make her proud."

***

Rowe's sweet, little hand rests in mine while my head rests on State's shoulder. A gorgeous cherry wood casket sits before us with a vibrant spray of lilies on top. Miss Tami's best friend stands before us, delivering her life sketch.

State scoots Rowe back on his lap and kisses the top of her head when her tears never stop falling. She turns into his chest and buries her face. My tears have dried up, and I sit heart broken and shattered in the church pew.

It's State's turn to talk. He sets Rowe on the bench next to me and stands up.

"Can I go with you?" She whispers.

"He's going up to talk," I tell her.

"I know."

State nods down at her. She grabs his hand and walks up to the microphone with him. I feel bare and lonely without the two of them next to me. Chills attack my skin and I begin to tremble. State's mom scoots over next to me wrapping her arms around me.

"Hello." State's voice booms through the microphone. "My name is Stayton Blake. I met Miss Tami when I was just kid on the streets. I was exactly her type. She helped me get through some pretty terrible parts of my life when I was a kid, but the funny thing is, she always had a knack for making me feel like a king."

He looks right at me while talking not reading a single word from a paper.

"She saved me when I was young, and then she saved me again. By chance, I ran into an old friend who I grew up with; Baylor. Miss Tami was the only who could get her to talk when we were young. She protected us and made sure we were always in the same class. Well, come to find out, she also ended up raising Baylor when we were separated. This is where she really saved me. She gave me the most beautiful gift ever. She gave back the other half of my heart. But knowing Miss Tami, she didn't stop there. She completed my world with Rowe and Miss Tami, herself. She showed me that there is a plan for the rest of my life. It was seeing her believe in me that has made me the man I am. I can only hope to inspire others the way she did effortlessly. I'll never stop making her proud or protecting her girls."

He bows his head and wipes away a few stray tears. I could tell they were coming when his voice cracked. He takes a red rose from the vase on the stand and walks down to the casket, placing it on top. He bends down and gently kisses the top of her casket.

Rowe tugs on his hand and he bends over to listen to her. He nods at her and then picks her up in his arms making his way back to the stand.

"I guess I'm not done yet." He offers the crowd a wide smile.

He bends the microphone down so it's near Rowe's mouth.

"Hi." She squeezes her eyes shut when she hears her own voice, but then starts up again. "My name is Rowe. I love Miss Tami. She was like my momma. Some bad men hurt me and she took me home. She made a castle of safety for me and gave me a sister."

She pauses to sniffle. State kisses her cheek and urges her on.

"Now I dance, laugh, and play all the time. I'm going to miss her bad. My heart really hurts, but I will be okay. Thank you, Miss Tami."

Rowe copies State's action, grabbing a red rose from the vase. He sets her down on her feet and she walks all on her own over to the casket. Her tears flow down her face as she places it by State's. She hugs the casket as her body falls into trembling sobs. State gives her time. Rowe kisses the casket and looks up at the crowd.

It's the first time in a long time I see the fear in her eyes as she scans the crowd. Her little fingers tremble. I stand up and take two steps until she sees me. I bend down and throw my arms wide open. She rushes into them burying her sobs into my neck.

"You're home, baby girl. I'll never leave you. Never."

Chapter 36

"Hey, baby."

"Baylor, I miss you."

"I miss you, too, State."

"We just got to our hotel."

"How is it?"

"Honestly?"

"Of course."

"It's bittersweet, Queen. I want you here and I want to be there. It just doesn't feel right."

"I know same here."

"Where's Rowe?"

"Napping. She had a hard day. We had a hard day."

I feel like shit for telling him that, but we've promised each other to be open, not holding anything back. We've vowed to not let life ever separate us again. I've had my fair share of meltdowns, as well as State.

"I can FaceTime later."

"That would be perfect. Oh, and I'm ready to drive to Arizona to kick that asshole in the nuts."

His deep chuckle fills the line. "Calm down. It's all part of the build-up for the big game."

"He's an asshole calling you out on social media."

"That he is…an asshole."

"I may have a voodoo doll with pins in his eyeballs, and his frank and beans."

"God, I needed to talk to you. I miss you so much." His deep chuckle tickles the depths of my belly

I pause for a second fighting away the urge to ask him to come home because I know he will. It was a hard decision to not attend the national championship game. State offered to buy Rowe a ticket, but it was all too much right after Miss Tami's passing. Rowe's body is still healing as is her heart, along with mine.

His mom stayed a week with us until I forced her to fly out to Arizona, and now Shayne is here. She's more than thrilled to miss the big game. State's mom has shocked the hell out of me. I now understand why State loves her so deeply. She's truly a dynamic woman. She's tried to apologize several times, but I always stop her.

It took lots of courage to admit what she did. Me, out of everyone, knows how terrible it is to run from the ghosts of our past. She broke the cycle and only wanted that for her son. We all make snap judgments. Right or wrong, it still happens. The fact she admitted it and opened up to me, means more than anything to me.

"How do you feel about the game?" I ask trying to refocus him.

"I'm fucking jacked. We are going to crush this."

"I know."

"Will you wake Rowe before four your time. I want to talk to her before I go into full-game mode."

"You know I will." I pause for a brief second. "State, you know I love you and believe the world of you. I have no doubt you'll kick ass."

"Thank you. I needed that." It's his turn to pause. "And a dozen naked selfies wouldn't hurt."

I full out cackle into the phone. "I'll see what I can do, man cub."

"I love you, Queen."

"Love you, too, I'll FaceTime soon."

I end the call knowing that we could go on forever with this little back and forth game of ours. I look over to Shayne perched on the couch with a bowl of popcorn balanced on her stomach while watching some dumb reality show.

"How's the hometown, horndog hero?" She asks not moving her attention from the show.

"Hanging in there."

"God, I can't thank you enough for getting me out of that game."

"You've mentioned that a thousand times now, Shayne."

"Seriously." She pops up into an upright position with popcorn nestled in her hair. "If I had to swallow another fucking game, I might have pierced my eyelids."

"Oh, Shaynee Poo, you have it hard for Ryder… and daddy issues."

She sends me the bird as I make my way to the kitchen to get the game day food prepped. It's not the traditional wings and dip, but more of a Pop Tarts and ham sandwich combo. I bring the plates out and go into Rowe's room.

She's snuggled deep in her blankets with her Rapunzel nestled in her arms. She's so sweet and has been through hell and back. It's taken a toll on her and she's been napping more than usual. I crawl into bed with her and begin to massage light circles on her back until she rustles around.

"Hey, baby. It's time to wake up."

She groans and rolls over.

"It's almost game time, baby. You need to get dressed and State wants to talk to you."

"Is he here?" She asks through sleepy lids.

"No, baby. He's in Arizona, but wants to talk to you before the game."

"Okay." She rolls back onto her belly. "Ten more minutes."

"I'll be back in a minute. I'll run a bath to help you wake up."

I swear she's stronger than I'll ever be. She's held me while I cried and even brushed away my hair. She's sung me to sleep while being the strong one. Rowe is the most amazing person I've ever met. I know she's destined for greatness and I'll be there every step of the way.

"The water is ready."

"Okay." Rowe props her sleepy self up in bed.

I hold my hands up to her and love it when she crawls into me. A large smile spreads across my face when I can hear Miss Tami scolding me not to pack her everywhere. She'll always be with us. I take Rowe to her bathroom and help her get in the tub. I squirt in some bubbles and then pass Rowe her favorite tub toys. Before long she's waking up, singing a tune, and playing in the tub. I sit back and watch her. Miss Tami left me with the best gift of all.

"Why isn't he answering?" Rowe presses her nose up to the screen with her wet braid swinging from side to side.

I pull her back into my lap. "Just hang on, it's been two rings."

The dial tone goes silent as the call connects.

"He's there. He's there."

Rowe peers into the phone on pins and needles waiting for him to answer.

State's sly grin fills the screen with a whole bunch of clatter in the background.

"Just a second, girls." He turns to the people behind him. "I'll be right back."

I see Coach Pete nod in the background . There's several seconds of him pacing through a long hallway until he enters a quiet room.

"Who is this calling me?" He waggles one eyebrow into the phone.

"It's me, Shrek." Rowe waves into the screen.

"Is this my princess?"

"Yes, it's me." She presses her face closer to the screen.

"Oh, I see you. Nice jersey."

She focuses the phone into the number seven across the front. "Where's the team?"

"They are all getting ready. It's the big game."

"Are you excited?"

"I am. I want to win and then get home." State's pearly whites shine through the screen.

"I don't want you to go home." Her face morphs into a sad one.

"Why?"

"Because you're so far away."

"My home is with you and Baylor."

She lights up and kisses the screen. "Then win that game and get home."

She throws the phone to me and hops from my lap.

"Hey." I smile and give him a wave.

"Hello, gorgeous."

"Oh, shut it."

I've never looked worse in my life. Bags under my eyes adorned with black lines. No hints of make-up and ratty-ass hair, yep, I've never looked worse.

"I'm serious. And I'm coming home as a champion, Queen." His eyes light up like they haven't in the past month.

"I believe you, State. You told me a long time ago, when we were young kids, you'd be a world champion and I never doubted you."

"Baby, do you remember our pink and blue mansions with no fence."

"Yep." I smile a genuine smile with hopes of the future lingering in sight. "With no fence and an Xbox."

"Yes, we never knew back then we'd fall hopelessly in love."

"I think I knew." I wink into the phone.

He only grins and doesn't respond, neither I do.

"But I'm thinking we change plans to one house with a white picket fence around it, add in Rowe and all the princess crap. Plus, I may want a dog down the road."

"And a cat," he adds.

"Possibly a goldfish," I reply.

"Deal, Queen."

"With bubblegum ice cream every night."

"Every night forever," he replies.

"State."

"Yes."

"Go kick ass."

"Okay, Queen. I love you."

"Always. Love you."

When the call ends and his deep pools of chocolate eyes disappear, I feel a pang of hurt for a second. Rowe distracts me by dancing around in her game day gear, chewing down on her favorite flavor of Pop Tarts. Shayne stands by her, twerking to a song playing in her own head.

They entertain themselves over the next hour before settling down. They take their places. Rowe fiddles with her bracelet listening to all the pre-game shit. Her face turns sour when the commentators favor the opposing team.

The pre-game intros into a special edition and the television is flooded with blue and orange. Familiar shots of the stadium come into view and then the headline flashes over the screen, "Who Really Cares?"

Several of State's teammates appear on the screen, saying their name, then repeating a random name after theirs.

Coach Pete finally fills the screen.

"Who Really Cares?" The three words flow powerfully off his tongue. "Look at my team and you'll see."

Childhood pictures blast across the screen, with the players repeating names in the background. A few players are zoomed in on and share their stories of beating the system and making it to college. Their story rings true and I find myself relating easily.

State is next on the screen in a pair of black gym shorts, twirling a ball on the tip of his fingers.

"I'm State Blake."

The camera then zooms into a picture of him and Miss Tami from our elementary years. He's sporting a black and swollen eye, but she's smiling proudly hugging him to her.

"She saved me."

He shares his story and it's similar to the others. A child who was forgotten because of drugs and violence, and he morphs into just another victim. However, it's a stark difference because he had her. I tune out the parts of his adoption and the years we missed together.

He repeats. "She saved me."

I glance up to the screen to see us in our Halloween costume, other random selfies, and then several of him and Rowe. The last one the special focuses in on is a picture of him and Rowe. He's wearing a crown, looking down at Rowe. The picture is an up close selfie of mostly her nose and eyes.

"She completed my world."

The final picture is of all of us at the pumpkin patch with scrolling text of, *In loving memory of all those who cared and saved the lost souls of the world. Miss Tami, you'll never be forgotten. I have your girls safe in my hands.*

The tears roll. I want nothing more than to be in State's arms hugging, kissing and loving the hell out of my gentle giant. Rowe prances around the room in a state of euphoria from seeing her and State on the television.

"Did you see my bracelet?"

I nod and wipe away the tears.

The popcorn and Pop Tarts fly as we watch the game. I wouldn't be surprised if the police come knocking any second. Our offensive is aggressive. Their defensive rises to the occasion. But by the second half, it's our defense scoring the points. State has several sacks and even tips the ball twice. Luckily, the ball ends up in his teammates hands and they run it in for a touchdown.

The camera loves his parents. Every chance they get, they focus in on his parents and gloat about the fact State was adopted and came so far in life. A few months ago, I would've become ill and despaired, but tonight I smile. It's sheer joy for State and his parents. They deserve this.

It's down to the fourth quarter and our offense is on the field. Ryder has had a tough game. He releases the ball and it lands into the defenses' hand. Yet, another interception. State leads his guys onto the field. It's evident they're exhausted, but their will is too strong to let go.

Two minutes. Two long, fucking, minutes are left on the game clock. I've learned so much can happen in football in the matter of one-hundred twenty seconds. Everything can be destroyed in that matter of time off the field, too.

The first play, State and his men stop the run. The second play the running back gains six yards. The third play the quarterback goes back and ends up throwing away the ball because of the pressure. Shayne and I leap into the air, cheering and screaming.

It's not until I focus back into the television that a player is down. The sea of blue alerts me then as the coaches run out onto the field. The network cuts to commercial and I don't say word. Shayne picks up on my nerves, so she helps Rowe in the kitchen to another cup of apple juice.

In Rowe's heart her hero has already won the game of his life. The score doesn't matter to her. But to me it's everything. State has put aside his football career to take care of us. If it's him lying injured on the turf…my world will quit spinning.

Commercials are over and it goes back to the game. State jumps up from the ground, waving off the coaches. Another player is lying down as well, but the coaches aren't focused on him.

"What?" It slips from my mouth.

"If he's injured and the time out is called he has to sit out a play," Shayne replies.

My fingers ache covered over my chest. "So, he's pretending?"

"Yes, he's hurting, but is refusing to leave."

The offense lines up. It's the fourth and final chance to try and tie the game. I watch State's helmet moving, following his actions.

"It's the princess play," Rowe squeals.

I nod to her and Shayne tells her something, but my laser vision is focused in on the TV.

"Gonna be a screen and he needs to read." It's the last words I hear from Rowe.

Everyone on the line goes for the run. I watch State stall for a second and I fear he's far worse hurt than anyone realizes. Like a predator, he watches everything before planning his attack. He leaps forward toward the quarterback when the rest of his team suckers in for the run.

The ball is still in the hands of the QB. He feels the pressure and fake pumps once, twice, and a third time. But all of Number Seven's cards are in…its go big or go home time. State lunges forward. He's right leg gives out, but he still sails in the air. The seconds tick by as hours. I hold my breath. He clobbers the quarterback, but the ball is nowhere in sight.

The fanatics in blue and orange who traveled to the game are up on their feet celebrating. The time clock has wound down. State is covering the quarterback. Game over. We win, twenty-one to fourteen.

But my game isn't over. I study the TV willing State to move. After a long while he rolls off to the side and I'm not sure if he moved on his own or was shoved off. Sprays of glittered blue and orange confetti blow up into the air.

My man is still on the ground. He's conquered the castle, destroyed all the dragons, and now it's his time to live his happily ever after.

"Just get up, State," I scream at the TV.

"Get up." Shayne joins me.

The confetti still falls and he lies there on the turf. My heart hurts and I'm ready to go pack bags for Rowe and I. He'll need his girls.

State rolls over onto his belly. He has several coaching staff on their hands and knees yelling into his face. In a slow motion he rises to his palms and knees. The television zooms into his face. We get a wink and a wave.

When State stands up on his own two feet, he causes the stadium to erupt in cheers. He's upright and walking, but I can tell he's hurt. State holds his helmet and limps over to the bench. Coaches surround him again, then it cuts to commercials.

"Breath, Baylor. He's okay."

"Jesus," I finally holler. "They're world champions."

The three of us dance around like lunatics in the living room. The trophy ceremony plays, State's awarded the MVP, and it's the first time I really wished I was there. I vow in this moment to never ever miss another one of his games, no matter the circumstances.

My phone buzzes on the table next to me. It's State's mom.

Martha: I'm so happy.

Me: You have no clue we are screaming like idiots.

Martha: I can tell he's dying to get off the field to call you.

Me: Give him an extra hug for me please (sad face emoticon)

Martha: I will, sweetie.

Chapter 37

I roll over to see it's only three in the morning. My body refuses to relax. I drift off to sleep for thirty minutes or so, then wake up. I ended up talking to State on the phone after the game, for nearly two hours, until I forced him to go celebrate with his teammates.

His ankle is swollen. It's not broken, but he's in pain. He'll be flying home later this evening and I have a feeling this may be the longest day of my damn life. I press play on my phone and let the mellow music lull me to sleep. It finally works after several songs.

Three hours of slumber float by. I sit up in the bed, deciding to give up on sleep all together. I run a hot bath and drop in a bath bomb. The color of the water swirls around with hues of pinks and blues, and a light shimmer. The floral scent fills the bathroom and relaxes me.

The door to my room creaks open. so I pull my shorts back on and ready myself to soothe Rowe. She must have heard me running the water. I round the corner.

"Rowe, why are you up?"

I look up and come face to face with State, my number seven. He covers my mouth muffling my squeal of joy.

"Shhhhhhh, baby. I wanted to surprise you." He drops his bag to the floor and hugs me.

"How is your ankle?" I kiss him. "Thank you for coming home." I kiss him again not giving him a chance to respond. "God, I love you."

"Is the water running?" He finally asks pulling back.

"Oh shit." I race into the bathroom. The water is high, but not overflowing yet.

I sit on the edge of the large tub and stare at State, who's propped in the doorway with his arms raised above his head and a sliver of his abs showing.

"My MVP." I can't contain my smile. "I really wanted to be there."

"I know."

"Tell me about that last play. I want all the details."

He steps up to me, nods for me to stand, then begins peeling my clothes off. The way his fingers move I can tell he's exhausted. Nothing about it is a sexual gesture. I help him slip from his clothes and then watch him gingerly get into the tub.

"I have a rub I can put on your ankle, baby."

He holds his arms up to me from a sitting position in the water. I carefully climb in and wonder for a second if we're going to send a shitload of water sloshing over the sides.

I nestle down into his lap, relax back on his chest, and let him wash the suds from the fizzy bath bomb over my stomach and up my chest. He tells me all about media week, the game, and even the last play. He said he felt something pop before he took off, and the pain was so unbearable he had to leap into the air just to get off of it.

The sports medicine team wrapped it up and iced it. He refused to get it looked at before hopping on the plane back home. Coach Pete and his parents are pissed. Something about causing more damage to it, but State was a determined man to get back to his girls.

"My appointment is at ten am today and then tomorrow there's a parade for the team at one."

"Sounds good, baby." I try to twist to face him, but he keeps my shoulders still. "Why are you so sad?"

"I'm exhausted." He leans down and traces the *S* of my tattoo with his tongue. "I'm hurt, broken, and sad, but mainly exhausted."

I hear his head fall back onto the tub wall. This time he lets me turn to him and he has tears rolling down his face. When he makes eye contact, he simply says, "I miss her."

"Me too, baby." I lay my head on his chest, sink my body under the hot water, and hold State.

Chapter 38

A year and a half later

"With the first pick of the draft Denver selects Stayton Blake. Defensive lineman."

I'm up on my feet screaming, and jumping up and down next to State. He rises slowly from his seat, buttons his suit jacket, and slowly smiles before he reaches down and kisses me.

He lets it linger with his hand on the back of my head pressing us together. The thin layer of my black evening gown does nothing to hide my sheer excitement for him.

"I love you, Baylor." He has tears forming in his eyes. It's pride. Years of dedication and hard work. He's done it. He won the Heisman award and now he's a first round draft pick in the NFL.

"Go enjoy the light, man cub." I slap him playfully.

He lets go of me and reaches for Rowe's hand. She has a bigger smile on her face than anyone in the building. The two trot hand in hand up to the podium. They've become a dynamic duo, on and off the field.

State wipes happy tears away with the back of his hand as they walk up to the front. He's not afraid to show the years of dedication flow down his face. He's made it all happen for us. We managed to get Rowe into a simple black dress. The commissioner hands each of them a new number seven jersey with Denver's logo on it.

A new chapter in all of our lives. It was the hardest decision of my life, but I knew the time was coming. I told State it didn't matter where he was drafted because I'd follow him anywhere. It was the three of us, in it forever.

He refuses to sell Miss Tami's house, our house for the last year and half, so he has a rental company renting it out to an elderly couple. We're all packed up and ready to have the moving company haul our life in their trucks when we get home.

I won't lie, I get violently sick when I think about leaving that place. My heart speeds up and my throat dries with panic. It's my home and always has been. I've had to tell myself I'm not leaving Miss Tami behind. It's something I have to work on every single day.

Last off-season, State and I tied the knot in the backyard with just a few friends and family. It was simple perfection. We haven't stopped believing in each other for a second of the day. We fall into each other when we struggle and collide with happy hearts during other moments. I wouldn't trade it for a thing.

I focus back up at State and Rowe on the stage in their new jerseys, and placing their hats on. It's the portrait of perfection. I grab the Yellow Seven UNO card from my purse and place it on State's empty seat. Soon they leave the stage and return long moments later. He places Rowe in her seat and scoots her in.

State peers down at the card before he sits and then glances up to me. He quirks an eyebrow and then picks it up. Staring to catch his reaction as he turns the card over in his hands. I swear I can hear him read each word on the back.

You're going to be a dad.

"Is this for real?" He doesn't look up at me.

"Yes, State."

He falls down into his seat never letting go of the card, his hand goes to the back of my head, pulls me in, and kisses me hard.

"What's going on?" Everyone at the table asks.

State finally pulls away from me and looks at the rest of our friends and family, complete with his parents, Coach Pete, and his family.

"We're having a baby."

The table erupts in cheers. Not one of us cares if everyone is staring at us.

Chapter 39

Saying good-bye is never easy. The house is barren. No sign of us living there for years. I peek into Rowe's room and see her sitting cross-legged in the center of the floor.

"Doing okay, princess?" I ask her.

"Yeah, just staring at the one crack in the wall one last time."

I take a seat on the carpet and sit just like her. I'm finding simple things like this harder to do as the days float by.

"I like that crack. I'd pretend it was the gateway to a far off fairyland when I'd play."

"I bet you'll find something like that in your new room."

She shrugs her shoulders. "It won't be the same."

"You're right. It won't be the same. It will be different."

"Yeah. I miss her."

"I miss her every second of the day Rowe." I clutch her little hand in mine. "But then I remember how hard she fought to make me a strong woman and that gets me through the day."

"Yeah."

"What else is bothering you?"

She just shrugs.

"Spill, princess." I poke her in the ribs that garners a smile.

"I don't want to hurt your feelings, sissy."

"It's okay, you won't."

I have a sneaking suspicion what's coming next. She's been thrilled about the fact I'm pregnant and never missed a beat.

She turns to me. "You know the baby?"

"Yeah."

"It's going to have a mom and dad. I won't. I'll never have parents. They didn't love me enough."

A creaking sound fills the room and I know State's behind us in the doorway, but he remains silent.

"I don't have parents. It's not the fact our parents didn't love us, it's that they made poor choices."

"Poor choices suck."

"Hey, look at me." I raise her chin with my pointer finger. "Poor choices do suck, but we would've never become family if they didn't."

She shrugs again. Her sad heart is killing me. State joins us on the floor and grabs her other hand.

"Baylor and I love you so much. Rowe, you're number one in our world and always will be. You are my kid."

She doesn't look up at us. I look at State and nod to him. We've had plans of adopting her, but never knew when to bring it up.

"We want to tell you something, but I need to see those pretty little eyes."

She looks up at him. The girl would walk on water for him.

"We'd like to adopt you. Do you know what that means?"

"Kind of," she replies.

"I want to give you my last name and be in your life forever."

"So, I'd be Rowe Blake."

We both nod.

"And you'd kind of be like my mom and dad."

"No." State shakes his head. "We *would* be your mom and dad. It will be your choice to call us whatever you'd like, but we'd be an official family forever."

She leaps between our bodies hugging both of our necks.

"I love you guys more than Pop Tarts."

"We love you, too," I tell her.

State and Rowe ensue in one final wrestling match on the floor of her bedroom, before we all join hands and walk through the house. We all silently say our good-byes before piling into State's car.

We've decided to road trip it across America to our new home in Denver, Colorado. There will be lots of firsts, memories, and laughs to cherish forever.

Rowe buckles up in the back without a fuss, as we settle in the front. A few tears roll down my cheeks.

"It's okay, Queen." He squeezes my hand. "It will be ours forever. It's just a piece of our past we get to cherish."

"Thank you for everything, State."

He begins driving down the road. I watch the only state I've ever lived in, pass by me. An hour into the drive and my bladder is throbbing.

"Are we almost there yet? I'm bored. I have to pee," Rowe announces from the backseat.

"What were you thinking?" State asks through a chuckle.

Epilogue

State's mom was right about one thing. I never finished earning my degree. I'm not bitter about it because it's simple, my life is sweeter than any career I thought I could ever have.

It took all of us a good six months to adjust to life in Denver. I love it here. It's like my soul was destined to be here. We're close enough to the mountains for a getaway and have tons of opportunities surrounding us.

Martha, myself, and State run a boys and girls club in the off-season. It's called, "Tami's" and is a place for young boys and girls from all walks of life to spend time. We help with homework, hand out food, and encourage their dreams. State's mom and I run it most of the time during football season and then State joins us in the offseason. The kids absolutely adore State.

"Baby, are you ready?" I look up at State dressed for a day at the park.

"I sure am." I hop from the bed and sneak a few gropes of my man. It's become harder to get private time with our demanding schedules. I never thought it would be possible, but he's gotten bigger over the years.

Before we get out of control, we both walk downstairs to find Liam and Rowe rolling around on the ground.

Yes, we have a beautiful baby boy who is a complete handful just like his father. He's a miniature version of State. Liam has always been off the growth charts. We named him Liam because of its meaning — resolute defender.

"Park time," I announce when I enter the living room.

Rowe and Liam are up on their feet running for the door. Willy, our adopted dog races right behind them. He's a rescue dog, small, and came to us broken and battered. Willy is now an official part of our family. He goes everywhere with us and even complies to being dressed up as a princess. Liam use to cooperate as well, but now that's he three-years old he resists a bit more.

The little man of the house adores his collection of footballs. Just like his daddy, he was born with a love for the game. I'm not sure how I'll ever be able to handle my little boy on the field. Rowe has developed my momma bear claw and little Liam has sharpened them.

Rowe and Liam walk hand in hand down the sidewalk, with Willy ahead of them. State and I follow close behind, also hand in hand. The large red picnic tote swings on his shoulder. He plays the sexy dad role very well. The other mothers at the park always appreciate the view and I only laugh, knowing he's all mine.

"Mom," Rowe hollers.

"Yeah, princess."

"Can we go?"

"Go for it." I wave with my free hand.

Our two kids, and of course Willy, race into the park heading for their favorite play structure. State and I find our perfect piece of grass, and lie out the blanket and ready the snacks.

I lay down first and then feel his body press up against mine. It's as good as a date night in this moment.

"You're on Willy poop patrol," State murmurs in my neck.

"Two blowjobs?"

"Deal."

I roll over and kiss him lightly. "Life is good, man cub."

"It's perfect."

"No pink or blue mansions." I lick his bottom lip.

"Nope, but a blue house with light pink trim."

I laugh at the statement because it's true as hell. State and I made sure we lived out our childhood fantasy. "You're my everything, State Blake."

"And I'll never get tired of calling you Baylor Blake."

His lips graze mine. I open up for him to devour my mouth. My man does it on command and just like the first time, I melt into him. It happens every time and I know it will be like that forever.

"Dad," Rowe hollers in the distance.

We both sit up to see her waving her arms in the air.

"Liam is peeing on the slide."

Our vision darts over to the tall yellow slide to see Liam peeing off the top of it.

"That's all yours," I giggle.

State's up on his feet, jogging over to our son. He swoops him from the top of the slide, kneels down on one knee, and gives him a speech. Liam bows his head taking in his father's speech. State has the perfect knack for handling both kids with gentle care. He ruffles the top of his crazy black hair, before pulling Liam's favorite football from his pocket.

It's a miniature neon orange version of his dad's football. They begin playing catch and running a few plays. It's eerily creepy how well the boy throws and catches a football at the age of three.

Rowe walks over to me, so I sit up and hold up my arms. She sits in my lap, relaxing her head back on my shoulder. I rock her side-to-side and kiss her temple. Rowe has her heart set on becoming a fashion designer, and I have no doubt my strong girl will become the best one in the world with her signature princess dresses.

"I love this life," she says, lacing her pinky in mine.

"Me, too."

THE END

Made in the USA
Charleston, SC
07 January 2017